MOUNTAIN STORIES

Ye Guangqin was born in Beijing in 1948, the thirteenth child of Manchu parents. At the age of twenty, during the height of the Cultural Revolution, she was seconded to work as a nurse in the western city of Xi'an. It was here that she developed a fascination with the culture of Shaanxi Province, and in particular, the fauna and villagers of the Qinling Mountains.

On becoming a full-time professional writer in the 1990s, she drew on her royal background to create historical tales of Old Peking as well as elaborating on local legends from her adopted area. Ye Guangqin's *Greenwood Riverside*, a bestselling account of the executed mountain bandit leader Wei Futang, was shortlisted for the Mao Dun Literary Prize before being adapted into a television serial.

Mountain Stories

YE GUANGQIN

Valley Press

First published in 2017 by Valley Press
Woodend, The Crescent, Scarborough, YO11 2PW
www.valleypressuk.com

First edition, first printing (February 2017)

ISBN 978-1-908853-81-3
Cat. no. VP0098

A CIP record for this book is available from the British Library.

Cover and text design by Jamie McGarry

Printed and bound in Great Britain by
TJ International Ltd, Padstow, Cornwall

Contents

Big Fu the Tiger

Cubs were raised annually in a deep, deep vale,
A wide berth being kept between tigress and male.
A village stood not too far from their lair,
The source of kine for those big creatures.
["Fierce Tigers" by Zhang Ji (*c.* 776-*c.* 830)]

I.

Big Fu died thirty-seven years ago in the springtime.

Second Fu is now a cadre in the animal protection division of the Qinling Nature Reserve. Next birthday he will turn forty-six.

This year's Wild Animal Conservation meeting is being held in the Qinling Mountains. Second Fu and I find ourselves reunited at Windy Grass Terrace.

Today, Windy Grass Terrace is a small, prosperous town in the heart of the Qinling Mountains. The 108 National Highway runs through it. There are deluxe hotels, karaoke venues, beautician's salons, foot massage parlours, and high-class bistros, as well as pretty girls who stroll along in the dusk looking for some, *ahem*, ardour … all in all, whatever may be seen in the big city can be found here too. Visitors have no cause to feel lonely, even if it is a foreign land to them. This small town in the depths of the mountains manages to keep apace with the times and, in common with everywhere else in China, is striving after a well-off life.

This is a source of relief.

Also it gives cause for worry.

The venue for the conference is "Big Fu Mansion," a Three Star hotel built on the mountainside. Set amid the exquisite landscape the white building strikes one as imposing and elegant. Moreover, it is well-run. In his introduction, the host states that the hotel is contractually managed by Second Fu's two younger brothers, Third Fu and Fourth Fu. Like the grand hotel, Third Fu and Fourth Fu are a stellar duo. They have been honoured among the "Top Ten Young Local Men of Achievement," and, what is more, have seen something of the world. I don't know the two Fus personally. I only remember them putting in an appearance at the opening ceremony of the conference. The two seemed as alike as a couple of peas. With large heads and round eyes, they glared at people much as a tiger eyes-up its prey. Their bearing was quite different from that of Second Fu, as though they were not the offspring of the same mother. Second Fu says that the boys are twins; a pair of animals who only know about money, but do not understand human nature. Second Fu has been my friend ever since our paths sixteen years ago when I went to the Qinling Mountains to conduct an interview. He loves literature, is loyal to his friends, and is of a sentimental bent, so his eyes easily become bloodshot with emotion. At that time he was studying in the Forestry Institute and had come home for the summer vacation. He followed me around the deep mountains for about one month. We built what was truly a firm friendship. I visited his home and met his elderly father and mother. They were both kindhearted senior citizens. Second Fu had seldom mentioned father and mother to me. He didn't even mention those two younger, pea-like Fus. What he spent most of the time describing to me were the exploits of Big Fu. During our first meeting he asked me to write something about Big Fu. In our later meetings, he further elaborated on this topic. This time his request has a greater air of urgency and cannot be deferred any longer.

At the banquet, with a face and neck reddened by liquor, Second Fu bangs the table and declares that nowadays famous personages love to have their autobiographies ghostwritten. Even those dog's fart entrepreneurs who possess nothing but money scramble to find a man of letters to record their memoirs.

Coming to this topic, Second Fu glances to where Third and Fourth Fu are seated further down the table. The two Fus bow their heads in an instant so as to avoid Second Fu's line of vision. Their expressions seem somewhat embarrassed. Everybody knows that there is a professional writer in residence, occupying the finest guest suite in the hotel. Every day the hotel lays on quality tea and cigarettes for him. The writer is composing a piece of reportage of around 80,000 words in length concerning the pair who is listed among the "Top Ten Young Men." Second Fu tells me frankly why nobody has written about Big Fu. "You men and women of letters are very snobbish. You will sound off about anybody who is prepared to give you money. There is no point at all in making wild boasts. Big sister Ye, if I give you money on Big Fu's behalf are you prepared to write about him?"

Second Fu eggs me on. Second Fu has drunk too much.

I promise here and now to write the memoir of Big Fu, a very great memoir.

Everybody raises a toast to Big Fu.

We also raise a toast to the Big Fu Mansion.

On returning to Xi'an I find that it is really tricky to write a memoir of Big Fu. I don't know where to begin. Foolishly gazing at the computer screen for a long time, I am unable to type even a single word. Thus, I lay Big Fu to one side and start to write about Second Fu himself.

II.

Second Fu's full name is Second Fu Li, and he hails from Birch Hills on the southern side of the Qinling Mountains.

Birch Hills is under the jurisdiction of Windy Grass Terrace.

It used to be known as a commune and was the most out-of-the-way government district in the Qinling Mountains. The commune had three production brigades, comprising fifty-two families. Scattered among six valleys a local fair was held between the fourth and seventh days of every month. Everybody would traipse through the valleys and mountains to Windy Grass Terrace high street where everyday necessities, including locally-produced honey, herbs, furs, and staple goods were being traded. Contact with the outside world was rare. Second Fu's hometown Birch Hills, is located on the slope of the northern bank of the River Xushui, where there are thick forests and grass. The locals make a living from hunting, digging herbs, and planting corn and potatoes, as well as perpetual green beans. Added to the high altitude of the mountains and the coldness of the climate, the destructive behaviour of wild animals mean their harvests are still limited.

Second Fu's family lived at the top of Birch Hills at a high elevation above sea level. There were no other trees besides this coniferous forest. Standing on the pinched empty lot before Second Fu's household, mountains over mountains and rocks over rocks were visible to the south, giving people a majestic and soul-stirring vista. Second Fu's family could not grasp this. They eked a hardscrabble and practical subsistence. Majesty was no substitute for food. Soul-stirring it might be, but they still needed something in their stomachs. Second Fu's pa and ma busied themselves all the year round trying to maintain a living. His pa traversed hills and valleys to dig herbs. He was a dab hand at foraging for herbs. He could find valuable Taibai Mountain hand-shaped ginseng, the rare single-leafed *kingdonia*, dogwood, and *Thunbergii* fritillaries. His pa always left early in the morning and came back in the evening. If found that he had walked too far he would bed down for the night on the mountains. Consequently, there were times when he would not return home for several days. All of the housework was dumped on his ma. Second Fu's ma was extremely capable. She came over here from Sichuan Province because of drought and, despite being petite, could endure hardships. She was adept at planting crops, mustering up pigswill, and gathering firewood. Her hands and feet being never idle, the local-born women were in no way her peers.

The climate in the Qinling Mountains has its own unique characteristics. While there may be drought outside, the interior can enjoy years of successive if modest harvests. In 1953, his ma decided she could no longer bear the hunger of northern Sichuan. She dragged herself along the ancient Tangluo Road to Birch Hills. She terminated her march at the household the Li family and then with Second Fu's arrival she became a mother. Second Fu's ma had a way with pigs. All Sichuanese excel at swine husbandry and know how to cure meat. His ma reared a pig every year, starting from the early autumn so that it would be fattened up by the following spring. The pig would be slaughtered at Dragonboat Festival and the meat hung from the rafters, lasting until next Chinese New Year. At the fair they would exchange the surplus for salt and rice. The cured meat was a crucial source of sustenance and fortune for the family. His ma showed the utmost concern towards the pig. She was not bothered if Second Fu skipped the odd meal, yet was perturbed if the pig were to go without.

Second Fu was known as Second Fu on account of a local custom. There was no First Fu or "Big Fu" ahead of him. Stemming from their respect towards nature, mountain folk had many of their own particular taboos. The firstborn child would never be called "Big." The eldest son would be named "Second." They offered the epithet "Big" to the tall trees, the rocks, the leopard, the bear, and other entities in the mountains. Those were all mighty and sturdy siblings. Becoming their "brothers" would endow kids with power and vitality. Hence, it was easy to cultivate and cherish a long life. Each of the infants in this district had their own "poplar tree brother" or "jackal brother" … Second Fu's big brother was "Biao," an alternative title for a tiger. Mountain folks dare not refer to a tiger directly by its name. They call it "Biao" or *big creature*.

Second Fu asked his pa whether he had seen a *big creature*. His dad replied no. His dad said that not since 1952, when a *big creature* was executed at Shahe Village in Chenggu County, had one been sighted among the Qinling Mountains. His pa called the hunting an "execution." His pa always employed new terms. That was his habit. He'd call a panda a "spotty bear" and the wails-like-a-baby fish a "giant salamander." He called climbing the slope "reaching above sea level" and the big sheep a "takin."

His pa was the Commander of the Production Brigade at Birch Hills. The Commander's language ought to be different from that of the ordinary people.

Second Fu felt sorry that his elder brother First Fu was only an empty symbol – there was no tiger in the Qinling Mountains.

In 1963 Second Fu was nine years old.

The nine-year-old Second Fu was in the second grade of primary school. The school was situated on the East River Terrace, three-and-a-half kilometres away from Birch Hills. Every day Second Fu went to school with his satchel just as the day was breaking. He would arrive at school when the sun had risen halfway up the pole. Within the school Teacher Zhou showed solicitude towards the mountain kids who had come from afar. He always arranged music as the first lesson. He would encourage the students to sing songs lustily at the outset as a means of allowing them to let off steam. The kids at East River Terrace School notched up a broad repertoire. Their best turn was a song named "Happy Festival." Actually the song had an urban tang, though was somehow much appreciated by the mountain kids:

Little birds lead the way,
The wind is blowing towards us,
We come like the springtime,

To the gardens and the lawns.
The bright red scarf
Bonny clothes
Flower-like blossoms
Oh jump, oh jump, oh jump.

The kids asked Teacher Zhou what a "garden" was. Teacher Zhou answered that the garden was the forest and the mountain landscape in Windy Grass Terrace. The kids then asked what "bonny clothes" were. The teacher replied that they were the clothes one wears during Chinese New Year when visiting relatives … The kids said that they understood, so they sang passionately. As they sang they felt as though they were wearing new clothes, and that in the forest sunbirds were soaring about their heads, magnolia blossoms were bursting open all around, and this made them feel elated. When the sun careened in the afternoon, Teacher Zhou would finish classes ahead of time and permit them to go back early. The children of the mountains all bore a heavy load of chores.

Second Fu's academic performance was desultory across the board, especially in maths. He could not recite his times table and failed to comprehend why two times three made six. The teacher worked hard to explain this to him, but to no avail. "If a pheasant lays two eggs," posed the schoolmaster, "how many eggs would three pheasants lay?" Second Fu responded with "Who knows how many? There are pheasants that don't lay eggs. Some eggs get stolen by weasels. Some pheasants rush all over the mountains and drop eggs willy nilly …" The teacher pointed at Second Fu's head and growled, "You … You …"

Second Fu returned home and asked his pa. His pa couldn't fathom out how many eggs three pheasants would lay either. His pa said, "Nobody can be certain about this. There is no need to be certain about this." Later on, when Teacher Zhou met Second Fu's pa and asked him to urge Second Fu to study mathematics harder, his pa said, "No need to put pressure on him. Your cryptic questions about pheasants made even my head ache. Our Second Fu will not become the brigade's accountant. There is no need for him to wrack his brains over this." Like him, his pa senses that maths is nothing. It's just as his pa says, "Go to school; learn several characters. Being able to write your name is enough. Even if you graduate from university you will still write 'one is one' and 'two is two.' You cannot write 'one' so that it forms a flower." Comparatively speaking, Second Fu was better at his Chinese Language course than he was at Mathematics. In Grade Two no writing course was set, but there was a course in Creative Description. Whenever Second Fu was engaged in this lesson, he became garrulous and gave free rein to his imagination. From looking at two or three pictures he was able to natter about what might be outside the border. For example, when confronted with a sentence like "The great wind breaks the spider's web" in pinyin Second Fu would describe it in a rather complicated way. He could tell you what species of spider it was, where it had woven its web, and what insect had been trapped in the web, how happy the spider was, and how terrified its prey was. He could say what kind of wind blew that day, explain how spiders try to protect their web against the wind, how insects scurry for their lives along the cables of the web ... Second Fu's descriptions were singularly vivid as if he had seen these things with his own eyes. His classmates and Teacher Zhou as well were taken aback by his narrative. His classmates said that he was good at spinning tales, but the teacher said that he had a tall imagination ...

When Second Fu was calculating the number of pheasant eggs or spinning tales about the spider's web, their family's dog Blackie would crawl under his desk. Blackie was a sharp mutt and ferocious with it. He would lunge at and bite anything, with bamboo mice, wild hares, and the village chickens being likely targets. Blackie had an oily, bright coat which reflected a kind of blue tinge beneath the sunshine. When he caught sight of a stranger he would squint his eyes, his throat would bellow, and, were the stranger caught off-guard he would lunge at him and savage their shins. Often those government cadres who came to the village would become his victims. The commune calculated that he had bitten about fourteen cadres, including one woman. The commune asked his pa to euthanize Blackie. His pa was, of course, unable to bear doing this. Second Fu had no heart to do the deed either. His pa insisted that Blackie must have been the offspring of a village hound and a dark leopard from Leopard Vale. Otherwise, he would not have been so wild. Second Fu also thought that Blackie had the blood of a leopard. Later on, when he grew up and enrolled at the agricultural university in Yangling, he learned that leopards and dogs belong to two separate families. They are genetically incapable of interbreeding. Blackie was Blackie. He was just an authentic country bumpkin of a dog. There was nothing wild behind his birth. However, at that time Second Fu and his father both believed that Blackie was the seed of the dark leopard. His pa delegated the responsibility of taking care of Blackie to Second Fu, so Second Fu would take Blackie to school with him every day. Blackie would run on ahead with the boy in tow. Sometimes Blackie would hare away and disappear, though Second Fu never worried for he knew that he would be there waiting for him somewhere up in front.

Teacher Zhou forbade Blackie from entering the classroom and announced that it was poor etiquette for people and dogs to share the same space. Blackie turned around and killed the three big bunnies that belonged to Teacher Zhou. The teacher became almost tearful from his sense of heartache. Blackie was unmoved by Teacher Zhou's sadness just as he was unperturbed about not being allowed inside the classroom. He started to show an interest in the schoolmaster's little daughter who wore floral trousers. Whenever the little girl peeped through the crevice in the door, Blackie would bump over and bare his teeth at her, which made her wail with fright. His daughter was more precious than the bunnies. After mulling this matter over several times, Teacher Zhou finally permitted Blackie to come into the classroom on the condition that he did not bring it into disorder. Second Fu gave him his guarantee and claimed that Blackie was no different from human beings, only that he had not been blessed with the power of speech. Blackie swanked into the classroom full flush with pride. His tail was raised high and he strutted in minute steps with Second Fu's schoolbag hung about his neck. The dog's face was both serious and solemn. Once inside the classroom, Blackie first smelt the corners of the wall with great care and then peed in all four of them. After he had confirmed his territory, he then encircled the lectern twice. Following this inspection, he inched his way under Second Fu's desk and began his lesson alongside everybody else. Three grades studied together in the same classroom. When Grade One was doing their homework, Grade Two would have their lessons. When Grade Two was doing their homework, Grade Three would have their lessons. There was no need for Blackie to write homework. He attended the lessons of all three grades. During those years, Blackie really did audit a plethora of lessons. If one were to write out his report card, he would surely meet the qualifications to matriculate from a three-year primary school.

III.

One day, Second Fu left home at daybreak as usual. Blackie, being lazy and sleepy, desperately did not want to go out. Second Fu's pa dealt him a hard kick and he wailed and sped down the mountain path. Second Fu's ma, with her protruding belly, dug out a number of baked potatoes from the stove. She caught up with Second Fu and slipped them into his pocket. This was to be lunch for him and Blackie. Second Fu's ma asked him to come back earlier so as to gather grasses for the pig. Second Fu promised to do this and pursued Blackie. The stomach of Second Fu's ma was waxing larger and larger by the day. She could no longer perform tasks like mowing grass for the pig. Second Fu was clear that after a few more months his ma would bring a Third Fu into the family. Second Fu had no brothers so he was plagued with loneliness. He hoped that his ma would go into labour prematurely so that he might meet Third Fu soon. Even so, his ma was in no hurry and insisted that the fellow in her belly was not Third Fu, but a girl. On hearing this, Second Fu was somewhat disappointed. He didn't argue with his ma, for he knew that neither he nor his mother could do anything about this issue. It was just like a cow making its delivery. No one was able to say whether it would be a he-calf or a she-calf.

The atmosphere at dawn was simultaneously humid and cold. The waning moon slowly descended behind the mountains in the west. It was autumn. The mountain lands were colourful, juxtaposing reds, yellows, purples, greens, Chinese pines, red birches, Chinese hemlocks, and bamboo wood … the east gradually whitened; the path then became half visible and could be seen to spool through the forest like a gentle thread. The streams were invisible, though the sounds of their running water could be heard as if somebody was crooning in a low voice in the depths of the mountains. The leaves of many trees had fallen. The red crotch fruit hung high in the branches, appearing crystalline and succulent. Once picked and bitten into, it would ooze with sweet and tart juice. The ripe wild chestnuts dropped to the ground in their hard casings, as delectable as small hedgehogs. The mountain bird whistled a long note overhead, the sound being sharp and clear like a hunter was about to slay it. After this, an alternative cry echoed all over.

The dawn chorus had commenced.

Among the grasses there was strewn the soil nosed by the mountain boars. The hogs had been searching for edible fungus. Behind the large rock lay a knot of long, yellow grass piled in the shape of a spiral; panda excrement. Second Fu found that the dung was still moist and emitted the smell of bamboo. He was thus certain that the spotty bear had spent the previous night on this patch. At the turn in the road, the bushes were broken and speckled with blood. Fresh and random as those bloodstains were, it seemed that a bloody and fatal fight had been staged here just before sunrise ...

At night the mountain forest was active, restless, and full of vitality.

Second Fu walked hurriedly, sweating. He did not understand what the matter with him was, but his heart was a little unsettled as though something was about to befall him. Second Fu often took this path by himself. He was familiar with every rock and tree along the road. Half a mile into the forest, came a fork that led on to Rear Valleys. Several of his classmates lived there. Their route to school was even longer than his, so they fell behind him, sometimes coming across one another at the fork. Once they rendezvoused, they would process to school in a grand fashion. Boisterous as squirrels scaling trees and bunnies plunging into holes, they could turn the entire forest upside down. That day Second Fu didn't run into any classmates from Rear Valleys. He walked by himself and felt a tad lonely. He gave a whistle and called out for Blackie. There was no response and it may have been that he had strayed far from him. Second Fu was furious and decided to eat a potato, so as to allay his nervousness, and to antagonize Blackie. Leaning back against a beech, he fumbled out a hefty tuber. The still-warm potato had been baked golden by his ma. Second Fu blew away the ashes which clung to it, broke open the flesh and plugged the big pieces into his mouth. The potato was burning hot, and so it made his tongue wriggle and caused him to gag with a straightened neck.

While he was eating seriously yet with contentment, he heard a rustling among the grasses beside him. Bowing his head, he discovered it was Blackie. It turned out that Blackie had not run on far ahead, but was still hiding at close quarters. Second

Fu glared at Blackie. He purposely tossed the potato in front of the dog and then caught it and pushed it into his own mouth. Blackie didn't react as he usually did when he was competing for food, instead paying no attention to the vegetable in his hand. Second Fu asked, "Blackie, when did you start to put on airs?" Blackie took no notice of him. His eyes were full of the panic of being captured. With his body trembling, he tried to cower behind Second Fu's body. Second Fu pushed Blackie forward and asked, "What are you doing? You've got my clothes wet with the morning dew off your body." Still no matter how hard he pushed him, Blackie refused to be moved.

The surroundings were miraculously serene. An ambience of the unknown appeared to engulf him. Second Fu felt that his whole body had been rendered soft and powerless. His biological instincts made him sense that the atmosphere around him was different and peculiar. His hair stood on end. A huge panic pressed down on him, causing him to struggle for breath. He even forgot to swallow his mouthful of potato.

Second Fu discovered a pair of eyes behind the bushes – gigantic burning eyes. Those eyes gazed at him. From the two eyes, Second Fu discerned a huge yellowish creature with black spots – a tiger! Second Fu was stunned. He wanted to run away, but could not stand up. He wanted to cry, but was incapable of making any sound. He wanted to shout for his ma, but could not open his mouth. He was unable to find himself. Blackie deposited himself in his arms and snuggled under his clothing. Shuddering uncontrollably, the dog was petrified to death. In actual fact, the tiger had taken note of Second Fu long ago. Second Fu had fallen into its view the moment he sat down to snack on the potato. Perhaps the tiger had had enough and was reluctant to trifle with such an insignificant wretch. The tiger had feasted his eyes on Second Fu and sensed that was enough. He yawned slackly. Second Fu being downwind of him, the smell of his breath was carried over on the breeze. He imbibed a reek sufficiently rank to make people gag.

Second Fu was only a few metres away from the tiger. He then did not know how to think and how to move. Having resigned himself to fate, he offered himself to the *big creature*.

A tug-of-war had begun between the two parties.

The sound of the children came from the little path. Second Fu's classmates from Rear Valleys approached him. While striding and chortling they beat the morning dew along the roadside. At the head of the group was Flower Bell. As she walked on, she picked fruits to eat, her mouth becoming dyed scarlet by the crotch fruit. She caught sight of Second Fu and asked him why he was sitting beneath the tree trunk. With his eyes fixed straight, Second Fu was struck mute. Flower Bell turned around and said to Zhang Jianshe at her rear, "You see. What's the matter with Second Fu?" Everybody pressed around Second Fu and wished to tug him up. Second Fu's face was blanched and his soul detached from his body. His pupils were fixed on the bush.

Flower Bell implored, "Second Fu, Second Fu say something."

A classmate named Wang Cheng said, "Second Fu looks like he's been hypnotized by mountain spirits. The mountain spirits that live in Beech Hills are very bad. They always make folks confused. They like to play jokes on people. Sometimes when people sit down to have a rest they forget where they are and where they are going. It is all because the mountain spirits play tricks. Whenever you sit down, you ought to grip a stick in your hand and point it in the direction you want to go. This way they can't pick on you."

Everybody chuckled and chatted about mountain spirits. They dragged Second Fu to his feet. A stinking smell emanated from Second Fu's posterior. He had shit his pants. They all said that Second Fu was good for nothing. Nevertheless, Second Fu's eyes were still fixed on what was behind the bush.

Flower Bell pushed Second Fu and said, "Is there something rare back there?"

Wang Cheng declared, "I will go and check." Zhang Jianshe said, "I'll go too." The duo ran to the far side of the bush.

There was nothing behind the bush.

Blackie stubbornly barked at the heap of grass. Zhang Jianshe made an inspection and told them that he had seen a leopard cat leap away up into a tree.

Wang Cheng called Teacher Zhou to come. Teacher Zhou instructed them to take turns to carry Second Fu home piggyback style. When Second Fu's ma saw the shit-filled pants, she lost her temper and exclaimed, "He was quite normal when he left home. How could he get into this state so quickly? Is he growing down?" Teacher Zhou said, "Second Fu must have run into something which caused him to lose control of his body." Wang Cheng suggested that he had encountered a mountain spirit. Second Fu's ma retorted, "I – your old ma – have never believed in those mountain spirits. The government has called on us to smash superstitions. How can you pupils still believe in mountain spirits? You ought to feel ashamed." Teacher Zhou asked everybody to help wash Second Fu and directed Flower Bell to soak his soiled pants in the stream. Covering her nose with her hands, Flower Bell slunk out with the garment.

The ma made a brewed a bowl of honey water. After drinking this, Second Fu gradually came around, though his head was still awash with sweat.

While everybody was busy with these things, Second Fu's pa remained silent. He sat beside the stove, smoking pipe after pipe with a blue face. His son's behaviour had made him lose face. To mess one's pants was not the response of a macho guy who got into a pickle. He was the Brigade Commander. How could his son mess his pants in the forest ... Even the bunny rabbits will be sniggering over this.

After Second Fu had finished that bowl of honey water, his pa asked Second Fu in a sullen voice what it was that he had run into.

The bare-bottomed Second Fu sat under the quilt. He leant

against the wall, his mood still inscrutable. Upon realizing what his father was asking him, he answered still with a note of fear, "Saw ... saw ... a *big ... creature* ..."

His pa was relieved. He spat and then said, "Do you know what a *big creature* looks like? You have never seen one before, so how can you be sure that it was a *big creature*?"

Second Fu said, "That was a *big creature*. I've seen one on a propaganda poster in the commune office."

His pa explained, "It has been a long time since there were any *big creatures* in the Qinling Mountains. Even if there were, I go through the mountains every day and so ought to be able to find some trace of one. All these years, I've glimpsed no sign." Second Fu recalled, "The *big creature* was really big. It was yellow with stripes. Its mouth was smelly. Its eyes were like a couple of bells."

His pa said, "The more you talk about it, the more real it seems. If it really was a *big creature* Blackie would have howled. Blackie is the best hound in these parts. That happened a very short distance away from here. How come I heard nothing? If you really did run into a *big creature* how come you got home safe and sound?"

Second Fu searched about the room for Blackie. Blackie was crouching by the stove, also gazing at him.

Teacher Zhou said that Second Fu possessed a truly rich imagination ...

Second Fu's ma wept.

His ma consoled Second Fu by saying, "My child did see a *big creature*. The *big creature* showed friendliness towards my son. He is my son's big brother and my son is his younger brother."

Flower Bell exclaimed, "Today, Second Fu ran into his big brother Big Fu."

Then everyone shouted, "Big Fu! Big Fu!" as if there genuinely was a Big Fu at Birch Hills.

Second Fu stayed on the *kang* for a whole month suffering from diarrhoea.

They sent for the doctor, but the doctor insisted that this kind of running stomach was necessary in order for him to replenish his life force. That entire autumn Second Fu's pa dug for milk vetch roots. Second Fu's ma suggested that his gallbladder had been damaged by the shock, so she asked all the people to search high and low for the gallbladder of a leopard. She maintained that this was the only remedy that would properly repair his own sick organ. Second Fu thought, "I'm not a thermos. How can that hollow thing inside me be replaced?"

For one whole month, Second Fu ate a lot of milk vetch roots until he had nosebleeds, his body itched all over, and his face assumed the complexion of that herb. His diarrhoea eased up, but then constipation set in. Defecating became a hard task. It was a pity that he didn't manage to eat the leopard's gallbladder about which his ma was nagging *ad nauseum*. A leopard's gallbladder was tricky to find. Not all of the leopards in the Qinling Mountains were willing to act as donors. Zhang Jianshe did send him the gallbladder of a dog. The half-grown dog belonging to the Zhang family from the mountains of Rear Valleys had stepped into a trap and died. Zhang Jianshe took the special trouble of seeing that the gallbladder found its way to Second Fu. Second Fu's pa said that the gallbladder of a dog didn't pass muster. Zhang Jianshe complained, "How come it doesn't pass muster? It says in the book that 'a dog's gall can shake the heavens'."

Second Fu's pa opined, "That is not a good expression. What's more, the dog from the Zhang family is still young and tender. It never saw much of the world. Eating its gall would be no better than eating Blackie's? Blackie is one hundred times better than him."

Blackie felt those words were tart. He gave a disdainful glance at Second Fu's pa and went out with a grunt, leaving a stinking fart behind him in the room.

Second Fu thought, "I can eat any dog's gallbladder, but not Blackie's. At this special moment Blackie really is good for nothing."

IV

Winter came and the first snow fell in the mountains. The dancing and floating snowflakes matted over the mountain slopes completely. Second Fu's pa did not go out to dig herbs. He was busy from head to heel conducting the national population census. The county government had sent census cadres down to validate each household one-by-one. His pa chaperoned them as they went from the eastern ridge to the western ridge, from the Temple of the Three Officials to Big Drum Terrace. The mountain people lived very sparsely. Sometimes they could validate only a single family in a whole day, so the speed of the operation was exceptionally slow.

When his pa went out on official business, his ma took care of the pig in the sty. She cooked feed and spread dry earth on the ground, and hung up grass curtains mindful that the pig should not receive substandard treatment. This pig had been driven over from the scientific research station of the commune. It was a foreign strain, a York pig, entirely white and large-framed with erect ears. The animal ate heartily and fattened-up swiftly. According his mother's estimation, the pork would be ready before the Dragonboat Festival. Next year they would ask his pa to go to the station and get another York pig. In the future their family would only raise York pigs. While his ma was busying herself over the pig, she would take out a stool for Second Fu and ask him to bathe himself by the door. Second Fu sat by the front door of the house, looking at how the mountains flashed within the bright falling snow. This made him very excited. At that time, he did not know the lofty words of Chairman Mao's poem "Snow": "The mountains dance like a silver snake/ The highlands slither like huge wax elephants." In his small mind, he felt intense pride about the scenery of his hometown. Under the snow, the mountain wilderness slumbered silently. The road disappeared, the forest disappeared. There was only whiteness – whiteness up on high and whiteness down below. The sky was clear and blue. The clouds floated, materializing as apparitions from behind the mountains to the west. They gradually dispersed as they wandered towards Birch Hills. When they reached over Second Fu's head, nothing was left at all. A black spot nuzzled the snow-clad slope. It nosed to the east for a time and then to the west. It was Blackie, finding a means of amusing himself.

From staring at Blackie in the snow, Second Fu's mind shifted to thinking of Big Fu. Where was that glamorous, great creature spying and stalking now? It truly was a deity descended from the sky. The beast came without any warning: magisterial, fierce, proud, solitary, and having absolutely the air of a king. Whenever Second Fu recalled the chance encounter with Big Fu, there was a kind of joy hidden in the midst of the panic. It was fate, after all. After all, Big Fu did not inflict any harm upon him. Big Fu just studied him as he likewise studied Big Fu – a peaceful communion. Could that be because they were brothers? Up until now only Second Fu had seen Big Fu. Nobody else had the chance. Even to the present moment, most of the people, including his pa, doubted the existence of Big Fu. This made Second Fu sense the force of fate at work; a kind of natural fate from which he could not extricate himself. Slowly, in his heart Big Fu developed a kind of brotherly longing for Big Fu. He had a species of unspoken yearning for Big Fu. He was expecting to hear news about Big Fu, to see his shadow being cast down, and to hear his voice. Again and again, Second Fu shouted from the depths of his heart, "Big Fu! Big Fu! Where are you?"

From then on, nobody sighted Big Fu a second time. There were no traces of Big Fu in the forest either. Big Fu disappeared as suddenly as he had arrived.

The sun shone brightly and the brilliant snow glared people's eyes.

Second Fu's health slowly recovered. Chinese New Year came around in the blink of an eye.

His pa wanted to kill the York pig. His ma argued that it was not fat enough. They should wait two more months. His pa said that with two more months this old Yorkie would be transformed into the spirit of a pig. Even now the pigsty was too small to contain it. His ma countered that they couldn't kill the pig simply because the sty wasn't big enough. The logic was that people could not move home on account of their rooms being too narrow.

Second Fu knew that his pa was fond of meat. They hadn't tasted the flavour of meat for a long time. The meat of the mountain boar and the roe deer his pa hunted was very coarse. Folks were tired of eating it. Second Fu also expected that they would slaughter the pig. When the pig was killed, it would slash the amount of time they had to spend on housework. At least his ma would be able to put her feet up.

Anyhow, his ma refused to slaughter it. She claimed that she would rather go without meat over Chinese New Year.

How could Chinese New Year be allowed to pass without them eating any meat? On the twenty-third of December, with a bag of dried edible fungus, Second Fu accompanied his father to visit the fair at Windy Grass Terrace. Their main purpose was to purchase meat for consuming during the New Year period. When walking along the mountain roads, Second Fu became conscious of how lying on the *kang* for two months had left his leg in a weakened state. He walked with great effort, forcing his father to stand and wait for him with his basket on his back. While his pa was waiting there, he would forage around for black edible fungus. Black edible fungus is different from white edible fungus. Although both are types of fungus and have the same diuretic effect, one is dark-coloured and the other is light-coloured. The black one is awkward to find as it leaves no signs above ground. Usually, the herb-diggers depend on their experience and instinct to detect it, and not every pain yields gain. The black one is twice as expensive as the white. One pound of dried black fungus is worth eighty cents. Second Fu and his pa sold nine pounds, making an income of 7.2 yuan. Second Fu could calculate the income more speedily than Old Zhang at the herb collecting station. Second Fu was not stupid; he was just unclear about the calculation involving the pheasant and its eggs.

On leaving the collecting station, Second Fu's pa had bulging pockets. They decided to have a good stroll around the local fair and buy something to use over New Year. 7.2 yuan was a sizeable fortune for Second Fu's family. Pork cost only forty cents a pound and wheat flour only thirteen. The father let Second Fu do the calculations. With the cash in hand, they could afford eighteen pounds of pork or fifty-five pounds of wheat flour.

It was the last fair before the New Year. Relatively speaking, there were more people on the street. All paths from every direction led to Windy Grass Terrace. Similarly, the streams of folk coalesced in the town from every direction. Old and young, male and female – most of them were familiar with each other and so exchanged greetings in bellowing voices, asking about each other's recent progress. Second Fu saw so many of his classmates on the street. Flower Bell and her ma both had oily red mouths. One glance at them was enough to know that they had just polished off bowls of spicy cold noodles. Second Fu knew that these two oily red mouths would be the talk of the town and they would not be wiped clean until everyone had taken note of them and they had returned to their village in Rear Valleys. For mountain folk, going to the fair and eating spicy cold noodles represented both something entertaining and an opportunity to brag. One bowl of spicy cold noodles would cost eight cents and a pound of salt even less! Second Fu also knew that Flower Bell and her ma could only afford to share one bowl between them. Her ma's shrewdness meant that they were able to put on airs on the outside, though not have satisfaction in their stomachs.

Second Fu saw Wang Cheng too. He was selling two pheasants. His small sister tugged at the hem of his clothes like a lean cat as she stood shuddering beside him. All the time she gawped at passersby. Second Fu thought that if in the future his ma bore him such a lean and unprepossessing sister, who would tug at his hems and loiter on the street, he would feel ashamed to death. Teacher Zhou set up a big trestle table in front of the commune gate. He had volunteered to write out New Year couplets for the local farmers to pin up in their homes. The first set was free, but three cents would be charged for the second one. Most farmers only requested one, though they had to bring along their own red paper for him to write his calligraphy on. There was no reason to let someone write couplets for you and have them donate paper into the bargain. Second Fu's pa brought a piece of red paper and cut off two narrow strips. He gave the leftover piece to Second Fu and let him take it over to Teacher Zhou. When Teacher Zhou realized how large the sheet was, he knew exactly what to write. Without saying a word, he took up his brush and wrote, "Heaven, Earth, Emperor, Beloved, Teacher" on the paper. This scroll would be displayed on the wall in the middle of the main room over New Year's Eve. As for the two strips of paper, his pa would not let Teacher Zhou write anything on them. Were he to do so, they would have to pay. Like the rest of the mountain folk, Second Fu's pa had his own method. On returning home he would trace around the mouth of a bowl to leave a series of black circles on the red paper. Once they were hung on either side of the wall, these too would appear bright and joyful. Who could deny that they were couplets?

After the "couplet" was written, Second Fu followed his father to the butcher's stand. Butcher Huo knew his pa and also knew that his pa was the Brigade Commander. His words inclined towards flattery. When his father said that he was going to buy five pounds of fatty meat Butcher Huo chose the best available. The fat on the joint was about one inch thick. Moreover, he threw in a pig's tail as well. Butcher Huo then asked his pa whether or not he wanted a pig's head. His father did not refuse him, but asked for half a length of pig's intestines. He told Second Fu to wrap up the meat and guts in the oiled paper they had brought from home and then bind an extra layer of pine boughs around it to mask the fleshy smell. This package he placed at the bottom of their carrying basket. Later Second Fu followed his father to the cooperative store. The shelves in the store were all empty. They now only sold salt and packing paper, not to mention some basic items of stationery. His pa bought two feet of patterned textile with his clothing coupon. The fabric was decorated with red flowers and green leaves. Clearly, this was for a girl.

His pa said, "Your ma will give birth this coming spring ..."

Second Fu understood that his pa and ma were of the same mind. They desired a daughter, but Second Fu didn't want a younger sister.

Second Fu hoped that his pa would buy him a green plastic ruler with scales on it. He opened his mouth a number of times, though didn't speak it out. After all, that would have been an item of great luxury for him. How could a kid from the mountains use such an implement? When his pa asked him what he wanted, he bit his tongue and said he wanted nothing. Second Fu thought that at least his pa would take him to the restaurant in town for a decent meal. That had been his purpose in following him out there.

As expected, his pa asked him what he wanted to eat. This time Second Fu was unabashed. He said that he wanted to eat two bowls of vegetable tofu. His pa was in a generous mood today and permitted him to have three or more. He was sure to have his fill today. While talking, his pa led him to a small roadside food stall. He ordered two bowls of vegetable tofu and one bread bun for Second Fu. For himself he purchased two ounces of Chinese spirits and a plate of marinated pig's ear. The vegetable tofu was in fact a kind of porridge made from tender tofu and rice, a popular local dish in the south of Shaanxi

Province. No rice or tofu was produced in Birch Hills, so it was rare for people from there to eat this. A bowl of vegetable tofu cost two cents. Second Fu could therefore eat as much of it as he saw fit.

When his pa saw Second Fu's eyes lingering over the marinated pig's ear, he pulled the plate nearer to himself and said, "Your stomach has just recovered. You can't eat this. If you got another runny stomach all of the money we spent on herbs will have gone to waste."

Second Fu felt that his pa was too stingy, so he deliberately forced his way through six bowls of vegetable tofu. His belly distended like his ma's and he was incapable of bending over.

At the neighbouring table sat an old man from Erlang Pit. His surname was Zheng and his home village was Thick Boundary Commune. When Second Fu's pa went to dig herbs in Erlang Pit he once lodged at Old Zheng's home. Upon seeing him, the old man was delighted and moved his food over to their table to share it with them. The liquor he drank was distilled in-house from dried sweet potatoes. At the same time he chomped on home-pickled bracken. Hard and desiccated, long bouts of chewing were required to break down the fronds ... Old Zheng prattled on at his pa and described how recently a forestry centre had been established there. The logging team had entered the mountains and recruited more than twenty burly men, his six sons being among them. They had become salaried government-sponsored workers. Even on rainy days when they were idle, they still received pay. What is more, they were also given labour protection insurance. Their working uniforms were cut from brand new, hard-wearing khaki.

Second Fu's pa said admiringly, "It is a pity that such a good thing could not fall our heads at Birch Hills. How come you folks at Erlang Pit are so fortunate?"

Old Man Zheng said, "Erlang Pit is blessed with fine woodlands. All the trees there are tall firs. It is a primeval forest ..."

Second Fu's father pa commented that the trees at Birch Hills are too much of a hotchpotch.

Old Man Zheng invited Second Fu's pa to visit Erlang Pit in order to observe those tractors that have no need to consume grass, to witness people building roads with explosives, and to see their sons' brand new working uniforms.

Second Fu's pa finished those two ounces of liquor with Old Man Zheng and then they ordered two more, and finally a further two. When his father stood up, his two feet twisted over each other like a housewife plaiting garlic bulbs for drying. As he spoke his tongue seemed enlarged. He almost forgot to pick up the carrying basket from the foot of the wall. Once the father and son were filled with food and liquor, the two strolled about the streets for half a day. They bought the items his father thought important. When they started back home, the setting sun was only half a pole in height above the peaks of Copper Ridge. His pa decided to take the shortcut through Leopard Valley. Despite having to tread up and down the valley sides that ought to cut the journey time in half. They could reach home before dusk.

This was the route which Second Fu and Zhang Jianshe had taken once before, so they were quite familiar with it.

On the way back, Second Fu walked at the front and his pa stumbled on behind. His pa would take one steady step and then three wobbly ones, so their pace was very slow. When Second Fu and his pa reached the bottom of the valley the sky had become morose and small flakes of snow had begun to fall. The flakes disintegrated into tiny particles of ice, which tapped against the grasses and trees on the roadside with a rustle. Second Fu and his pa walked alongside the small stream. The almost-invisible road was clad with years of shed leaves. It was soft and easy under one's tread. The moss was thickly-piled and hirsute upon the rocks, blunting away the sharp edges. One walnut tree had been scratched by a panda and its bark bitten away, exposing the whiteness and making for a heart-wrench-ing sight. By the bank of the stream was amassed the dung of leopards. That pale complexion and solidified texture were the hallmarks of faeces from carnivorous animals. Walking further on, there was a swaying plank bridge. After that bridge was crossed and a slope was mounted, the family home was not far along the ridge from there on foot.

Behind Second Fu, his pa was wheezing. The unstable pa nearly lost his footing while crossing the bridge. Second Fu led his father step-by-step over the pass. The forest grew even darker and a gust of wind swelled up. Snowflakes were stirred upwards and the fragments slapped against their faces. That was excruciating. Second Fu realized that this wind had come too abruptly and without any forewarning. His back was permeated with cold sweat and his two legs started to become tender. Second Fu had experienced this feeling before. He was no stranger to it. He sensed that the creature was nearby, peering at them from close quarters.

Second Fu felt his runny stomach coming on.

One missed step and his pa bumped into Second Fu. His pa asked him why he had ground to a halt. Second Fu almost murmured into his pa's ears that "Big Fu is coming." His pa awoke from his stupor. He carefully inspected his surroundings, smelling in firmly with his nose. Second Fu noticed that the top of his father's head was drenched in perspiration. After a while, his pa relaxed and told him that it was not Big Fu but the black leopard from the forest. Second Fu maintained that it was Big Fu and there could be no mistake; he knew about it. His pa said that the black leopard had detected the scent of the intestines inside the basket. The leopard had been following them stealthily as they got down into the valley. He had been on their tracks for one-and-a-half kilometres. While complaining that Second Fu hadn't wrapped the intestines and meat up tightly enough, he pushed his son forward. Second Fu wondered how in that drunken state his pa could know that the leopard was following them. His pa told him that his body was intoxicated but his heart was sober. If a small weasel were to pop up its head in the forest, not even that would escape his attention. In order to confirm his judgement, his pa boomed out down the slope, "Go back! Don't follow us! There is no portion for you."

Another gust of wind whipped up.

Second Fu shook coldly.

Second Fu and his pa advanced. Unknowingly, the pair sped up. Second Fu said that his pa should have brought his rifle with him. His pa replied that if they had gone to the fair with a firearm the people at Windy Grass Terrace would have guffawed at them.

Climbing to the top of the ridge, the vegetation grew sporadic. On one tract of damp ground were several distinct, plum-like paw prints. The prints radiated dignity and deadly might. They were heart-stopping. His pa squatted down and measured the prints with his hands, not saying a word. Second Fu thought that in actual fact his pa knew everything. He had mentioned the black leopard only to pacify him lest he would be struck with terror once again.

v.

The primary school broke up for the winter holiday ahead of time and the start date for the next term was not yet fixed.

Big Fu was the cause of all these problems. Second Fu's pa wrote a report to the commune and they passed it onto the county government: the paw prints of a Southern China tiger had been found in Rear Valleys, Birch Hills and the Temple of the Three Officials. According to the observation, the tiger must be an adult specimen more than 400 pounds in weight. It may have migrated from Erlang Pit.

Two days after the Lantern Festival brought the New Year festivities to a close on 15th January, a hunter from Broken

Stone Roller Village by the name of Constant Happiness Shi reported to Second Fu's pa: the tiger had eaten somebody.

His pa asked him whom the tiger had devoured. Constant Happiness said that he didn't know, but the tiger had eaten somebody for sure.

Without any word, his pa picked up his hunting rifle and dashed to Broken Stone Roller Village with two members of the militia. Blackie, who enjoyed raucous situations, went out with them simple-mindedly. The dog, however, knew one thing – that the power of the master fortifies the bearing of the hound.

Broken Stone Roller Village stood near to the greater range of the Qinling Mountains. In former times it used to be an important stopping-off post for those travelling along the Ancient Tangluo Road. During the years of the Republic of China (1912-49), it was plagued with bandits. The ringleader of the bandits in Hanzhong, Three Springs Wang, massacred 103 people in the course of one night. The corpses were laid to the back of the village. Blood seeped down from the slope and the whole river was dyed scarlet. Those who survived escaped to other places faraway. The community was abandoned. Walls tumbled down and houses collapsed, leaving a scene of desolation. Later on, a pack of drought-fleeing beggars trekked along the ancient road from the north. They stayed here for three or five days and then left in a hurry. This place seemed forbidding. People believed that it had the strong vapour of the underworld. The wronged spirits of those hundred victims still hovered at large because to date nobody had avenged their loss.

Last summer vacation, Second Fu and Zhang Jianshe went to Broken Stone Roller Village for an adventure. They didn't run into any wronged spirits, only the moss-covered remnants of houses and walls and a stone tablet slumped among the wild grass. Since their education was limited, they could recognize none of the characters incised into the tablet. Wang Cheng, on the other hand, had a little knowledge. He recognized a huge letter denoting an "official." A few of them sat on the stone tablet for a long time and moaned that there was nothing interesting here. It would have been better if they had gone to the main street of Windy Grass Terrace and listened to Blind Pang singing his ballads. On his return from Broken Stone Roller Village, large itchy sores started to erupt all over Second Fu's body. His pa said that these were known as "ghost wind welts" and his ma blamed the stealthy wind for causing them. That there were fierce breezes in that area had nothing whatsoever to do with ghosts. From then on, Second Fu and his mates never frequented that place again.

This time his pa went there armed with a hunting rifle. It appeared that Big Fu's luck might be outweighed by danger.

Second Fu didn't know how he had managed to kill time for that whole day.

His pa returned under the cover of night. His pa said to his ma that the *big creature* had a voracious appetite. He chewed people whole, leaving no splinters of bone. His pa talked about what had happened over the dining table. This seemed to cause his pa acute distress. Judging from his pa's description, there was a half-collapsed earthen brick house in the east of the village. The right and rear walls had already given way, leaving only a shabby door and window frame. To the left of the room was a *kang*, though half of it had crumbled.

When his pa arrived, he discovered ashes on the ground. Someone had been warming himself there. The worn cotton quilt had been shredded into pieces. Small fragments of cloth were everywhere. On the snowy ground outside there were the traces of a fight. The footprints of a man and the paw prints of a tiger mingled pell-mell. On the approach to the forest were sprinkled human hairs and bloodstains ...

His ma listened with goosebumps all about her person. She asked, "Is our York pig ok?"

His pa grunted, "You are only bothered about pigs! Something that affects human lives has happened in the mountains.

We must inform the commune. Tomorrow I have to go to Windy Grass Terrace."

His ma didn't know who had been eaten by the tiger. His pa said that the scraps of cloth gave the impression of having come from a patched-up garment. The victim may have been someone who migrated there from the north to escape the drought. His ma said that no matter who has been eaten it was a pitiful thing. She went on to say that Second Fu had been lucky. He had dangled his life before the eyelids of that creature. No wonder Second Fu had been frightened in that way. His pa said that if the *big creature* were not done away with, the primary school could not resume classes. If any of the kids ran into danger, he as the Brigade Commander would not be able to shirk his duty.

The news of the tiger eating a man soon spread around the villages. When evening came every household would secure their gate tightly. What had been backwaters to begin with were now even less populous. If people had to go outside, they would do so in groups of three or five, brandishing some kind of weapon. Everybody processed along the road with caution just like those common people did on the tiger-infested Jingyang Ridge, as described in *The Water Margin*.[a]

His ma added three wooden fences to make the perimeter of the pigsty higher so it became one head taller than Second Fu. His pa said that his ma was doing things blindly. He said that no matter how fierce a tiger might be it would still be wary of people. The tiger would not descend on farming families. It had its own territory and didn't charge about randomly.

His ma said, "The best thing would be for him not to come at all, but if that ten thousand to one chance goes against us …"

His pa said, "It won't happen. Even if it does, Blackie won't stand for that."

Second Fu thought that his Pa was expecting too much of Blackie. His pa didn't know the truth about Blackie. Still, he was unwilling to blurt this out to his pa. That dog was theirs.

They should keep face for it. It was better that his pa slowly got to know about Blackie for himself. At this moment, Blackie was tugging at his pa's trousers with a sloppy mouth. He had just made his way over from the pigsty.

Flower Bell's home was located in Rear Valleys. Big Fu had gulped down half of their cow. Flower Bell's grandpa dropped in on Second Fu's pa with the cow's bell. Full of accusation, he demanded that he tackle the menace.

Second Fu's pa said, "You've come to me. What means do I have?"

Flower Bell's grandpa said, "You are the Brigade Commander. If you don't have the means, who does?"

Second Luck He from the Temple of the Three Officials also visited Second Fu's pa and claimed that his sheep was gone. It was a big, sturdy ewe, though vamoosed with not a sound that evening.

"How do you know that it was taken away by a tiger?" Second Fu's pa asked.

"What else could have done this!" Second Luck He snarled.

The cow from the Flower family, the sheep from the He family, the pig from the Li family, and the chicken from the Zhang family – so many losses were slung on Big Fu's shoulders. Not being content with just picking off the wild animals from the mountains, Big Fu did indeed stoke up a hearty appetite. In a matter of days he had swallowed half a cow, then eaten a whole sheep ...

Soon afterwards, Big Fu paid a call on Second Fu's home.

That day, Second Fu's pa had gone to the commune to attend a Three Scale Meeting for cadres. The Three Scales of the meeting referred to the commune, the big brigade and the small brigade. That meeting was exceedingly important for it was about the sending the Four Cleanups Movement groups to the villages.[b] The working group was about ...

His pa didn't come back that day, even after dark.

Experiencing some discomfort, his ma went to the *kang*

without even feeding the pig. She stroked her protruding belly and said that she might be ready to deliver tonight. She asked Second Fu to be on the alert even while he slept and if anything were to happen he should go down the slope to call for Fourth Girl's grandma. She then cursed Second Fu's father and pronounced, "May your pa die outside. Going to those endless dull meetings – worth no more than a fart. He never cares about his family." His ma then asked Second Fu to remember that in the future he could do anything he liked as long as he didn't become a cadre … Second Fu pleaded with his ma to take it easy and told her that he would never choose to be a cadre even if someone threatened to beat him to death.

Second Fu woke up after midnight. He heard his ma humming. He asked her whether or not he should go and call for Fourth Girl's grandma. His ma answered that it was still early and they ought to wait until daybreak. As soon as those words were spoken, they heard a bumping sound outside. It was the noise of a heavy object dropping into the pigsty. His startled ma sat up. She pushed away the quilts and called out, "Second Fu, get up. The big creature is coming." Second Fu shrank beneath his quilt.

His ma was indeed bold. She picked up the stick used for propping the door closed, kicked the door open, and went out with a loud shout. Second Fu saw that blood was trickling down from her body. The responsibility of a man and the duty of a son prevented Second Fu from staying in the room any longer. He leapt over to the rear courtyard naked, discovering that the gate of the pigsty was tightly closed, though the fat swine had vanished. Big Fu had hoisted a live pig out over the top of the fence with his mouth. How accomplished this Big Fu was!

The pig was his ma's root of life. His ma's heart ached over the pig. She screamed and made desperate chase through the night. Second Fu was worried about his ma. He was hot on her heels. The mother and son raced over the freshly-ploughed cornfields behind their home, ran around the pond, and made pursuit along the small path on the fringe of the forest. They were shouting all the way, utterly insensible as to their own safety.

Although he had a pig in his grip, Big Fu moved swiftly. The nape of the pig's neck was clamped into the jaws of the tiger. The pig did not even emit a murmur. Big Fu advanced with ease. Now and then he would turn around and glance at the mother and son who were chasing after him. Sometimes he even paused so as to select the route which would be easier to drag his prey down. No matter what might transpire, he had no intention of surrendering it.

Second Fu and his ma were already fatigued. The distance between them and Big Fu widened and widened …

Second Fu's pa sat in the meeting for half a night and he came back to Birch Hills at daybreak. When he saw the familiar house in the early morning sunshine he extinguished the pine taper he was carrying for light. The relief of having reached home made him happy. He shouted volubly towards the house several times.

Blackie dashed out like an arrow towards the home, barking madly. Blackie's abnormal behaviour unsettled his pa. He peered at the top of the house and at once noticed that something was amiss. Where was the kitchen smoke that should be creeping through the tiles? Where were the rowdy chickens that should be in front of the house? Where was the shadow of his wife stalking in and out of the door?

The home had taken on a terrifying tranquillity.

Second Fu's pa dashed to the front door, which turned out to be latched on the inside. He shouted for Second Fu for a long time without any answer. He was in such a state of worry that his timbre altered. Blackie was barking at the rear of the house. His pa then suddenly remembered something and dashed to rear of the dwelling. There he discovered that the back door was wide open and that the pig was gone from the sty. Across the courtyard was a mixture of footprints – those of human beings and a tiger, smeared with gory apostrophes. Following the footprints through the soft fields, his pa could discern his wife's treads and those of his son mingled with the paw marks left by the tiger. They wound towards the mountain ridges. His pa poked at the blood on the ground and then rubbed it between his finger and thumb. He could then confirm that it was human blood, and so let out a loud call and took several strides in that direction before turning back and heading for the commune.

VI.

Two people had disappeared from Birch Hills. How could the tiger create so much trouble! It wouldn't do.

The commune at once deployed Lai Guangyi, Lai Guangmin and six other militia men to dash over after Second Fu's father to Birch Hills. They were armed with two rifles and a handgun.

Second Fu's pa was hungry for revenge, so he accelerated up in front, easily outpacing the militia. None of the militia spoke. They all knew that no matter how fast they went the mother and son would still be dead. Children and women always lose out when they take on a tiger. Needless to say, that particular woman was on the brink of delivering.

After covering several ridges and slopes, there was no trace of the tiger. The group then walked along the mountain ridges to the west. In this way, their line of vision could become broader and they would be able to observe the slopes on both sides. The southern slope was dense with forests. The northern slope was full of wild grasses and scattered rocks and dead lumber. Second Fu's pa asked them to pay greater attention to the northern slope and said that the tigers like sunny slopes as opposed to gloomy forests. Thus everybody looked to the northern slope, not missing a blade of grass or a stump of rock.

It was Blackie who had first hit upon this abnormal situation. Originally he ran ahead of everyone, but then suddenly he made an about turn. Weaving himself between the legs of Second Fu's pa, he refused to proceed further.

Second Fu's pa said in a low voice, "There is something up in front!"

All of the militia was well-trained. They were not hoodlums. Each one of them observed the lay of the land and chanced upon a big rock behind which they could shelter. They soon detected Big Fu about fifty metres away among the grass. The sated Big Fu crouched there cozily like a pussy cat. With his front paws covering his mouth, he was basking in the delicious sunshine.

Cheng Decai said, "How can that be a tiger? It's a huge cat."

Second Fu's pa didn't care whether it was a huge cat or not. He tilted his rifle, ready to fire. Cheng Decai stopped him and warned, "This big creature is not simple to handle. If one shot doesn't kill it, it's sure to agitate it. If that's the case none of us will get out of here in one piece. We should come up with a strategy."

They started to discuss strategy behind the rock. They finally agreed that since handguns and hunting rifles had limited fire power, they should try to dispatch it at close range. The two rifles were the first to discharge. The rest of them were on the alert with their sticks like Wu Song making ready to fight with the tiger.[c]

The tiger was slumbering peacefully. If he knew that so many people were wracking their brains over him, he would be flush with pride.

Lai Guangmin and Cheng Decai each gripped a rifle. Both of them were crack shots. They had won red flags in the county-level militia contest. If the two of them launched their attack, there was not a chance of them missing. A distance of fifty metres was small beer to them because they had been trained to shoot over a range of 200.

Second Fu's pa said, "When I say 'ready fire' you should shoot at the same time. We must succeed. Failure is not an option."

The two men agreed.

The two rifles aimed at the sound asleep Big Fu.

Second Fu's pa asked, "Are you ready?"

The two guys said, "Yes, ok."

Second Fu's pa said, "Ready – fire."

Cheng Decai's rifle discharged, whereas the bullet remained lodged in Li Guangmin's weapon.

Cheng Decai lived up to his reputation as a crack shot. He had aimed at the tiger's head and the bullet struck in the exact spot. Beyond everybody's expectation, Big Fu did in fact belong to the cat family. The members of the cat family have their own fixed sleeping position. Its massive paw was shielding half of its head, so Cheng Decai's shot struck the foot.

Big Fu stood up with a start. He roared and swung his front paw, not knowing what had just happened. His roar caused the earth and the mountain to shake. The sound was sullen, angry, sad, powerful, deep, and penetrating. It roused the birds and made the trees shed their leaves. It seemed that the whole forest was shuddering. The crack shots did not know where to fire next. The contests had required them to hit black and white targets. They had never encountered something with such animation.

The disgruntled Big Fu lost his temper. He angrily swung around again and then again. His tail swept powerfully through the air once and then twice. While the grass was scythed down in large bunches, a shrubby tree was dashed in two. All at once, dust pervaded the surroundings. Rocks were cast into motion. Big Fu repeatedly reared himself up straight and then bumped down. The agony of its paw was difficult to bear. He soon discovered the group behind the rock. Without hesitating he roared resonantly and bounded in their direction.

Those behind the rock became addled. Great danger had appeared. Cheng Decai yelped desperately, "Fire! Fire!"

All of the guns fired simultaneously.

The assorted guns shot all at once directly at Big Fu. Big Fu stumbled and ground to a standstill on the middle of the slope. It was in that moment that the people could clearly see the tiger's pure and bewildered eyes, so full of miscomprehension. If we use the original words reported by the journalist at that time, the look in its eyes had been "etched into their hearts ... Lai Guangli was to feel deep regret ..." The wounded Big Fu gave up on his attack and turned and withdrew to the east. He could not run any more. With great difficulty he made his retreat.

Lai Guanyi's shot struck his forehead. Big Fu had lost his self-control. He let out his last long roar and slid to the bottom of the valley.

The bitter and painful roar shook the souls of the hunters. Those people behind the rock remained motionless for a long time. They appeared impotent and had neither the haughtiness of victors, nor the visceral joy of somebody who had found revenge. Their brains were empty. It was the intervention of the heavens that had forced them to hear Big Fu's last farewell. Their offspring and the offspring of their offspring would never hear such a voice. They would never hear it ...

An hour passed. Second Fu's pa pointed out, "We cannot hide here forever."

Lai Guangmin said, "We don't know whether he's dead or not."

The party clambered up from behind the rock. They jostled and tried to push one another in front so that they might be the one to look down the slope. The bushes through which Big Fu had slid were crushed down to form a deep groove. There were many trees at the bottom of the valley and there was no sound, nor could they see anything. Cheng Decai told them to pelt stones and toss sticks down there. They dropped so many projectiles, though still no noise could be heard from below.

They all sat there waiting. What they were waiting for nobody could tell.

Another hour passed. Cheng Decai said, "We must go down and take a look."

Everybody looked at each other, but no one was willing to volunteer.

Second Fu's pa proposed, "Let Blackie go. Blackie is bold. He has the blood of a leopard."

Blackie never thought that Second Fu's pa could have had such an ulterior motive. He wouldn't go. He stood at the opening of the groove made by Big Fu, refusing to budge no matter how hard Second Fu's pa tried to drive him. Second Fu's pa lost his temper. He asked Cheng Decai to help him. Each of them grasped a pair of Blackie's legs and on a shout of "One, Two, Three" prepared to throw him down to the bottom of the valley.

Blackie gave a lamentable yip and the sound was ugly on the ears. He didn't know how to curse. If he did he would wish that his "doggy blood would drench his head." They swung him several times and then Blackie was thrown. Blackie traced an artful arc with his body through the air. He fell with a shrill, despairing howl.

Everybody looked down to the bottom, expecting that Blackie would relay some information. Hardly had the two throwers relaxed themselves when Blackie crawled up from a few metres away. When he reached the top he didn't look in the direction of the human beings, but turned around and ran away. He had seen through what men were.

An everlasting barrier had been erected between Blackie and Second Fu's pa. This barrier would persist until the two of them departed this world and was never to be breached.

The group of people came to the bottom of the valley. They saw Big Fu lying between two rocks, his body outstretched to a massive length and his eyes closed as if he were enjoying a cozy sleep. More than thirty years later when a journalist wrote an article entitled 'The Fate of the Last South China Tiger in Qinling' for the *Xi'an Evening Post* his closing summation was on how: "The tiger's face was covered with blood. His angry eyes were wide open and he was fixed in a squatting posture ... Lei Guangyi and the others could not relish any joy now. The dead, but not restful shadow and the regretful eyes of the tiger were etched into their heart." When Second Fu talked with me about this report he said that the writing had been coloured by the emotions of the journalist. It was strongly idealized to boot. If one were to produce a television drama on this subject, these effects could be made to convey a symbolic meaning. The fact was, though, that the tiger was simply lying dead between two rocks on the valley floor.

I believe in the veracity of Second Fu's words, but I can understand what the journalist was driving at as well.

The tiger was carried to Second Fu's home and laid out on the ground outside the house. Second Fu squatted beside him, stroked the creature's disordered fur and limp body and limbs. Big Fu's corpse was still lukewarm. Second Fu said in his mind that this was Big Fu, his elder brother ...

His elder brother was dead. He had died in a truly miserable manner. Could his elder brother be held to blame? He was not at fault for he had to eat in order to survive.

The weeping of an infant was to be heard from inside the house. It turned out that when Second Fu and his mother had chased over onto the mountain ridge, they discovered the two legs of the pig that Big Fu had left over from his meal. The mother and son carried them home. Hardly had they arrived home, when his mother went into labour. She bore him a pair of twin brothers. From then on the family had a Third Fu and a Fourth Fu.

The patterned floral cloth his pa had bought at Windy Ridge Terrace was obsolete.

VII

The following paragraphs concern the aftermath of Big Fu's demise. It may not be necessary to write about these matters, yet I feel that it is better to give the reader a more rounded account. Writing this gives me no sense of pleasure.

On the second day, Big Fu was strung up on the eaves of Second Fu's house. Butcher Huo was personally to dismember the beast with Second Fu's pa as his assistant. They were going to skin and gut the tiger. Folks came over from far and near, even those from Windy Grass Terrace and Thick Magnolia Blossom Village dropped by to be spectators on this rare situation.

Big Fu's cadaver was hung vertically for its full length. His four paws swung powerlessly.

Under the chairmanship of the Communist Party Secretary, the clerk was required to write a solemn record:

... Male, weight: 225 kilos, body length: 2 metres, tail length: 0.9 metres ...

What a big brute!

All the people exclaimed, gasped, and gave praise.

Butcher Huo had skinned countless pigs, though this was the first time he had to flay a tiger. Despite being dead, the tiger still possessed sufficient power to dwarf the people around him. Huo's hand which bore the knife shook. He pondered matters for a while and then reached for a bowl of liquor, which he sprinkled before the creature as a sign of reverence. He murmured some sort of incantation, which no one could hear even the gist of.

The peeling proceeded from the mouth of the tiger and then the chest was exposed. Within the time it would take to eat a meal, a perfect and intact tiger pelt had been removed.

The bystanders formed a semi-circle. They watched in silence and nobody coughed, let alone spoke. The wind was whooping in a way that made hearts feel heavy ...

Butcher Huo's knife stabbed into the tiger's larynx. Blood

gushed out. Fourth Girl's grandma caught the liquid in a small plate. Courteously she carried it into the house and daubed the character for "king" on the foreheads of Third Fu and Fourth Fu. The two small babies with bloodied heads started to kick and cry loudly. Fourth Girl's grandma said, "Grow up, grow up smoothly and peacefully. Your elder brother is protecting you."

In the courtyard Big Fu's belly had been sliced open. All of the people suddenly lurched forward. Each of them prodded for some blood and wiped it onto their bodies. They all wanted to have some good fortune transmitted to them from the tiger. The Party Secretary asked them to keep their distance so as not encroach upon the workspace of Butcher Huo and Second Fu's pa. The Party Secretary asserted, "The tiger is the property of the state. The state has the right to decide how it is treated." Of course, as a local state official he also had to take into account the interests of local people. He was not about to let local people get the short end of the stick.

Big Fu's stomach and intestines had been dragged out and scattered on the ground, becoming caked with dust. Second Fu's pa took out the green gallbladder especially and cautiously placed it on the stone beside him. The gallbladder was the size of a baby's head.

Soon the huge Big Fu had been transformed into a mound of hide, skeleton, and reddish flesh.

The meat and pluck were divided among the local families who had been menaced by Big Fu. Each would be awarded three pounds of fat. The bones were sold to the herb-collecting station with every pound being appraised at forty-eight yuan. Apart from the skull, Big Fu's skeleton weighed forty-nine pounds, having a total worth of 2,352 yuan …

Everybody went home contentedly with the meat from Big Fu. When they were all gone, Second Fu's pa suddenly thought of the gallbladder he had left balancing on the stone, but when he went to retrieve it the organ was no longer there. The father told Second Fu that he didn't care about the fat and meat. He only wanted the tiger's gallbladder. Heroes possess the gall of a tiger. This was its most precious component. It was hard to obtain. On hearing his pa's sentiments, Second Fu helped him to make a speedy search for the thing.

Second Fu and Zhang Jianshe saw that Blackie was chewing some unpalatable repast on the other side of the door. His doggy face had been dyed green. The two scrabbled to remove it from Blackie's mouth and found that the object was what was left of the membrane from the gallbladder. Second Fu's pa was livid and got ready to beat Blackie. However, Blackie leapt so high and squared up to his master.

Second Fu's pa roared, "You've eaten the tiger's gallbladder. You bastard dog! How dare you."

Blackie barked at Second Fu's pa without any sign of weakness.

Second Fu thought, "A gallbladder from any creature is surely not delicious to eat. Blackie's swallowed Big Fu's gallbladder with a grimace. He has decided to take on my pa and make him furious."

Second Fu believed that his father deserved it.

The meat of the tiger was rank. Later on when I visited Windy Grass Terrace some folks told me that tiger flesh was far less delectable than that of a wild boar. The flavour was sour. I met one of the cadres by the name of Wang who had once come over here to conduct an inspection. He said that during that period of time their commune always staged meeting which lasted until the middle of the night. When they were hungry they would boil noodles because there was no catering. In spite of its bright yellow glistening appearance, the piece of tiger's fat they sliced and diced had no taste in the mouth. Still it exerted some sort of strong heat, since while they were eating they had to remove their cotton padded coats.

I once asked Second Fu about this, but he denied that tiger's flesh or tiger's fat ever passed his lips.

The tiger's hide was later commandeered by the Animal

Research Institute and fashioned into a taxidermy specimen. Whoever sees it can exclaim that this was the last tiger to have walked among the Qinling Mountains.

No one knows that his name was Big Fu.

On Camera

I

"On camera" is a piece of jargon used in the media circle. It actually means to make an appearance on the film screen. If you mention this word to ordinary people most of them will not understand it. If you mention it to a peasant he will be more perplexed still.

At the moment I am talking to a peasant about the problem of being on camera.

The peasant I am speaking to is the Village Head, Old Man Defu. He is sixty-three this year. As per the cadre system he should have retired long ago. Defu still remains in post, mainly because they cannot find a suitable successor. This village is too poor and lacks rain and running water, so nobody is willing to take on the role. Upper Mirth Village used to be the encampment of Li Zicheng (1606-45), the peasant rebel who became emperor. It was from here that Li Zicheng quit the mountains and rode directly to the imperial palace. Ninety per cent of the villagers have inherited the spirit of Li Zicheng. To quote the words of the Curator of the County Cultural Centre, they have "a strong rebellious streak" and "a vigorous battling spirit." Those who have had contact with people of Upper Mirth Village know that the villagers are easily incited to take up anything that can serve as a weapon. When some matter crops up, they will come to bloody blows first and then discuss it later. What is more, their tussles follow a unique patter, which includes scratching, biting, jabbing, grabbing, kicking, shaking, beating, and wrestling. They employ all these skills very adeptly and to perfection. If one were to deploy a national-level martial arts squad to fight with them not even they would be able to win. No matter how capable you are, should one of the locals refuse to fight with you there is no alternative way of dealing with him. On this point, they have inherited the spirit of Li the Insurgent King. Maybe Li Zicheng fought with the Ming Imperial Court in this way and thereby proved victorious. In Upper Mirth Village whoever wishes to be the Village Head must be fully-prepared to be beaten by other people. It is said that since Defu became the Village Head his scalp has been sliced open four times. There are forty or fifty stitches from the top to the bottom where it has been sewn back together. Someone claimed, "If the Village Head shaved off his hair, his head would look like a basketball. It has segments clearly picked out on the surface."

Our camera team came here from Beijing. We have been shooting footage for several days. We chose this place as our location simply because our Director Upright Li was rusticated here for three months during the Cultural Revolution. By the fourth month, he was violently driven away. According to my estimation, Upright Li was himself a troublemaker. When he was young, activities like stealing chickens and dogs and plucking off the shoots from the farmers' garlic proved too tempting for him to avoid. His forcible ejection from Upper Mirth Village must have been a case of "it takes more than one palm to make a clap." Li Zicheng was not entirely to blame. When Upright Li recalls what happened at that time his heart still flutters with fear. He says, "Barren mountains and untamed rivers produce wild people. The villagers there are really wild." "Wild and unruly folks are surely no match for you, Upright Li," I remark. "In recent years, you've been running rings around everyone in the media circle, and to great success! You've given us full proof that you did in fact stay in this village for a while. You are a trickster too."

We selected this spot as the location for the TV serial *The Sun is Still Red* because we were satisfied with the scenery here. The more barren and unruly the mountains and rivers are, the more splendid the scenery will be. The more inaccessible and un-trodden by traffic the less interference from modern civilization there will be. Today, such locations are becoming increasingly difficult to find.

Upright Li must coordinate the crowd scenes in Upper Mirth Village.

The hitch is that Upright Li dare not meet the Village Head Defu face-to-face. Perhaps the old man has some hold over him. He has asked me, the scriptwriter, to go and negotiate these matters. He said that the peasants have an instinctive closeness and trust where women are concerned, while his reputation in the village is the pits. Were he to approach Defu maybe there would be no way of pulling things off.

I said, "As far as shooting a TV series goes, if something is a goer it's a goer, if it's not it's not. The two parties should engage in discussion. Neither the village nor the team should make the situation hard for one another."

Upright Li replied, "If it goes like that it will be great."

II.

When Defu hears that I want to invite the peasants of Upper Mirth Village to appear on camera he blinks for a while and says nothing. I am afraid that he may not catch my meaning, so explain it once again with gesticulations, "It is just a crowd scene. No acting skills needed. Anybody can do it. As far as pay is concerned, the team will not treat the folk unfairly."

After having thought about it for some time Defu seems to finally cotton on. He hacks repeatedly and then says slowly, "Let everybody appear … on … on what?"

I say, "On camera."

"Ah, yes, on camera. It's a good thing," Defu comments. "For the villagers this is their only chance in maybe a hundred or a thousand years. *Print* their activities on camera and let all of the folks in China see them. Such a fortune usually only drops down on those big stars in the city, so how can we not let it fall on our heads? Upright Li, that little weasel, might have gotten to be a great ... great ... great what?"

I say, "A great director."

Defu adds, "Ah, right, a great director. This means that he still remembers us."

"This is a big scene," I say. "Extra people are needed. It's a crucial part of the drama."

Defu replies, "I see, I know this. I've watched the TV. Now there are more than fifty TV sets in our village. Everybody knows what it's like to shoot a TV drama. This can help the spread of cultural civilization. It echoes the calls of the folks higher up. The villagers should wholeheartedly support it."

"This is for the best. You can enlist all the people. We will pay five yuan per head per day."

"How can you act like such a good comrade? You are the one taking pictures of us. How can we ask money from you? Last year a photographer came to our village. He charged twenty yuan for taking photos – still shots – but this time you are making moving pictures. Don't mention money, it will drive a wedge between us."

I say that this may be improper.

"It's nothing serious," Defu insists. "This is Upright Li's thing. We should help him. Let's do it like this. Play it as if it were a village festival. If you only lay on a meal for the villagers that will be fine."

"That's normal," I explain. "When shooting a TV drama the team will also provide a meal for the extras in the crowd, as is customary. This is included in the budget."

"But you intend to load cold meals into plastic boxes and fetch them over from the county town," Defu hazards. "If you make us eat that it's playing us for fools. It's better for us to do all the cooking together. You can have a few steamers full of buns and cook a big pot of cabbage with tofu. Farmers' meals cannot be compared with what is eaten by those stars. There's no need to make loads of dishes and soups as long as we can fill our boots."

"Then let's do as you say. You can let the accountant submit your expenses slip to the team."

All of the matters are easily arranged and stand in good order. Defu sends me out to the village committee and, standing on the step, he shouts, "You tell that little weasel Upright Li that he should come for a stroll around the village when he's free. Nowadays nobody has the will to settle their dog shit scores with him."

I ask him what dog shit scores Upright Li has left unsettled in the village.

"As far as the hens in the village are concerned, he stole away seventy or eighty of them in one month. Then none of the families in the village could have eggs and all the village roosters were made into bachelors."

I say there is no wonder that he was branded a "weasel."

III.

The shoot is fixed for Monday. On Sunday I receive the word. It is said that Upper Mirth Village has slaughtered a pig and a sheep; several strong men went to the county town and brought back 200 pounds of tofu together with a cart laden with fresh produce. A number of women ground wheat the whole day long and have spent two days steaming buns. The buns are massive, being almost half-pounders. The pork and mutton are stewed separately. A huge pair of pots for meat steam with fragrant aroma. The 200 villagers busy themselves preparing for a big feed, with the real prospect of appearing on camera tomorrow. Added to that, every family has relatives from other villages lodging in their houses. These people will not only take part in the shooting, but also try to claim their share of Monday's feast.

The situation is pressing.

The film producer tracks me down and says, "You've promised that Upper Mirth Village will be paid its expenses according to what they have consumed. Now they are fully-prepared for their big eat. What should we do about the per capita fees and the cost of the pig and sheep they bought?"

"What can I do?" I ask. "They insist that they are not used to the boxed meals eaten by our crew. I thought that they genuinely might not be used to them. I didn't expect that they would play tricks on me. I've already reduced the payment from ten yuan to five for each person. I think we've gotten off lightly there. Defu has not asked about labour costs, only about the cost of the meal. He really is very cunning …"

The producer says, "Peasants have their own kind of small-mindedness. We can never beat them where playing tricks is concerned. Why didn't Upright Li come to Upper Mirth Village on his own? Simply because he has seen through all of this."

"So that's how it is? If this is the case, we will deal with it tomorrow – play it by ear. Just as long as we don't get into a fight."

"Fight?" the producer exclaims. "Even ten teams our size are no match for those offspring of Li Zicheng!"

The next day after breakfast, the crew goes to Upper Mirth Village in two baker's delivery-style vans.

The vast and empty riverbank is the chosen location. When we arrive there the place is already darkly jammed with people. A guy named Lock tells us that he has been waiting here since before daybreak. All of his family have come along and hope that they can appear on camera.

Fog hangs above the land. People cannot see around clearly. In the midst of the fog Defu walks towards the van. Upright Li jumps out in a hurry to greet him. The two first shake hands and then pat one another on the shoulder, pummelling each other like they are cut from the same cloth. Upright Li asks Defu whether he has used the same mobilizing tactic that worked when recruiting hands to excavate the local reservoir. "Do people really need mobilizing?" Defu wonders. "No need to call out loud. Every last one of them is trying to elbow their way to the front. The village sees this as a chance to stick their fingers in some cultural civilization. The village committee has been discussing it over a couple of nights." I notice that Defu's attire is unusual today. Where his beard had formerly been is shaved and he is wearing a new felt hat and leather shoes. The small white collar of his shirt pokes strategically out from beneath his Mao suit. This deliberate touch of refinement is the handiwork of a woman. The producer has perhaps already sensed something from the manner in which Defu is dressed. He stands silently alongside him patting his chin with his hand.

The fog gradually disperses. Everything all around becomes clear. The people on the riverbank are exposed beneath the sunlight. We are greatly shocked when we catch sight of the group of extras Defu has recruited.

The peasants have come to appear on camera.

The most eye-catching of the lot is Defu's mother. She is perhaps ninety years old. Flanked by her grandson and his wife she stands unsteadily at the forefront of the crowd. Her satin coat hangs over her shoulders, the arms not being threaded through the sleeves. This has been done so that nobody can fail to notice its plush sheepskin lining.

All of the men are wearing brand new clothes. They dare not move their hands and feet since they are conscious of their delicateness. Every last one of them is as reticent as newly-unearthed terracotta warriors. The props manager distributes some specially-made pitchforks and sticks among them. Holding these props in their hands, while wearing brand new clothes the people are overcome with a comical feeling, a sensation of being neither fish nor flesh. An air of insincerity is all-pervasive.

The several guys who wear suits are perhaps the village *fashionistas*. Naturally, they are unwilling to rip the brand labels off from their sleeves. They refuse to handle any of the props in order that they might retain their grace. As soon as the film camera focuses in their direction they channel the image of the modern dandy.

The women are all in floral dresses. The younger ones have without exception powdered their faces. The aged ones have combed their hair brightly smooth. The bolder specimens sport hairpins. Most striking of all are the kids who are being carried around in people's arms. They dot the crowd with their light purple and yellow colours.

Upright Li says to me, "You can take charge of arranging everything for the shoot. Call me when you've finished." After those words, he disappears.

I pull Defu to one side and query, "What are you doing? All of you look slick and shiny. We cut a deal that we would recreate the conditions of the 1960s. It's the 1960s, you know? We are staging a fight with hand-tools between rival villages. We are not putting on a nineties fashion fair for the countryside."

Bearing the whites of his eyes, Defu maintains, "I didn't ask them to dress like this. They did it by themselves."

"Why did you let this happen?"

"I am the Village Head. Wherever I go I am the representative of Upper Mirth Village. I should not appear too humble on camera or else I will lose face in front of others. What is more, you didn't tell me beforehand that you were putting on a fight scene."

"All of you are scared of losing face, so you've concocted this riot of colour. Just think of it. In the 1960s you were too hungry to even raise your heads. How could you afford these leather shoes, suits and fur overcoats? Listen, get rid of these new clothes. Put on what you would have been wearing in the 1960s. This is no joke!"

"I'm afraid that stuff is hard to lay our hands on."

"If it is hard to find just put on what you wear at ordinary times. Don't dress like you are attending traditional festivals."

Defu passes on the word to others, but nobody is willing to relinquish their personal glamour.

"Doolally!" Defu's mother blurts out. "Who doesn't wear new clothes when they are having their picture taken? If we wear old clothes it sends out an unlucky impression of us."

"This isn't taking a picture," I point out. "This is making a TV drama. Honourable Grandmother, please sit up there on the slope and watch this boisterous scene. Don't add to our troubles down here."

Defu's mother starts, "If I cannot leave a moving image of myself now, I will never have a chance in the future. How can I just sit by and watch that boisterous scene?"

The producer loses his temper. He raises a loud speaker and shouts into the crowd, "Women and kids, all of you leave!"

The women start to dive into the crowd and secrete themselves behind the men. Nobody departs.

The producer shouts a number of times but still nobody will leave.

It is windy and cold along the riverbank. Some kids start to cry. The two parties are engaged in a tug-of-war, with neither prepared to yield. I am suddenly put in mind of the situation in a movie when the Japanese soldiers enter a village and threaten the residents. This is somewhat like singing a different tune but with the same skill.

I find Upright Li in the van. He is sleeping with his head covered. I relate to him the situation. Upright Li says, "You see, you've really botched things up. A few strapping chaps alone won't be enough to put matters in good order. Wait and see." With those words he jumps from the van and comes to the scene.

Now blue-faced, Upright Li says, "Women come out. This is men's business. Why should women come over to interfere? Third Auntie, Ershun's mother, Sixth Sister-in-law, you all come out and stand on the slope. You few guys in suits come out. You and you and you …"

A smattering of people does break from the crowd.

Upright Li grasps a few handfuls of earth and flings them at the crowd. The people try to dodge them. Those in bright clothes flee, protecting their kids. The children run up to the slope. Curses fly all over the riverbank. Most of them make reference to Upright Li's past misdeeds.

Patting the earth from his body, Defu walks over and asks, "Upright Li, how can you be such a barbarian? All of these years have passed and you've just stayed the same. You've not made a jot of progress."

Upright Li smiles and shouts at the onlookers, "Is there anybody here from Lower Mirth Village?"

Several strong young guys bound out from the crowd of onlookers.

Upper Li instructs, "Go down. Beat them up!"

"You'll give us money?" one guy asks.

Upper Li shoots a glance at Defu who is alongside him and says, "Defu will shout you a meal."

Those guys have all been finding things tedious and are looking for the opportunity to kick off. They rush to the riverbank and discover a few tough rivals who they are prepared to take on.

Here, Upright Li tells the cameraman to zoom in on the heroes and just use the rest as the background. The cameraman nods and says yes.

"Ready … and action!"

With that order both parties begin to fight. Within seconds Upright Li shouts that they should cut. The reason is that they are not taking it seriously. The key problem is that the people from Upper Mirth Village begrudge getting their new clothes dirty. They run with their eyes staring into the lens of the camera. Once the lens is focused on them, they immediately put on airs and pose with smiles upon their faces.

Upright Li asks, "Are there any more guys from Lower Mirth Village?"

Several more fellows bound out from the crowd.

Upright Li says, "In the early 1960s Upper Mirth Village and Lower Mirth Village fought over water on the riverbank and somebody was killed. At that time, people battled desperately. People from Lower Mirth Village beat Water-carrier Chang from Upper Mirth Village to death, so Upper Mirth Village sabotaged the water supply to Lower Mirth Village. This feud goes back a few generations. Now, we just want to reenact the situation at that time. So, we must take on the spirit of those years past and the lust for revenge. You should display this to the full right here. Ok. Ready. Action!"

Defu who is standing behind me shouts loudly, "You bastard, you are inciting the masses to fight!"

Upright Li says, "I'm just stirring up their emotions so that they can get into role quickly."

Defu protests, "How can you stir things up like this? Relations between Upper Mirth Village and Lower Mirth Village have gotten much better in recent years. It took long negotiations involving the county government. This can't be all ruined for the sake of appearing on your camera."

"Don't you interrupt my shoot. If we miss the chance, do you know how much money we'll lose for this one day? 24,000 RMB! If you were to sell off all of your belongings would they fetch 24,000?"

"I don't care whether it comes to 24,000 or not. You can't drag that skeleton out of the closet and expose Upper Mirth Village to the whole nation like that. We did have fights in the past, yes, but you can't make fun of us like this. Dirty linen shouldn't be hung out. You bastard. You once stayed in Upper Mirth Village, so how can you not understand this?"

"I want to tell everybody about the past experiences that the farmers have had. Tell them to the future generations, so that the peasants will be able to overcome their limitations and rebuild a brand new national mindset."

"Whether the national mindset is brand new or not, there is no need for you men of letters to talk about this. We can remember our own lessons in our hearts. Naturally, we'll pass them onto the future generations as well. But we won't have this laid bare on the TV. If your old man was thief would you bang the gong and put up posters to tell everybody about it?"

"People can only make progress when they are prepared to face up to their mistakes. My TV series won't specifically point out that the village is Lower Mirth."

"We don't want to pull off our trousers and let others look at our piles."

Upright Li doesn't take any notice of him and continues to direct the shoot.

The people in the produce and props department act as the cheering squad. They wave their arms and shout loudly, "Come on! Come on! Upper Mirth Village, come on!"

But all the folk on the riverbank act like a football team that cannot be rallied. They fight for the sake of fighting. Some of them even pause to watch the quarrel between Defu and Upright Li.

The film camera automatically shuts down. It is obvious that the shoot cannot continue.

Suddenly, Defu grabs the loudspeaker from Upright Li's hands and shouts to the crowd, "All you folks from Upper Mirth Village come out! If there's anybody who won't come out, I'll fuck your ancestors! Men have faces; trees have bark. We cannot bring disgrace on ourselves!"

The people rush up. Some of them run towards the film camera with bricks in their hands. When Upright Li sees what is going on, he shouts loudly to his crew, "Run for it!" Realizing the danger in that situation, we rush towards the van as if competing in the 100 metre dash.

The people behind us are in hot pursuit.

Some handfuls of flung earth find their way down the back

of my neck.

The cameraman, who is running comparatively slowly, is struck by a brick leaving his ankle black and blue.

Our van makes a frenzied escape like a hare being coursed.

Behind the van somebody whistles by way of seeing us off.

IV.

The whole group, myself especially, are consumed by a panic that has gone on for several days. Whenever I hear the sound of the local dialect, I get the jitters in case it is the people from Upper Mirth Village coming over to ask for their food and labour expenses. If there were not 1,000 extras present on that day, there must have been at least 800. That's a big sum of money. Upright Li complains about me not having told the villagers what exactly we were trying to do. My response is, "Big scenes are normally just shot there and then with no need to tell all those extras about the particulars."

Upright Li says, "All the people in Upper Mirth Village have become dull under Defu's leadership. They can't even understand the meaning of 'Come on!' None of the men in the village – damn them – know how to fight ..."

The cameraman pulls up his trouser leg and comments, "So their combat skills are not good enough!"

I say, "They proclaim that they are Li Zicheng ..."

"That's the *Emperor* Li Zicheng," the producer emphasizes.

Three days later, the accountant from Upper Mirth Village comes over. I make excuses to avoid him. I hide in the barn behind the hostel, where there is no heating. I shake because of the cold, managing to tolerate this for two hours. When I get back to the room I see that Upright Li and others are chewing on chicken. I ask, "Why didn't you call me over when you knew there was chicken to be had?"

The cameraman says to me, "The chicken was sent over by

the Upper Mirth villagers to their former neighbour Upright Li. They still remember how much Upright Li loves chicken."

I ask the producer how much money have they paid to Upper Mirth Village.

The producer explains, "The villagers declined to accept any fee because they didn't get to appear on camera after all."

Looking at Upright Li's greasy mouth, I exclaim, "You are now in their debt again?"

"I'm always in debt to them."

"Dare you go back to Upper Mirth Village again?"

"Absolutely not."

A Panda Named 'Little Mite'

By the time Fourth Girl leaves Colourful Duckweed's home at Oak Weir the forest-strewn mountains have already become completely buried in heavy snow. This is the first round of snowfall this year. The drifting flakes descend without sound, landing on the groves of pine-flowered bamboos which carpet the mountains, as well as on the thick bushes now lashed impenetrably together, and on the coniferous forests of the summits. They metamorphose into fascinating works of art which dangle down beneath the trees. Fourth Girl has appreciated this kind of scene before albeit in a pictorial newspaper. She cannot fathom why that picture moved her to such an extent that she should have committed it to memory and should still frequently recall it now. Upon coming into contact with the reality and finding herself in that precise situation, she doesn't feel moved; on the contrary, she is overcome with a kind of all-too-familiar indifference and nonchalance. She knows that were it not for the coating of snow the seemingly pure-white path that snakes beneath her feet would be a shambles. It is customarily the preserve of orangey-yellow grass, sharp stones, blackish-brown cowpats and dirty messy slushy puddles. In the summer there are gadflies, gnats, snakes, and land leeches that adhere themselves to the tips of blades of grass, waving at passersby. Of course, all of that is now gone. Everything is white and flat. Everything seems very serene and not at all dissimilar from the pages in the pictorial. However, this is not the scene in the photograph. They are not one and the same and that is that.

There is no wind. The mountain hollow feels positively balmy. Snow is swirling, but the air is free of chill. Having walked for a rather long while after quitting Colourful Duckweed's home, Fourth Girl's face is still ruddy. She carefully relishes the exotic aftertaste in her mouth. It is the first time in her life that she has enjoyed such a flavour: sweetness combined with bitterness and a milk-like aroma blended with a kick of herbs – so wonderful and so indescribable. When Colourful Duckweed initially tried to cram that substance which resembled a piece of Shaanxi takin's dung into her mouth, she did her damnedest to dodge away. Unable to fend her off, she had to allow the stuff to enter her mouth. She didn't dare breathe out through her nose nor did she dare waggle her tongue. She was afraid that she might spit it out with a "*Wah*!" sound. Next, the "takin dung" melted in her mouth and she experienced that unique feeling and imbibed that exquisite taste. No tree in the mountains could bear a fruit that was like this and no grass in the mountains could ever give off such a scent. Fourth Girl asked Colourful Duckweed what on earth she had given her to eat. Colourful Duckweed replied casually that it was chocolate.

Chocolate!

Fourth Girl probed into what chocolate meant.

Colourful Duckweed replied, "Chocolate is chocolate and it has no meaning."

Fourth Girl persisted, "How can it mean nothing? Everything under the skies that has a name must have a meaning to match: the crotch fruit looks like a man's crotch; the chicken-claw vegetable looks like a chicken's claws. What is this chocolate?"

Colourful Duckweed answered, "Chocolate is a kind of foreign sweet, a kind of sweet that Mickey Mouse eats."

"Does this Mickey the Mouse eat rice raw like other mice?" Fourth Girl pried.

"Mickey Mouse not only eats rice raw," Colourful Duckweed responded, "but plays the piano and dances as well. Mickey Mouse is in fact a type of big-eared rat raised by Americans that is able to talk and wears clothes."

Fourth Girl had never imagined that there could be such a

thing as a talking mouse. In the mountains she would more often than not encounter bamboo rats. Those rodents are podgy and large with tiny ears and silvery grey fur. They bore holes wildly like a blind man and mainly gnaw at the roots of bamboos which stand in the same row. The bamboos then die off row-by-row. In Fourth Girl's imagination, were a bamboo rat to suddenly talk to her, she would be scared half to death. It would be more disturbing still to know that the critter also eats *cho ... colate*.

Her query about chocolate stands unanswered, having only received a cursory explanation. This foreign Mickey the Mouse is perhaps bogus, but the chocolate he is said to enjoy has genuinely gone into Fourth Girl's mouth. This should be an authentic foreign flavour – unadulterated. Fourth Girl must admire Colourful Duckweed from the bottom of her heart because she knows about Mickey the Mouse. Had Colourful Duckweed always stayed at Leopard Terrace in those ancient forested mountains secluded from the outside world like her, she would not have been able to see that Mickey the Mouse either, much less to have feasted on chocolate. When all was said and done, Colourful Duckweed was given just such a chance. Her paternal aunt in the provincial capital found her a job as a home-help and she left the mountains in a stately manner. Naturally, the things she was able to eat, wear, watch and listen to were quite different from those in the mountains. Only half a year has passed by. Not only has her demeanour changed, but even her accent as well. Now when she talks, she frequently spouts "yeah-yeahs" and copies the intonation of Southern China. In this way she conveys to others the impression that she is well-educated, wise and well-nurtured and that even her reproaches must be beguiling. None of the girls at Oak Weir or Leopard Terrace can emulate her in that respect.

When she reaches this particular thought, Fourth Girl doesn't know why she should sense such a stream of indescribable melancholy and a kind of gentle sadness inside. The mood, which

66

escapes explanation, has been constantly lingering in her heart and mind of late. It surfaces in strings and locks that can be neither disentangled nor cast away. She doesn't envy Colourful Duckweed's good opportunity. Going outside to be a home-help entails nothing more than washing the laundry and cooking. Fourth Girl too has the knack of being able to perform these things so is in no way at a disadvantage. When Colourful Duckweed stayed at home, she was the spoilt and pampered child in that household – she only needed to reach out her arms to be clothed; she only needed to open her mouth to be fed – and had to undertake no household chores whatsoever. Nevertheless, she went outside this time and came back home a notable. She brought back home chocolate in addition to so many eye-opening items for the mountain girls. In truth, that paternal aunt had originally come over to seek out Fourth Girl. Fourth Girl is diligent, intelligent-eyed and good-looking. According to the conventions of kinship, she should call Colourful Duckweed's paternal aunt "Third Aunt." Third Aunt had a mind to bring Fourth Girl to the provincial capital, though Fourth Girl couldn't leave. Her mother has long been stricken with illness. Whether it is winter or summer, she will sit warming herself by the fire pit the whole day long. On some occasions her clothes have actually caught alight, but she doesn't extinguish the flames straightaway. Mother's heart is in a mess; her heart is not here.

People say that Fourth Girl's mother was not like this in the past. When she was still a maid, Fourth Girl's mother was regarded as a beauty in Oak Weir – a village situated a couple of miles away. She had four years of schooling and can read. A quarter century ago, Fourth Girl's father was already the Village Head. Back then he was not addressed as "Village Head" but "Brigade Commander" and thereafter as "Team Leader." It has only been in the past few years that it was decided he should be addressed as Village Head. Notwithstanding what his official title is, her father has always been the biggest boss in this vicinity and has always wielded the most authority. Twenty-five years ago, a beauty from Oak Weir could aspire to marry a Brigade Commander and had no better alternative. If her family was thereby able to strike up a kinship link with the largest fish in this small pond, that beauty had played her part and there was no cause for pity. Thus, everything advanced as expected and the beauty from Oak Weir became the wife of the Village Head at Leopard Terrace. After their marriage, the belly of the Village Head's beautiful wife grew swollen several times. First she gave birth to a daughter, who, alas, died just three months afterwards. Later, she carried a daughter again but when the foetus had barely taken on the shape of a human, she suffered a miscarriage in the bamboo groves on the middle of the slope behind her homestead. The third one was another daughter. She survived but was a simple-minded soul. From morning to evening, she ran frenziedly all over the mountains and simpered with a drooling mouth. No matter what man she bumped into, she called him "Father." The beauty was worry-stricken and so was the Village Head. Even so, this was not regarded as an unsettling business here and everyone took it as a common occurrence. When she was eighteen, the Village Head's third daughter married Dragon She from Oak Weir. Dragon was poor and so did not care about the third daughter's simplicity; he explained that it was ok as long as she could give birth to a child.

Fourth Girl was born in 1978, at the point when China had barely implemented its policy of Reform and Opening-up. In that year a photographer came to the mountains. Foisting a mortar-barrel-like contraption upon his back, he hung around in the ancient woods for a not inconsiderable period of time. At first the mountain folks treated this as a novelty. Sporting a small white sunhat and a bushy beard, the photographer wandered here and there, tilting his mortar barrel in the direction of cats, dogs, wild boars and leopards. When each photo was being taken they only heard a click and never saw a bomb being fired out afterwards. The wild animals still strolled about the slopes as ever before but satisfaction was written all over the photographer's face. They thought it was unbelievable yet tedious at the same time and so left the photographer to do as he pleased.

The photographer lodged at the Village Head's home for the better part of one month and the Village Head's wife cooked for him every day. Their fond third daughter of course addressed him as "Father." The young photographer felt uneasy and his face turned red and then white out of embarrassment.

At the beginning of the next year, following the photographer's departure, the mother gave birth to Fourth Girl. By the age of barely one month, Fourth Girl could laugh and roll her eyes to figure people out; her body radiated intelligence. The mountain people were surprised. Some detected the shadow of the photographer about her brow. Some said that while the photographer boarded at the Village Head's home, there was one time when the Village Head went to the township for three days to attend a meeting; something must have happened during that three-day-long period. In actual fact, there was nothing incriminating and all of this was blind guesswork and nonsense. It was a good thing that Leopard Terrace had nurtured the quick-witted and capable Fourth Girl. The Village Head spoke of her in aggrandizing terms to the effect that she might be capable of achieving anything, and so did the fellow villagers. The Village Head was the sun that shone over Leopard Terrace and Fourth Girl became the moon.

While Fourth Girl grew day by day, her mother simultaneously withered with every passing day and often fell into a trance-like state. People said that Fourth Girl's mother had transmitted all of her essential force into Fourth Girl and that Fourth Girl's precocity stood as testimony to this. There were those who claimed that Fourth Girl's mother was pining after that photographer. The photographer, who was gone and never to come back had hooked up the soul of Fourth Girl's mother and spirited it away. He came and went like a wind, not even leaving his address behind. But, to clarify this point, as Leopard Terrace falls within the boundaries of the nature reserve, plenty of people are inclined to visit and then depart. Who out of this number would ever think to leave their name and address at a small mountain village with a population of no more than 100? There was no need.

Fourth Girl's mother gave Fourth Girl a younger brother called Hare. Hare received this name because of his hare lip. His two front teeth stuck directly out through the cracked upper lip of his mouth, reminding people of a hare. Hare's full name was Universe Shocking Li. That scholarly name was bestowed upon him by an expert from Peking University who came here to study the local fauna. Fourth Girl's father had not the knowledge ever to hit upon such a gloriously resonant name. The expert meant to infer that Hare would attain something momentous after he had grown up and that his name would redound throughout the four seas. Despite having been born with a disability, he was neither simple-skulled nor feeble – he could add and subtract rather proficiently with the aid of his ten fingers and ten toes. Young guys are something to be feared, the expert thought. How can I predict what they might become in the future? Perhaps a few dozen years later a big shot might emerge from this mountain hollow. When the expert was about to depart, he informed Fourth Girl's parents that they should have no further children. He said that Universe Shocking Li's hare lip represented a serious augury about the family's genes. If they kept on having children, they were destined to savour the bitter fruit from the tree that they themselves had planted and the consequences would be unimaginably catastrophic. Fourth Girl's father replied that he was the Village Head and a Communist Party member. He should, of course, take the lead in following the state's family planning policy. He had three children, but two of them had left the production line with imperfections. The only fully-finished product was Fourth Girl – a daughter. According to the lore of the mountains, he should go on siring. Waving his hand, the expert admonished him by exclaiming "Don't ever do that! Don't ever do that!" He went on to say that the hare lip could be cured. The hospitals in Beijing had specialist departments dedicated to performing reparatory procedures. If the operation were a success, the child would be as good as new and nobody would be able to detect this former defect. Fourth Girl's father complained, "How can children from the mountains have the good fate of being able to go to Beijing? I would consider myself lucky to get to the county town, never mind Beijing. A round trip there is about forty miles. I need to scale Lordship Ridge, Soul-confusing Ridge and cross Ghostly Wind Valley. I might run into wolves, pythons, tigers and leopards and it is never an easy journey." The expert said, "Your words sound too puzzling. We too have to scale those same ridges and cross those same ravines to pass in and out and I haven't seen anything bad befall anyone." Fourth Girl's father responded, "Who are you and who are we? How can we compare ourselves to you?"

Fourth Girl, who was standing nearby listening to the conversation between her father and the expert, felt rather nonplussed with her father. She wondered why her father, who was after all the Village Head and a very charismatic and influential personage in the village, allowed himself to be shrunk in stature when faced with this professional man. What was wrong with Hare? She wondered if it was predestined that he should never go to Beijing. She should go outside. Go outside to earn money. When she had the money, the first thing she would do would be to take her brother to Beijing to have his condition treated. The expert had said that if the operation was a success, her brother would be as good as new. It was her responsibility to help her brother become as good as new.

Now, with two pieces of chocolate in her pocket, Fourth Girl is scooting back home. She wants to bring her brother the candies that the Mouse enjoys and to let him share some foreign flavour.

She skirts around the rock which lies horizontally by the roadside. Not far away stands the compound of Old Man Li the Second. Old Man Li the Second's household is the westernmost outpost of the village and reaching his homestead is tantamount to having reached Leopard Terrace. It is not clear when exactly he came out, but the yellow dog belonging to Fourth Girl's family has come forward to welcome her. Perhaps he has been waiting for her by the rock for some time. His hips girding and his tail wagging, the yellow dog trots in front of Fourth Girl and repeatedly turns his head to look back at her. Fourth Girl presses down upon the candies in her pocket and says, "This is not for you!" The yellow dog lets out a sneeze and pitches forward.

Fourth Girl also picks up speed.

Fresh paw prints in the shape of Chinese plum blossoms have been left in the snowy ground by the road. The yellow dog gives them a sniff and passes over the marks without fear. Fourth Girl too skips casually across them. They both know that the ageing she-leopard has come down from the mountain ridge to the gully for some water. The she-leopard must be too weak. In recent times she has rarely hung around Leopard Terrace Village. When her paw prints are no longer visible here, that must mean that she has died. Fourth Girl thinks, "The paw prints say that it is her. That beautiful solitary spirit is still alive!" Rustling sounds are to be heard from the depths of the bushes. The yellow dog halts in his tracks and directs a glimpse over there. He then lets out a lazy "woof" and strikes a posture that indicates that they are not in any danger and the sound isn't even worth being heeded. Fourth Girl gives him a kick and the two run to the village.

From the bottom of the gully come the children's excited whoops and cheers. Hare's inarticulate yells are mingled in with that mix as well. His voice is high-pitched and piercing. Before Fourth Girl has had time to react, the yellow dog has shot to the bottom of the gulley like an arrow. What's going on?

Fourth Girl plucks apart the thick branches by the road to look down. Hare and several other children are leaping and bounding between the stones at the bottom of the creek, brandishing their hands and shouting. The stones are perilously slippery and there is snow. The children are absolutely soaked. The yellow dog, meanwhile, has joined the crying mob and become its most vociferous member.

Fourth Girl goes to the creek. Seeing that she has arrived, Hare rushes over in feverish excitement and declares loudly, "Sister, a spotty bear! There is a spotty bear over there!"

The locals call the panda a "spotty bear" – the name has been passed down from generation to generation. Mountain folks think that spotty bear is a more accurate name than "panda." What is a panda? The name for the Giant Panda (*da xiong mao*) in Mandarin literally means "big cat bear." What is a spotty bear? A spotty bear is a bear. Those black and white creatures which frequent the mountains and wilds can only be bears but never cats. A cat is a meowing animal that coils up on the bed or nestles alongside a fire pit. No matter how hard you try, you can never drive felines up into the mountains. A spotty bear is a mountain spirit. They run a mile from any place that has the aura of man. They step backwards to free up space for the strong and great humans to perform their activities in. They are always stepping backwards, stepping backwards so that they have been pushed to the furthest reaches of the high mountains and the depths of the ravines.

Fourth Girl pats the snow from her brother's body and asks reproachfully why he has become wild and crazy like this over a spotty bear?

Hare responds, "A ti-neee, very ti-neee little spotty bear …"

Fourth Girl questions him, "What spotty bears have you not seen? Spotty bears are to be found scurrying all over the mountains wherever there are forests. No matter how small he might be, he is still very fierce. Don't tease him. Come, follow me home."

Hare is reluctant to go home.

Fourth Girl sweet-talks her brother, "I secretly buried a few taros by the pond today. They were not quite ripe then, but should be ready to eat now."

"But the spotty bear has got stuck in a crack between two stones and it can't move," Hare insists.

Fourth Girl warns, "Then you shouldn't get close to it. An older spotty bear is most probably watching from nearby."

"The ti-neee spotty bear needs taking care of," Hare implores. "Sister, you should save him."

Fourth Girl gazes at her disabled brother and a jet of warmth surges in her heart. Hare is a kind-hearted kid – a child who is a little timid and has a slight inferiority complex. Were it not for his unusual lips, he might have behaved differently. When her train of thought has led her to this point, she wraps her arm around Hare's shoulders and says, "Escort your Sister to go and take a look."

In a rapturous mood, Hare promises he will. He accompanies Fourth Girl and they take two or three turns before reaching a pile of stones by the creek. Pointing at a crevice in between two boulders, he says, "Sister, there he is!"

Fourth Girl spies a furry ball clamped between two stones – it is stained all over with mud and water and is so dirty that the eyebrows and eyes of that furry ball cannot be made out.

Fourth Girl says, "Perhaps he is dead?"

On hearing her words, the children led by Hare immediately refute them. "He is alive! He just stirred now."

Fourth Girl's wary eyes scan rapidly across the nearby mountains. The forested mountains are serene and wreathed in snow and fog. Beyond a range of 100 metres nothing can be seen clearly.

The yellow dog, who doesn't know what is good for him, is still barking.

"Shut your stinky canine mouth!" Fourth Girl snaps at him.

Having been given a tongue-lashing, the yellow dog immediately gags his mouth, retreats with a shrivelled head, and slinks behind the children.

Fourth Girl tells the children to stop shouting and gathers them together to wait quietly for a while at a secluded spot. Not until she is sure that there is no mother panda nearby does she let them scoot to the front of the boulders.

The baby panda has been stuck in the crevice for quite some time and is breathing his last. The mother panda has already left and surrendered her final efforts after her baby. Fourth Girl pushes and pulls for half a day but still fails. The baby panda remains stuck fast and motionless in the crevice. One of his legs is apparently already broken – the consequence of his struggles.

Fourth Girl busies herself there until her head is drenched in sweat. Still she fails to get the baby panda out. His broken leg being jammed into the narrow crevice, the baby panda doesn't allow anyone to touch it. Lacking any other option, Fourth Girl turns her head and says to Hare, "Go bring Father here."

Hare turns to the yellow dog and commands "Go, go bring Father here!"

The yellow dog darts to the village, his hips girding.

Father soon arrives. He knows a method. He suggests, "Ease him back out by retracing his steps. Since he has found his way in there, he can also find a way out. Don't tug blindly but drag him backwards from behind so his body follows the most convenient route out."

Fourth Girl disagrees, "But his leg is broken. Can we still drag him?"

Father says, "We can't bother ourselves with that problem now."

Fourth Girl helps her father drag the creature out. The baby panda doesn't put up a struggle but leaves himself at the mercy of the father and daughter.

Father surmises, "It may be the case that the 'little mite' won't survive even though he has been rescued."

"You little mite" is a pet name given by mountain folks to their favourite kids. For people outside that area it means "a tiny dear one." Father calls the baby panda "Little Mite", which means he has taken him as a child just like Hare.

After the efforts of nine bulls and two tigers have been exerted Little Mite is finally recovered. The rescued baby panda lies motionless on a glossy slippery stone. The yellow dog approaches, takes a sniff at him and raises his head to bark once at Father. Father concludes, "Maybe it is a goner."

Hare disagrees, "No, Father. Look, his eyes are still open."

"He's not much bigger than our family cat," Fourth Girl comments. "So pitiful."

Father adds, "Hasn't been weaned yet, so he can't survive."

The twilight is gathering and plumes of kitchen smoke are swirling up above many of the village households. Father goes back home with Little Mite clamped under his armpit. Fourth Girl and Hare follow in tow. Fourth Girl can see the wounded leg of the baby panda dangling down from the crook of her father's arm swaying to the rhythm of her father's footsteps. It is simultaneously absurd and unbelievable.

II.

Little Mite has settled down in a corner of the room where a thick blanket of rice straw has been padded down for him. That rice straw was fetched by Hare. Originally he also wanted to spread out a coverlet there for Little Mite. Father said, "Leave it there. Is there any place where it wouldn't bed down in the wild? What's the good of a coverlet?" But Hare's reasoning was that in the past Little Mite had been nurtured upon his mother's chest. What could be softer than his mother's bosom? Little Mite's broken leg has been bound in bamboo splints by Father, who concluded that "Fate will decide whether he pulls through or not." Now, Little Mite lies in the corner, silent and breathless like a heap of uncooked tattered animal hide. Fourth Girl simmers a wok of rice porridge for him but is unable to pour any of it into his mouth. Finally, Mother gets to drink all the porridge.

During this time, Uncle Wang, Uncle Qinglai and Third Maternal Uncle come to see Little Mite. After one glimpse, they all shake their heads and conclude that this "little mite" is at most three months old and cannot survive without the mother spotty bear.

Father is smoking by the fire pit. Staring at that pile of "tattered hide," he pledges that tomorrow a meeting of the Village Committee will be convened.

Unable to fall asleep, that night Fourth Girl tiptoes to the corner where Little Mite is lying. Little Mite is still crouching down there in the same posture and nothing has changed. Fourth Girl gives his soft fur a stroke; Little Mite lets out a gentle grunt. Fourth Girl detects a thread of faintly-discernible warmth. With the aid of the dim light reflected by the snow outside the window, she is able to spot an attractive pair of sparkling black-button-like eyes. Suddenly, she feels that her nose is turning sour. Unable to speak, she combs her fingers time and again through the shaggy hair beneath her hand.

A small moist nose dabs gently at her hand. She lowers her head. It is the yellow dog. The perisher has crawled into the room who knows how ...

That next day, Fourth Girl's father summons a meeting of the village cadres at his home. The attendees mostly came there the night before. Among their number is the young Deputy Village Head named Mountain Forest Li along with Uncle Wang, Uncle Qinglai and Third Maternal Uncle. According to their customary rules, when a meeting is held at a committee member's home, the host – no matter who he is – should take charge of the prerequisite spirits and tea. There isn't a great deal of expenditure, save for the cost of several mugfuls of corn-distilled spirits. Every household at Leopard Terrace distills spirits from corn, and this should last one winter and one spring until the new corn is harvested the following year. The spirits are drunk without any accompaniment. People sit around the fire pit and a large enamel mug is passed around perpetually. This one takes a mouthful and that one takes a mouthful. After one mugful has been exhausted, another serving will be ladled out and the mug passed around again. The authorities have criticized this kind of meeting many times and enjoined them to rectify their working style because the final decisions made at such village meetings always turn out to be nonsensical. In the end nobody remembers what the original intention of the meeting was. Whereas city cadres ride home from a meeting in their *Santanas* many has been the time that the children of these village cadres have had to carry their fathers back home.

The mountains are high and the emperor is far away. The authorities can criticize if they like but the cadres at Leopard Terrace still refuse to hold a meeting unless there is spirits. They cannot imagine what wise and correct decisions could possibly be reached at a wine-less gathering. Today, as he raises an enamel mug at the Village Committee meeting, Fourth Girl's father declares that they have two key issues to address: the first one is they should do their best to save the spotty bear and let the spotty bear feed. The "little mite" will never die under their watch. The second point is that they will send a memo to the nature reserve as soon as possible. They are the unit officially in charge of rescuing spotty bears. The state has allocated so much money to them. For what? Not so that they can relieve the spotty bears' sufferings and help them survive their hardships at a critical moment?

The others all echo, "Yeah!"

Mountain Forest Li is the lone voice of dissent, "Save my arse. Just let it slide. Those that backslide will backslide and those that are meant to die will perish – this is the inescapable law of nature."

"In a few years it will be your time to die," Qinglai mouths in a low voice.

Mountain Forest Li brushes him off and persists, "Haven't the dinosaurs become extinct? Haven't the sabre-toothed mammoths become extinct? Haven't the local South China tigers become extinct? This is the process of natural selection, which is beyond our control."

Fourth Girl's father throws a glance at Mountain Forest Li.

The other cadres all throw glances at him too.

Nobody takes up his words.

Third Maternal Uncle says, "We should find someone to send a memo to the county government."

Mountain Forest Li retorts, "The heavy snow has sealed off the mountains. No man can get out there, so how can a message be delivered?"

Fourth Girl's father says, "A man can't get out there. Then we can use the wireless set. Haven't they left us a modern piece of kit?"

Mountain Forest Li ripostes, "The water in the stream is frozen solid and no electricity can be generated that way."

Uncle Wang reminds them, "Use the dry batteries then. They gave us a few dry batteries – they're all stashed away in the book-keeper's glory hole."

Mountain Forest Li responds, "The book-keeper is an amateur. He's only gone and left the dry batteries by the windowsill. The damp has spoiled them all."

No one opens their mouth now.

Finally, Fourth Girl's father pipes up, "Since you chaps have voted for me, I should keep the affairs of you chaps close to my heart. In the past when the supreme instructions needed to be relayed to Leopard Terrace, we never waited overnight. Qinglai acted as the liaison guy and he knows that."

Qinglai echoes, "Yeah. Even though it might be raining knives I would still run to the commune and bring back the instructions …"

Mountain Forest Li adjusts his seating posture impatiently.

The others all know what Fourth Girl's father is driving at by saying "keep the affairs of you chaps close to my heart." Those words of blame were aimed exclusively at Mountain Forest Li. Recently Mountain Forest Li has become obsessed with building several clay brick cottages on the southern slope and making the preparations necessary for growing shiitake mushrooms in the next season. The local shiitakes are elegantly-shaped, authentically-flavoured and thickly-endowed with flesh; one pound of them brings home fifty to sixty yuan.

Their topic turns from the affairs of "you chaps" to the technical studies on how to plant medicinal dogwoods and how to grow edible fungi and then wanders onto how the wild boars have been making a mess by uprooting their taros and how the bears have been damaging their corn. They bellyache about wild boars and bears both being classed as national treasures and listed as animals under Second Grade State Protection. The government doesn't permit the public to hunt them. If people were to hunt them, they would be breaking the law. However, shouldn't those who are forbidden from hunting be seeking compensation from the government? The little people don't deserve to be given the short straw. The state has also passed a law to protect private property. Wild boars are the private property of the state. Aren't taros the private property of the peasants?

Mountain Forest Li explains that the county government takes charge of doling out compensation. The state, it seems, has a fund exclusively designed for that purpose and the villagers can go and claim it. Mountain guys should not always have to lower their heads like straight arrows. There is even a song that goes like this, "Leap into the fray when you have to." Rendered into the local tongue, it means "Reach out your hand when you have to" – to claim compensation while singing the tune loudly. Only by this means can their claim obtain a result.

Fourth Girl's father disagrees, observing that this move is not advisable and demands that the cadres shouldn't go outside and make jackasses of themselves.

Then they ramble on about how the sow belonging to the family of Old Man Li the Second went outside looking for an illicit mate and gave birth to a litter of long-legged, long-snouted wild piglets, each of whom gnawed at their mother's nipples until the teats were mangled. Little Dong came over from the nature reserve. He tagged every baby pig with a number, took photos of them and allowed Old Man Li the Second to neither slaughter nor sell them, claiming that he was making a study of what-was-that? – hereditary mutation. The study of that mutation produced no research findings, but the mother pig belonging to Old Man Li the Second's family had still suffered an ordeal …

The Village Committee sometimes deals with concrete issues and with ideological guidelines at other times. The meeting convened in the interests of the panda drags on and on until there is no end in sight.

Fourth Girl has ladled out spirits seven times for them.

The committee members still show no signs of wrapping up.

Little Mite is still holed-up in the corner and seems to only let out one breath in half a day.

Fourth Girl is on a knife-edge. She knows that Little Mite won't survive the night if immediate measures are not taken.

Mother comes in with a nursing bottle in her hand. The nursing bottle was used by Hare when he was still a baby. Milk couldn't be directed into the mouth of the disabled Hare unless a nursing bottle was used. The nursing bottle was brought back home by someone entrusted by Father. Among all the children at Leopard Terrace, perhaps only Hare has ever been bottle-fed.

Catching sight of the nursing bottle, Fourth Girl knows what is in her mother's mind. She rinses out the spirits-ladling enamel mug in her hand with fresh water and then tells Hare to hurry to Old Man Li the Second's home at the entrance to the village to fetch a mugful of ewe's milk.

Hare is swift-footed. In no time, he has brought home a mug brimming over with ewe's milk together with Old Man Li the Second's promise, "As long as it is for the baby spotty bear, you can go milk the ewe anytime."

Fourth Girl pours the still-warm ewe's milk into the nursing bottle and raises it to the mouth of Little Mite. Little Mite doesn't react. Fourth Girl teases Little Mite's mouth with the rubber teat. Little Mite turns his head away.

Their supply of corn-distilled spirits having been suspended, the wine-eager committee members adjourn the meeting automatically. Soon they find out that the contents in the wine container passed around by them have altered – hard liquor has been exchanged for ewe's milk.

The key issue concerning Little Mite is therefore raised again. The committee members decide to go to the grass-roots level to deal with the business on the spot. They leave the fire pit for the corner and crowd around Little Mite.

Little Mite refuses to take in any food.

Now being the centre of all the Leopard Terrace cadres' attention, Little Mite keeps his eyes half open and half shut.

Third Maternal Uncle says, "We can only toss him to the back ridge to feed the she-leopard."

Uncle Wang concludes, "There might be no more baby spotty bears in this mountain range."

Qinglai persists, "We should find a vet and form a rescue team."

Fourth Girl's father says, "We should first work out a way to pour the milk into the mouth of this 'little mite.'"

Mountain Forest Li disagrees, "Still let nature take its course."

Amidst the committee members' remarks, Fourth Girl's mother gathers up the baby panda without a sound and clasps him to her bosom gently like she had done in years long past with Fourth Girl and with Hare. It is a mother cradling her baby; it is the transmission of life and love. Little Mite has apparently sensed something and opens his eyes slightly for once. Fourth Girl's mother takes over the nursing bottle from Fourth Girl's hand and squeezes several drops of milk onto the mouth of Little Mite. His memories having been refreshed or rather his instinct to survive having been revived, Little Mite grabs the rubber teat in his mouth nimbly and sucks slowly. However, after several mouthfuls, he stops sucking.

"Why's he stopped drinking?" Third Maternal Uncle inquires.

Qinglai explains, "He must still be too weak."

"As long as he is willing to open his mouth, he will survive," Fourth Girl's father reassures.

III.

As Father had predicted, after drinking the milk several times, Little Mite can totter a few steps. Hare slices some tender bamboo shoots from the slope for him to eat. He declines this and will accept only milk. Within two days, he has regained his vitality. As well as his food intake skyrocketing, he now runs amok all over the compound and climbs up and down without one moment's break. His wounded leg evidently doesn't inhibit his mobility much. Unlike a man, he doesn't need to groan for several months tormenting his bed. Soon, a crisis engulfs the provision of ewe's milk from Old Man Li the Second – demand is exceeding supply. The milk consumed by one spotty bear surpasses that required by a number of lambs. Old Man Li the Second no longer repeats, "You can go milk the ewe anytime." His face has become sullen. More than once when Hare has gone to milk the ewe, he comes back empty-handed.

Father summons Old Man Li the Second to his home and, pointing at Little Mite, who is running wild, observes, "That is a national treasure. It is more precious than you and me."

Old Man Li the Second replies, "I know. After I have kicked the bucket, nobody will be bothered. But after he dies, the news will be relayed to the provincial capital."

Father enjoins him, "Those few sheep of yours are not worth as much as one spotty bear."

Old Man Li the Second retorts, "It's the other way round. My sheep can be sold; they can be exchanged for money. Who would dare try to sell a spotty bear? Anything that can't be changed into money isn't worth one coin, like the dung beetles in the grass."

Father tries to enlighten him, "Old Second, why is your brain only obsessed with money now so that you don't have even the least bit of proletarian consciousness? Your father was an old soldier in the Red Army, who joined the Twenty-fifth Regiment in fighting the Nationalist Forty-seventh Regiment here. Why can't you follow your father's example by making a small contribution to the revolutionary cause?"

"Contribute what? My ewe's milk?"

"Exactly."

Old Man Li the Second grumbles, "Then who will make a contribution to me!"

Father concludes, "Done, done. Old Second, you're over and done with. Studying over the facts in detail confirm that you are descended from revolutionary martyrs. Even so, you have single-mindedly crawled into the jaws of money. How much milk must one baby spotty bear consume that you could become as stingy as this?"

Old Man Li the Second retorts, "How hellish it is to be descended from revolutionary martyrs? The kin of revolutionary martyrs cannot stride into communism ahead of time. The kin of revolutionary martyrs still have to buy salt at a rate of two yuan per pound. It is no big deal for me to supply milk for one or two meals. But this 'little mite' does not need to be weaned off milk until he is two or three years old just like a baby. My loss is too great, isn't it? I'm not a householder who specializes in breeding spotty bears."

Father replies, "Does every word you speak have to be money-oriented? Let's do it this way: No matter how much milk this 'little mite' consumes, write it down in the account book. When it is sunny and the authorities come to take him away, send them the bill."

"If that's the case, I will charge them four yuan for every pound of milk."

"Everything has its limit. Not even human milk would be as expensive as that. Don't bring shame upon Leopard Terrace."

"The government has money to burn. It's a waste if I don't charge them like this."

"Suit yourself."

While Father and Old Man Li the Second are discussing Little Mite's food and drink Fourth Girl is simmering vegetable porridge on the kitchen stove – she cooks vegetables and corn-flour together into a sticky paste. She understands that the milk from Old Man Li the Second's ewe can't last for long and Little Mite's diet must be adapted according to the situation.

As the price of the ewe's milk is being debated, Little Mite follows the yellow dog to mill around the fire pit amidst the aroma of the corn-flour paste. Dragging his wounded leg, he stumbles at almost every step and staggers in pursuit of the yellow dog. The yellow dog dodges about in an impatient manner in an effort to avoid this creature that is neither-fish-nor-fowl and has bamboo slips about his leg, which clatter as he moves. The two circling animals form an intriguing scenario.

The corn-flour paste is scooped out into an earthen pot and served. The smart yellow dog darts over, followed by the clumsy Little Mite. Regardless of how Fourth Girl tries to restrain him, the yellow dog sticks his snout into the earthen pot without hesitation or manners and starts to chomp away, vulgarity written all over his greedy face. Little Mite hesitates. He wants to come over to the earthen pot as well, but he doesn't know what he should do after that.

Fourth Girl drives away the yellow dog and fetches Little Mite to the earthen pot. Little Mite sniffs at the pot and obviously doesn't know what to do. Hare comes over and presses Little Mite's mouth into the pot. He surmises that Little Mite will then also reach out his tongue and chomp away like the yellow dog ...

Little Mite hasn't opened his mouth. His face is completely stained with corn-flour paste.

Mother says, "He is still too young. You should feed him."

Fourth Girl thus uses her fingers to daub the paste into Little Mite's mouth.

After several wipes, Little Mite has committed the flavour of the paste to memory. Later on, without being summoned, he will follow that string of fragrance over to the earthen pot as soon as it has been placed on the floor.

Attended upon by people – or strictly speaking, being attended upon by Fourth Girl – Little Mite has gradually regained his sense of self. He likes drawing close to people, likes romping together with the yellow dog and likes Fourth Girl scratching the dishevelled hair upon his head. When the children come to search after Hare, he will roll to and fro under their feet and from time to time clutch this one's leg and grab at that one's foot. In high spirits he might even mimic the way the yellow dog wiggles his hips and amuses the children so that they hoot with laughter. Fourth Girl comments, "How can this 'little mite' still be a spotty bear. He is a spotty dog from head to foot."

Every villager sends their leftovers to Fourth Girl's home. As things proceed in this fashion, Little Mite is apt to run outside and roll ball-like across the courtyard whenever he hears the gate squeak. This frightens the assembled geese and chickens so they flap their wings blindly and with animation.

Now that his wounded leg has healed, Little Mite is becoming livelier and more intelligent. He has taken up the pastime of chasing people who he knows will offer him delectable foods. At any time, they can conjure up foods that are beyond his wildest dreams – foods that could never be appreciated in the world of spotty bears. By now, his diet boasts no significant difference from that of the yellow dog – leftover noodles, leftover steamed corn breads, raw sweet potatoes, well-cooked taros, and anything else in fact. The milk from Old Man Li the Second's ewe is no longer sufficient to set him on his way and it has occurred to nobody that he might eat bamboo too – perhaps he himself has forgotten that bamboo is even edible. Hare often feeds milk toffees to him. However, after he has eaten the sesame cracknels someone else fed to him, he loses his interest in milk toffees because sesame cracknels are crispy and crunchy whereas milk toffees get stuck to his teeth – he doesn't like sticky foods.

Before she returns to the city, Colourful Duckweed comes over to see Little Mite. She says that Little Mite is different from both the toy pandas on display in the shops and the pandas in the zoos in the city. With their blackness clearly picked out from their whiteness, toy pandas are rotund, slippery and soft. Little Mite is too grubby, like a small muddy ball. What is more, he frequently bites at people and grabs at their trouser legs. He is not as lovely as those stuffed pandas on the shelves. She continues that the pandas in the zoos appear very dignified and very elegant and remain standoffish towards people, unlike Little Mite, who thrives on the attention of the crowd and doesn't display the least bit of restraint as pandas are supposed to have.

Fourth Girls says nothing. She thinks that a dirty panda with teeth is a panda true to the name. Similarly, those short-sighted annoying bamboo rats are bamboo rats. Were those rats to get into the hands of city slickers they would surely adjust the behaviour of their mouths and faces too.

The authorities have passed on the word that the people of Leopard Terrace will take care of Little Mite for the time being.

When spring arrives and the snow on the mountains has thawed a little, the county government will send hands to transport him to a panda breeding base. Old Man Li the Second, in particular, inquires about the remuneration. The authorities respond that everyone is responsible for the rescuing of endangered wild animals that are on the brink of extinction. But of course the state won't shortchange the peasants. They add that it is the first time that local residents have saved and protected so young a panda and that this is unprecedented for the county to boot. Accordingly, they must be extremely cautious. The baby panda has already been registered at the forestry ministry. Should any incident him place him in jeopardy, not only the Village Committee of Leopard Terrace would be reprimanded and punished but officials from the county government as well.

From that point onwards the atmosphere somehow starts to crackle with tension. Little Mite is kept under strict supervision. Originally he had been allowed to roam free in the courtyard to run awhile and chase the yellow dog, the pair gamboling together. Now for the most part he remains closed behind the door of the utility room where the agricultural implements belonging to Fourth Girl's family are stored. The yellow dog is Little Mite's friend. Unwilling to let Little Mite stay alone in desolation, he doesn't roam far but frequently stalks in front of and behind the utility room; if necessary, he will bark several times at the cracks in the door.

IV.

It is slowly growing warm. The authorities have sent hands to carry the panda out of the mountains.

In the courtyard of Fourth Girl's family, several fellows are assembling a wooden cage, hammering nails noisily. Half a dozen young men have been hired as the carriers, being paid fifty yuan apiece.

The panda which is soon to hit the road is now akin to a daughter about to be married off. People at Leopard Terrace have suddenly become inordinately attached to the little life that is no more than half-a-year old and they turn out to see him off with fresh taros and hard-boiled eggs.

Hare bathes Little Mite in a special way in the creek by poaching the shampoo Colourful Duckweed sent to his sister. That whole bottle of shampoo, the cap of which had not even been unscrewed, is all spent on him. After the bath, Little Mite is clean and refreshed and exudes fragrance in every direction – it is almost no longer a spotty bear. Hare thinks that the spotty bears "on the shelves whose blackness is clearly picked out from their whiteness" are probably no better than this. Hare's original intention was that the spotty bear which is to depart from Leopard Terrace should not be too shabby and should embody how the local people take pride in their appearances.

That afternoon, all the members of the Village Committee play host to the personnel deployed by the authorities at Fourth Girl's home. Sitting around a squat table, they drink wine and dine on mashed taro, venison cooked with air-dried bamboo shoots, and stir-fried dainty mushrooms – all prepared by Fourth Girl. The cadres eat to their heart's content and drink until their faces are bright red. They exclaim that, living such a life in such an environment, the people at Leopard Terrace are wayward immortals that stand aloof from worldly affairs, folks who must enjoy their eternal life and are immune from ageing. They indict urban life for being too heartbreaking and too depressing. The air is polluted. There is too much infighting. Wives and children and the soaring prices have deprived them of even one moment's peace.

Fourth Girl judges that these guys are drama queens who still bemoan how their lives are in tatters though life in fact has smiled on them.

Old Man Li the Second is standing stubbornly beneath the eaves with his ewe in tow. Fourth Girl's father goes out several times and tries to persuade him to go back home. He won't. Fourth Girl's father instructs him to demonstrate the elegant demeanour of the offspring of the Red Army, to be broad-minded and noble and not to haggle over every pound with their superiors. Old Man Li the Second doesn't buy that and retorts that his father was his father and he is himself. He requests that the Village Head should not willfully lump them together.

The Village Head comes back in and raises the problem of the breeding-fee with caution.

Qinglai the Village Committee member says that Little Mite feasts on ewe's milk, honey and white steamed buns every day and the daily expenditure is enormous.

The superiors jape, "Are you providing for a crown prince? Giving him milk and honey every day? He couldn't gorge like this even if he were the emperor's son. Don't make up excuses to extort money from the seniors. Leave things be. You will be given the amount of money that is due to you. Seek truth from facts – that's the working method upheld by the Communist Party."

At this time, nobody knows how Old Man Li the Second has managed to enter the room with his ewe in tow. He invites the superiors to inspect the ewe's teats, saying that the once-heavy milk sack has become a sagging shrunken leather bag and for the sake of Little Mite, his two lambs have both had to go into the wok to be simmered into soup. How can he not request that the government compensate him for his loss?

The superiors are stuffing themselves until their heads spin and their faces burn. The sudden appearance of a big ewe cheeses them off. Their faces sink, they yap, "What hell is going on? Is there not one scrap of organizational discipline?"

Fourth Girl's father orders Old Man Li the Second to beat it. Old Man Li the Second doesn't. He states that not only will he refuse to leave but there are several other compensation-seekers outside the door who want to come in as well. The bear has trampled their beehives and pilfered dozens of pounds of their honey. With no income this year, the little people will be forced to drink the northwest wind.

The Village Committee member Third Maternal Uncle refills the cadres' wine cups while sweeping his small eyes across their number and asking loudly, "Which family has not had their beehives trampled on by the bear? Why have I never heard tell of that!"

Someone outside picks up on his words and a few still want to come in but are intercepted by Qinglai.

The cadres answer, "The people's losses will be compensated for and the animals should also be protected. Our economy is developing but the wild animals in the mountain forests are slowly dwindling away ..."

Someone outside cuts in, "Who says *dwindling*? There is a plague of takins in the mountains and they go out onto the roads to protest in herds and gangs. There've been plenty of traffic accidents on the roads but you still blindly protect them and don't allow us to go hunt them."

Old Man Li the Second says, "I don't want to talk about the takins. I only want to discuss the spotty bear that you are whisking away. He has polished off thirty-six and a half pounds of my milk not to mention robbing me of two lambs."

Old Man Li the Second's ewe knows how to act in unison. She releases a pool of hot urine and expels a floor-full of ewe pellets very properly at this time. The air in the room is clammy and immediately becomes malodorous.

The cadres sweet-talk him, "You guys should be attuned to the country's difficulties and share the government's tribulations. Here we are at an old revolutionary base with an excellent tradition of making contributions ..."

Father shouts for Fourth Girl and asks her to clean the floor as soon as possible.

Fourth Girl is coaxing Little Mite in the utility room. Little Mite, who is behind the locked door, has become irritable and restless after hearing the clinking sounds of axes and chisels and

91

having caught sight of the ferocious-looking white-stumped big wooden cage. He keeps on pacing around and even Fourth Girl cannot draw near to him. The handles of pickaxes and iron shovels, the thresher, the ladder ... he has chomped most of the wooden articles completely out of shape. Panting heavily, he now rams his body against the grain silo. The silo sways and is about to fall apart; it cannot withstand one more strike.

Little Mite is demonstrating his bearish temper to the full.

Ceaselessly calling out "Little Mite," Fourth Girl cadges a big chunk of freshly-dug yam bean from Hare's hand and offers it to Little Mite. Tender crispy yam bean is a specialty in the mountains, being as sweet as sugar cane and as refreshing and fragrant as peanuts; after one bite, the juice will slither down along the eater's hands. Yam bean is a favourite of both the children and Little Mite; Little Mite is no different from the kids in this respect. Nonetheless, at this moment, Little Mite repudiates that kindness. Furiously he pinches the yam bean that has rolled to his feet into a pulp and then pulverizes it by sitting down on it hard.

Hare comments that Little Mite has become angry.

Leaning against the doorjamb, Fourth Girl tries to mollify, "Little Mite, I know you don't want to leave. I don't want you to leave either. Even so, life is better outside the mountains. Men go outside and water flows outside – this has been the rule here since ancient times. How many old Red Army soldiers left this place to become high-ranking officials in Beijing? Whenever they went out, none of them wanted to come back again. This proves that life is much better there outside than here in the mountains. But why don't you want to go out? Outside the mountains there are mice that can talk and chocolate that is more fragrant than sesame candies, cement roads that are as flat as a mirror, and high-rises. Don't you want to take a look? I know: you are scared, as scared as I am. But in fact you are much better off than me. They will bring mountain bamboo directly to your mouth. You can eat it sitting there or lying down or in whatever way pleases you. There is ewe's milk in endless supply; you can drink however much you want. Nobody wants to risk doing anything to upset you. Everyone has to sweet-talk you and provide for you. You are a national treasure! Little Mite, what is it that you still feel attached to? To the mountain wastelands and the wild ridges? To those miserable days when you were stuck in the gap between two stones … Go, Little Mite, go. If I were you, I would go away. I wouldn't lose my temper …"

Tears unconsciously trickle down Fourth Girl's cheeks. Her melancholy and sorrow, having been pent-up for so long, flow out slowly in the form of those tears. She senses that she is not talking to the spotty bear but to herself.

Hare looks at his sister blankly.

Little Mite totters over and squints at Fourth Girl. He then clutches her leg without much thought. Believing that Little Mite has been moved, she bends down to stroke his clean glossy fur. She wants to sweep him up in her arms like her mother did when she fed him the ewe's milk.

As she bends down Fourth Girl detects that something has gone awry. At first she senses the strangeness in Little Mite's eyes and then she feels the pain in her leg. Next, blood slithers down from the bottom of the leg of her pants. She is terrified. She knows how good the mouth under her feet is. Every item among those pickaxe handles and handles of iron shovels and the legs of the ladder – which have all been bitten into splinters – was stronger than her leg …

Fourth Girl's face becomes deathly pale.

Like a rabbit Hare rushes to fetch his father.

Father comes and so do the cadres and her third maternal uncle and his gang.

People yank at Little Mite, but Little Mite won't unlock his jaws.

Father demands, "This 'little mite,' what's wrong with him today?"

Qinglai probes, "He must have spotted the cage and gotten vexed."

"It's because you put him in a prison," Mountain Forest Li concludes. "A man, never mind an animal, would bite after being locked up for days on end."

"An animal is an animal," the cadres comment. "Its brutal nature will never go away."

Fourth Girl's mother pats at the panda's head and cajoles, "Let go with your jaws. Why throw a tantrum?"

Little Mite releases his jaws and with a sweep climbs the ladder to the small attic of the utility room. Then, clattering and clanking, he punches and kicks out hard there again.

A few bloody punctures have been left in Fourth Girl's leg and blood is gurgling forth.

"Go to the hospital," the cadres instruct. "Find several guys to take it in turns to carry the panda and to carry the girl as well."

After giving Fourth Girl's leg a pinch, Father says, "Nothing serious. The bone is not fractured."

On hearing Fourth Girl's father say that the bone is not broken, everyone present lets out a sigh of relief. They all know Little Mite hasn't thrust the heft of his jaw into it. They have each of them seen how a spotty bear gnaws at a bamboo – *ka chow, ka chow*. It should not be difficult to chew up a leg.

Third Maternal Uncle says that they should move Little Mite to another place. Or else he still can't quiet down at the sight of the cage in the courtyard. Tomorrow, providing that this piece of cargo has been packed off safe and sound, they can put their hearts at ease.

Qinglai agrees that he has a point.

Scanning those agricultural implements that have been bitten into splinters, Father too says that they should move Little Mite to another place.

The men therefore go back to the main room to continue their wine and to discuss how to pacify Little Mite tonight.

Mother rips apart one of Hare's white shirts and bandages up Fourth Girl's leg with it.

Nobody notices that Little Mite has slid down the ladder and fumbled his way over here. He pillows his massive head on Fourth Girl's leg.

v.

After their discussion, the cadres decide that Little Mite will be moved to the book-keeper's glory hole in the office of the Village Committee. Comparatively speaking, the book-keeper's glory hole is the best-defended place – there is an iron gate with two locks and a wooden window with iron bars. Of course, they have learned a lesson from the devastation wrecked upon the wooden wares in the utility room, and instruct the book-keeper to remove his desk, chairs, benches, and anything else into which Little Mite could sink his teeth. The book-keeper is displeased and yammers on about who is to shoulder the responsibility should anything happen as a consequence of this key financial department being moved.

Qinglai explains, "That 'little mite' will stay in your office for one night only. He will hit the road tomorrow morning as soon as the dew has lifted. Just show a little tolerance."

The book-keeper grunts that it is too troublesome to move things to and fro.

"All the wooden-handled tools in the Village Head's home have been mauled by Little Mite's mouth and he doesn't call it *troublesome*," Third Uncle reprises. "You are only being asked to move your desk and you complain it is troublesome. How can you have the nerve?"

The book-keeper bites his tongue.

After supper, Fourth Girl's father tells people to manhandle Little Mite over there.

That night, leaning against the head of the bed, Fourth Girl looks out at the courtyard through the window. The courtyard is full of moonlight, which cascades down like water is being sprinkled. A black silhouette is strolling in a leisurely fashion across the mountain slope opposite. Fourth Girl surmises that it must either be the she-leopard, a black bear, a takin, or perhaps something else … A single bank of cloud coasts over and eclipses the moon. The she-leopard is gone. So too are the black bear, the takin and everything else. It is a dark blur. The wooden cage stands out in the darkness. She doesn't know why the wooden cage should appear so incongruous in the midst of that serene night in the mountain village. Early tomorrow morning, Little Mite will be caged up so he can be conveyed to the outside world which lies beyond these overlapping mountains and waters. He will see many novelties that can't be observed by Fourth Girl at Leopard Terrace. He will see many more rarities than Colourful Duckweed has ever observed. He will no longer be a spotty bear. As Colourful Duckweed has said, he will become a toy on a shop shelf or a proud exhibit that a zoo can use to rake in money …

When her train of thought reaches this point, Fourth Girl's eyes brim with tears.

Mother asks, "Does your leg still hurt?"

Fourth Girl shakes her head.

Mother says, "Tomorrow, Little Mite will leave. This is the last night that he will stay in the mountains."

Fourth Girl observes, "Tonight, Little Mite must be very sad."

Mother agrees, "Wild animals are all intelligent. They have a kind of telepathic bond with the mountains. You see, how he kicked up a fuss today. It was really creepy."

Fourth Girl says, "Mother, after my leg heals up, I will go out as well. I have reached a deal with Colourful Duckweed."

"After my daughter has gone out, she will never come back again."

"Mother, I shall come back."

96

"You are all cheating me …"

Early the next morning, the book-keeper scoots to Fourth Girl's home in a hurry and reports to the Village Head, "The spotty bear has run away!"

Father hastens out while slipping into his clothes, murmuring without stopping, "How was he able to run away? How could he?"

By the time Fourth Girl's father arrives at the book-keeper's glory-hole, many people are already standing there both inside and out. Among the crowd Mountain Forest Li is mouthing off loudly, "Run away! That's great!"

Examining the window frame that was chewed apart by Little Mite, Third Maternal Uncle bleats, "… How come we have forgotten that it is a spotty bear …"

Touching the iron bars that were scattered all over the floor when the window frame was bitten into splinters, the cadres comment, "Incredible, really incredible!"

Father kicks the yellow dog that is crawling here and there among the crowd and rebukes, "You kept watch on him every day. What were you doing last night?"

Finding himself on the side of right and consequently having strong lungpower, the yellow dog barks at Fourth Girl's father several times.

Fourth Girl's father reproaches, "Son of a bitch, you still dare to talk back. Go search for him. Go out and search after him for me!"

The yellow dog turns his head and runs away.

The yellow dog runs directly back home.

At home Hare is talking to Fourth Girl about Little Mite.

In the ensuing summer, Fourth Girl departs from the mountains – Colourful Duckweed has written to her telling her to go out.

Several more years pass by. The population in all the other places is surging. On the other hand, the population at

Leopard Terrace merely dwindles – down from ninety-four souls five years ago to eighty-one now; the young people have mostly gone out, leaving behind only the elderly, the weak, the diseased and the disabled. According to the expert in demographics who comes along to conduct investigations, within forty years, Leopard Terrace Village will perish naturally. Each of the expert's students is overcome with excitement at this prediction. They declare, "Returning the mountain forests to Mother Nature and to the wild animals. This is the progress of society. This is the great achievement brought about by the improvement of the natural ecological environment."

Fourth Girl's father shakes his head. He says, "If our village perishes, who can the spotty bears seek refuge with? In the past few years, the spotty bears have mastered the rules. All the sick, starving and dying spotty bears flee here. Leopard Terrace will stand no matter what happens – stand in the depths of the mountain forests, stand at the end of the high mountains and steep gorges."

The students are perplexed. They cannot work out whether it is the human beings or the animals that have evolved.

Anyhow, Fourth Girl has never come back.

What You're Seeking Left No Trace

I

The regular fortnightly gala for patients in the Psychiatric Hospital is getting underway in the entertainments room.

The eyes of most of those in the audience remain vacant.

In the midst of the wide-eyed spectators are a few members of staff in white gowns, who silently pay close attention to the patients.

The onlookers sit in their melancholy postures, with no one interacting with anybody else. Everyone seems to be sealed up with the acute worries they have to bear. The programme of turns to be exhibited on the green carpet in middle of the room holds no appeal for them. The acting is of absolutely no concern to these people, nor are the earnest actors. Not a single performance manages to elicit applause no matter how wonderful it is – every individual soul in that group is locked within his or her personal world of isolation. Were that not so they wouldn't have to be here in the first place.

A young woman is performing a ballet routine adapted from the famous *Pas de deux* in *The Nutcracker Suite*. Although she is dancing solo, her devoted expressions and skilful movements make others sense the presence of a partner who exists only in her heart. Her eyes are clear and lofty; her face, pure and winsome. There can be no doubt that she is an outstanding dancer; nevertheless, the loose blue gown with white stripes discloses upon first glance that she too is a patient undergoing treatment.

Gu Ming, the lead physician, sits pokerfaced at the rear of the crowd, casting a chilly stare at the dancer. The nib of his pen slips under the name of the young dancer but makes no mark there. The youthful doctor Xiao An has, however, already deposited a tick after her name. This is a sign that the patient is making a recovery. If three ticks appear in a row, the patient is considered ready to be discharged from the hospital.

Noticing the director is looking at her, Xiao An says, "She dances rather well and is well on her way to recovery."

Gu Ming doesn't make any response, instead casting his eyes back onto the dancer.

The dance is drawing to an end. The swift spinning pirouette showcases the ballerina's extraordinary artistry. A trickle of applause emanates from the staff among the audience. Xiao An retraces that tick even more thickly.

After a delicate yet still very professional reaction to the curtain call, the young lady steps back to her seat with an intoxicated expression on her face. Staring outside the window in silence, she doesn't even slip off her pink ballet pumps.

Xiao An sneaks a look at the director's record sheet – a rough cross has materialized beneath the girl's name.

A man with whiskers approaches the centre of the room. He is clad in the same white and blue outfit, buttoned up askew, with one foot bare. A nurse rushes from across the room in his direction and helps him put on the other shoe. He blurts out with a shy and girlish laugh, "Surely I can't manage this." He is ready to step away immediately but finds his way barred by the nurse. He stands there, rubbing his hands anxiously, "Do I have to?" Getting an affirmative answer from the head nurse, he thinks for a while and murmurs, "How about I sing you a bit of that revolutionary opera *Fighting on the Plain*? I'll do the part of Li Sheng." Receiving no response from the audience, he adds, "I'd better not bother if you are not interested."

Gu Ming proclaims, "Just sing it, Old Wang. I love that piece."

Old Wang then begins to sing,

You listen—

A boom like roaring spring thunder,

This is Zhao Yonggang, the son of workers and farmers, known to everybody on this plain!

His footprints cover every inch of Mount Taihang,

The railways shake their whole length with his anti-Japanese stand.

The man you're seeking left no trace,

He beat you like an invincible army, hardly to be guarded.

Freely as fish swim in the water and birds fly in the woods,

Where the ordinary folks are, there is Zhao Yonggang!

This section of the *erhuang* and *erliu* melodies[d] is dispatched in excruciating fashion by Old Wang the patient – the correct key cannot be found. There is hardly any applause for him, even from the staff. They are not at all familiar with *Fighting on the Plain*; actually it means nothing to anybody under forty. They have no idea what Old Wang has been uttering.

Gu Ming is the only one to clap.

Dr. Gu Ming is familiar with the opera as when he was an "educated youth" rusticated to a farm he happened to be cast as Zhao Yonggang.

Old Wang salutes him with folded hands and a nurse leads him offstage, his face a picture of embarrassment.

Gu Ming makes a tick under Wang's name.

Xiao An is left puzzled by this.

All the skits that follow abound with pranks and din.

II.

Having clocked off from work, Gu Ming cycles back home, humming the line *The man you're seeking left no trace* repeatedly until he has scaled the stairs to knock at his door. He seems unable to get that line out of his head.

Gu Ming's wife, Xie Yuqin, has stayed at home ever since she applied to be signed off from work on medical grounds. She doesn't in fact have any illness but taking compulsory redundancy was her only alternative. At her age, the chances of finding other employment were considerably slimmer. It was more reasonable to wrap things up completely: she cited a strained back as the grounds and then retired.

Xie is so pleased to welcome her husband back home. The tea is freshly-brewed, supper is cooked presently and a pair of slippers is pushed in the direction of his feet. Gu Ming changes his clothes and sits at the table. He hasn't had chance to tuck in when the yellow kitten they have only recently adopted leaps onto his lap, raises its downy head and meows at him.

Gu Ming's thoughts still linger on the operatic aria that Old Wang performed and he chants to the kitten with his head wagging, "*The man you're seeking left no trace. He beat you like an invincible army, hardly to be guarded…*"

"Eat up," Xie prompts him. "Why are you singing to the cat?"

Gu Ming explains, "You know Old Wang at our hospital. He's on the mend. That's what he sang today."

Xie doesn't grasp the opportunity to chatter on about Old Wang but tells Gu Ming, "The neighbourhood committee held a meeting today. It was reported that the District Women's Federations have chosen to commend couples who have been married for over twenty-five years. They are going to offer them two towelling coverlets as a reward."

"We're hardly short of towelling coverlets ourselves," Gu Ming points out.

"But we meet the requirement of twenty-five years of matrimony," Xie answers.

Gu Ming remarks, "These old women just try and take every opportunity to remind the world that they still exist."

"You shouldn't put it that way," Xie continues. "This happens to be an honour as well. Old Zhang across the way and our downstairs neighbour Aunt Song have already sent over copies of their marriage certificates."

"The Women's Federations do this as a means of trying to discourage divorce but actually divorce is not such a bad thing."

"Not a bad thing? You think it is something good!"

"I didn't say that."

"The thing is we should find our certificate. It has been missing somewhere in our home for years."

Gu Ming doesn't want to hear any more about the towelling coverlets and hums that line again over his beer.

Xie's mind is still on her marriage certificate.

At this moment, Xiao An drops by. She hasn't had supper yet. Her mouth waters upon seeing that red bean porridge prepared by Xie. She just sits together with them at the table, not eating a morsel. Xiao An has come to arrange the discharge of the ballet dancer. When she saw that Gu Ming had written a cross earlier that day, her resolve seemed to weaken. She is no longer sure whether the release form should be filed.

"Her situation is rather serious," Gu Ming states. "She hasn't found a release from her own personal drama. To put it another way, she is not aware of who she is and where she is."

Xiao An sits there without saying a word; caring simply about the porridge. Finally she asks, "But why did you write a tick next to Old Wang's name? What he sang sounded a muddle, totally incoherent."

"How incoherent?" Gu Ming replies. "The lines are meant to be like that and Old Wang phrased them acceptably. Didn't you notice that he's already regained some awareness of his surroundings? He didn't want to sing when he found that no one was clapping. This is precisely because he realizes that he doesn't sing well and is afraid of being teased by others...What does that infer? That is how normal people think and behave..."

Xie has no interest in their discussion about patients and slips away to Gu Ming's study for the certificate.

III

It has been three days since Xie began her certificate-hunting quest, but she still hasn't found it.

Her face has turned green with anxiety.

It is certainly not on account of those the two towelling coverlets. The certificate was originally put away safe and well, so wherever could it have got to? At last Xie's endeavours have come to be motivated purely by the sake of finding it.

The home is now in utter disarray. Even the milk bottle that was once used for feeding her daughter has been scooped up out of the broken old basket. Coming back from work, Gu Ming cannot even find a spot on which to stand. The dust chokes him to point of sneezing. No longer is he waited upon with hot teas and warm dinners. Even Sandy the kitten has been scared into hiding. Gu Ming calls after it for a while both inside and outside the apartment; after a time, Sandy stumbles out from under the cupboard with ash all over its head.

He then peers at Xie who, with a cloth wrapped about her head, is on the balcony checking through the "Talk about the Picture" exercise books their daughter read as a girl.

"Why are you poking about here?" Gu wonders. "These have been bundled-up ready to be sold."

"Maybe the certificate found its way into these books," Xie answers.

"The kid has already entered university," Gu notes. "How could it have got here?"

"The more remote we go, the more possibilities there are," she reasons. "Think how ridiculous it would be if the certificate turned up in your brand new investors' handbook."

"You've made a proper mess here over two pieces of paper," Gu complains. "Is it worth it?"

Xie continues, "I'm just curious as to how a pair of big, picture-sized documents could go missing. So weird!"

Gu muses, "It seems like I've seen it somewhere."

Xie stares at him. "Where? Think it over."

"I can't," Gu replies. "It's just slipped me by. It's been ages."

"What a fool you are," Xie retaliates. "You only remember your mental patients. We met a cadre on the street that day and you claimed he was a former patient of yours. He didn't admit it himself but you took it so seriously and even pulled back his collar to check for a birthmark. That was so embarrassing! Now you ought to have been of some use but you said it slipped you by. What do you want me to say?"

"I've got it. The last time I saw it was when the shockproof shed was being built. Yes. The shelter. Your mother said the paper was sturdy and wanted to use it to patch up the window. I said no. That's our marriage certificate! "

"Then?" Xie asks.

"I have no idea," admits Gu. "You shouldn't be asking me. Ask your mother."

Xie is irritated and screeches in a high-pitched voice, "If I could ask my mum, I wouldn't be standing here! Are you looking forward to me dying?"

Gu Ming is familiar with how tempers can fray when people search for lost possessions so knows it's better not to cheese her off. He consoles her with the observation, "We've been together for dozens of years. Who can say we are not a couple?"

Xie insists, "The point is that we have the certificate. I was formally taken by you. It is not as though we moved our bedding together and then made do."

Gu asks, "Who said we just made do?"

"Then where is the certificate? Xie probes. "We are making do if there's no certificate."

Gu Ming doesn't know what to say and so changes the topic: "What are we having for supper?"

This unexpectedly provokes Xie to still greater anger. She raises her head: "Have anything you like. I'm not touching a bite until I find it."

"What's the use!" Gu exclaims. "If you really want to take

it so seriously, let's go to our work units to have a certificate printed off. They are the same."

"It's no use having that certificate from our departments," Xie persists. "They offer any certificate as and when required. Even for Xiao Liu's beriberi. Everyone knows that the certificates from our working unit are worthless. What is a marriage certificate? A marriage certificate has legal effect and is issued by the government. How can it be approved by our working unit?"

"Then you go to the notary's office to have a certificate printed off there," Gu suggests. "That would to all intents and purposes be the same as a marriage certificate."

Xie pipes up, "Now this is quite useful. How come I didn't think of it?"

Xie kicks away the stack of old books and prepares to cook. "Thanks goodness for the notary's office," she thinks. "There is finally a place to ask for justice. Otherwise, I would never be able to confirm my marriage to Gu Ming."

IV.

The next morning, Xie goes to the hospital seeking out Gu Ming who at present happens to be dealing with the ballet dancer together with Xiao An. It turns out that the dancer tore off and ate her buttons, believing them to be walnuts. Nurses attempted to coax her to the radiography department for an X-ray but she wouldn't budge. Dancing non-stop, she whirled between patients' beds with doctors and nurses. They tried hard to bring her under control and a couple of nurses smuggled her over to radiography.

Xie follows Gu into the office and declares, "How could that beautiful girl be a patient? What a pity! She seems healthy."

Gu says, "It is a kind of environmental fixation."

Xie asks for details.

"Sort of like reaching a dead end without being able to find a way out."

Xiao An interrupts, "Actually everyone has some degree of that. If we take it lightly it can be labelled 'nervous temperament.' Should it intensify then it is classified as a disease."

Xie protests, "A disease is a disease. How can you say everyone has it?"

Meanwhile, Old Wang is in the process of being discharged from the hospital. His wife fetches him over to say goodbye to Gu Ming.

Xiao An gives him a one-month-discharge note. Gu Ming tells his wife to escort him around and not to return to work too fast. Wang's wife says that they have no money for travel.

Their oldest son is preparing for the entrance exam to senior high school. If he is admitted to a key school they will be required to stump up a large sum. Their son must never work as a boiler man like his father. He ought to be an intellectual.

"It's good to work," Old Wang adds. "I don't want to travel." These days he owes so much to his wife; she has suffered a great deal.

With red-rimmed eyes, Old Wang's wife blurts out, "Don't say that. We are a couple."

Xie then interjects, "Do you have your marriage certificate?"

The wife answers, "Look how my sister puts the question. We got married on 9th March 1980. Yes. How could you say that we don't have our certificate?"

"I mean is your certificate kept somewhere, safe and sound?" Xie asks.

Old Wang and his wife look at each other, unable to answer the question.

Xie asks again, "What did I say? You are shocked? Just like us, go find it soon."

The couple doubt each other and depart.

Gu Ming asks his wife what she is doing here.

Xie reveals, "A marriage certificate cannot be certified by the notary's office."

Gu asks, "Why?"

"A working certificate and a household registration card don't count," Xie carries on. "They only accept an official marriage certificate."

"Then it is a dead end and there is no other way?"

"People in the notary's office said if the marriage certificate is lost, we should go to our original working unit for the document. If they offer the certificate, the notary office will do."

Gu Ming is puzzled for a moment and says, "Our original place of work? That's in Aksu, Xinjiang…"

"How about going there?"

"Over twenty years have passed. Those colleagues must now be scattered all over. That working unit was disbanded. Whom should we look for then?"

Close to tears Xie asks, "What would you suggest then?"

"Just forget it" is Gu's reply.

"Forget it?" Xie cries. "No way!"

"We have no option. We can't rustle one up."

"You can forget. I can't. I'll get the notary certificate."

Now becoming somewhat aggravated Gu pronounces, "Go ahead if you have nothing better to do. What an idle life."

Xie retorts, "And that's your attitude towards the laws of the land! What do you mean by 'I have nothing better to do'? This is our business. I am doing it for our sake."

Gu goes on, "It's too late to go on thinking about the certificate. What did you do before?"

"This is what I was about to ask you," Xie replies.

Xiao An passes a glass of water to Xie, signalling that Gu Ming should rein himself in.

Gu claims, "I don't mind about the marriage certificate. I'm going to Jilin for a meeting tomorrow."

"Psychiatric research again?" asks Xie.

"Of course," answers Gu. "What else can I do?"

Xie inquires about who will accompany him.

"Xiao An is also going."

"You go to your meeting. I shall do whatever is necessary to find the certificate, even if it means going up into the sky or down to the sea."

"You are taking this so seriously!" Gu counters. "Only two towelling coverlets. I can buy you a pair."

Xie asks, "How could your mind still be so confused? The towelling coverlets are of no consequence. What matters most is the status."

Gu Ming asks her to what status she is referring.

"The legal status of our marriage. Without the certificate, what sort of relationship do we have?"

"What sort of relationship? Your parents didn't have a certificate either," he observes. "They shared their entire lives and died together."

Xiao An continues, "It's no joke at all. A lot of my friends cohabit without a certificate and they have a fine enough time. They enjoy such freedom. If they decide they don't want to carry on, they can step away easily. Very flexible."

"That is the modern style," Xie observes. "Living together without getting married. What a disgrace! The government and your work unit will never support you."

Xiao An explains, "Now that no one recognizes your marriage, it's much easier for you... you are older unmarried people. You can either register for marriage or look for a new partner. How wonderful that is!"

Gu Ming chuckles.

Xie gasps, "It's getting even more absurd!"

v.

The old grannies from the neighbourhood committee are practising their fan dancing. Among their number, an absent-looking Xie makes a few mistakes. The coach calls out her name but she still cannot keep the pace. Aunt Song alongside her asks what the matter is. Xie says she has got a headache.

"You have a doctor at home so shouldn't have to worry," Aunt Song reassures her. "Let Doctor Gu examine you."

"Don't mention that doctor," Xie's answers. "The man you're seeking left no trace."

"Out on another trip?" Song asks.

Xie replies, "You bet. Jilin. " She continues, "Aunt Song, you have given a lifetime of service to the neighbourhood committee. What would you say if a couple doesn't have a marriage certificate?"

Song replies, "That's easy. Cohabitation without legal marriage."

Xie asks, "But if they had a certificate then lost it?"

Song says, "Reapply in the district where it was lost."

"What? It can't be reapplied for?"

"Ask the original issuing unit to offer a certificate of loss."

"What if this certificate can't be obtained?"

"If that's the case, then the marriage does not exist. The relationship has no legal protection."

After the talk with Aunt Song, Xie feels the growing significance of this business. She looks stunned. She starts to regret not having paid much attention to that piece of paper before. Now without it, everything seems untrue and of no account. The kid will be rendered an illegitimate child no matter whether it is in college or still being fed on milk powder.

Xie goes back home unhappily. She doesn't cook but throws her frame onto the bed, her mind teeming with thoughts.

She is overcome with an unprecedented pang of peril: now that her marriage with Gu Ming doesn't have a certificate of legal protection, they are actually free and have the right to choose again. She is retired and as an older woman and a housewife, the chances for her to choose and be chosen seem limited. On the other hand, Gu Ming is the lead physician and enjoys the greatest success in his career. He could certainly find someone one hundred times better than her in every respect… The youthful doctor Xiao An who always went to their home seemed to be a potential threat. The expression she had when she looked at Gu Ming was not entirely trusting either… Why does she always have to accompany Gu Ming? How many times have they been away together? The age gap would not pose a problem. This was the new trend – a sophisticated youthful lady with an older man. Moreover, old men like to play around with younger women. Who knows? Maybe Gu Ming had that intention as well. Men always like the new and hate the old. Something might be going on there already. Take his attitude towards the certificate as an example. He neither became worried nor anxious over it. He even said "just forget it." What did that mean? Did he want to forget the certificate or the marriage? If it were the latter, she bet that he would like to forget it soon. That gem of knowledge was imparted by An – "if they don't want to carry on, they can step away easily." Her marriage to Gu Ming was in just such a flexible state. He might have started playing another tune while she was still concentrating on finding the certificate! Stupid, really stupid. Couldn't be more stupid!

Xie turns over in bed and sinks into a deep state of contemplation.

Having mulled over the matter thoroughly, she realizes that it is just possible that she has never actually clapped eyes on that certificate. When they went to get registered at the office, she, as the leader of the "iron women team" at the time, was busy leading the crowd to dig a tunnel in order to set a record for labouring continuously for seventy-two hours. The certificate was handled by a female secretary. Unwise, extremely unwise! She was too young and reckless… She must have just taken everything for granted. If things went on like that, the very existence of the marriage certificate would soon stand open to question. Gu Ming, it must be noted, was aware of all this. He might have hatched a second plan since then. No wonder when she was searching almost everywhere for the certificate, he kept on singing *The man you're seeking left no trace. He beat you like an invincible army, hardly to be guarded.* Hardly to be guarded! It turned out that the invincible army had made its ambush more than twenty years earlier... He even sought to trick her and said that her mother had used it to paste up windows. That was all a ploy. Bullshit!

A fear-stricken Xie now sits up in a cold sweat. Staring at the black and white wedding photo, she feels so lost.

On that photo, she is shown smiling shyly while Gu Ming appears to twist his lips into a grin with his thoughts being elsewhere.

Xie murmurs to herself, "So it has taken me up until now to work this out."

VI.

Xie has it her own way. She decides to request a new marriage certificate from the sub-district office. In that way she can vouchsafe the family and bring an end to her worries. As for their twenty-fifth anniversary and the towelling coverlets, they don't matter. Those were "adding more flowers to the corsage" but what she is in need of now is "fuel for snowy weather."

At the office, she is told by the staff that marriage registration had been transferred to the district level. She goes to the district and is told there that this is pretty straightforward – only letters of introduction are needed from both working units.

Xie wants to be absolutely certain so asks, "So easy? Any other documents needed?"

The member of staff responds with, "No. But a photo is needed. That will be pasted onto the certificate."

"That's easy."

Xie is elated, thinking that it is finally going to be resolved. Nothing could be easier than obtaining a letter of introduction from her working unit. They were even able to issue a certificate for beriberi, let alone provide her with a marriage certificate. Besides, her marriage to Gu Ming is common knowledge there, so it would just be a matter of going through the procedures. But it would still be necessary to mention it to the leaders first.

After Xie tells them the details, the leaders cannot help laughing, "How amusing it is!" But this is no big deal at all so they ask Xiao Li in the office to issue a letter of introduction.

Old Zhang, one of the leaders, says "If this is how things are, I ought to find my certificate back home. God knows where it's been put. I thought it was only a piece of paper but now that Xie has told us this it seems so important."

"My certificate has gone," Old Zhang continues. "Ten years ago I rowed with my wife and she tore it up in a blazing temper. But who is to say we are not a couple?"

"Who did take it seriously back then?" Xie asks. "Especially people of our age. The commitment we made was more significant than the paper. At that time, we thought nothing would happen to us once we got married. But now, it seems we should think about it from other angles …"

A few colleagues who are also in the room overhear that Xie is going to "marry" and clamber to try and get a share of wedding sweets. One of them even draws up a list for an office whip-around. All of this now seems true.

"What a to-do!" Xie complains. "We are an old couple and just want to go through the motions. Don't tease me!"

The crowd says that re-registration is a form of marriage as well and so some happy celebrations are called for. They tease Xie gleefully about the registration.

Xie's good mood is discomfited by her meeting with Xiao Li at the office.

Xiao Li asks her, pointing to the letter of introduction: "What should I write here? First marriage or remarriage?"

Xie answers, "Remarriage of course."

"If that's so," Xiao Li explains. "The first marriage should have been annulled through divorce. And you ought to have a certificate for that."

Xie doesn't have the divorce certificate. She is overwhelmed with shock.

Xiao Li suggests, "Maybe you should just write 'first marriage.'"

Xie disagrees, saying, "What about my daughter if I write 'first marriage'? Does it mean that I gave birth out of wedlock?"

"Your daughter is over twenty years old," Xiao Li observes. "Speaking scientifically, that should make you a single mother."

Xie is at once filled with irritation, being unable to stomach either the prospect of pregnancy before marriage or of being a single mother.

Xiao Li pushes the letter forward in her direction, insisting, "You just put whatever you like then!"

Xie has no idea what should be written.

VII.

Xie has been under the weather for a few days. She skips the fan dance practice and her mind appears to be wandering. The woman murmurs to herself whenever she catches sight of the wedding photo on the wall. When her daughter comes back from university she finds her mum humming *What you're seeking left no trace...* all day long. This makes her rather anxious. She does not know what has happened to her so tends to her needs with caution.

When Gu Ming arrives home from his trip, the daughter is in the kitchen making noodles for Xie. She tells Gu Ming, "Dad, go and see mum. How come she has turned into the fool Keiji Yokomichi in that Japanese movie?"ᵉ

Gu Ming enters the bedroom; Xie is propped up in a trance. Gu says, "Still after the marriage certificate? Have you finished?"

Xie doesn't want to speak with Gu Ming. Tears well up in her eyes.

Gu comments, "You stay at home all the time and stew over things to the point of making yourself ill. You'd better go out and find something else to do tomorrow."

"I shall do after I am through with the certificate. Otherwise my daughter will be made an illegitimate child."

"What are you talking about? I think you are close to becoming a mental case yourself – just like my ballet dancer patient. A one-track mind that can't be brought out of itself."

Xie points to the photo on the wall, pronouncing, "Look at you, that false smile on your face. Just like mercenary boiler man in *Taking Tiger Mountain by Strategy*.ᶠ What were you thinking when it was taken? Don't think that I don't know it!"

"You go tell me what I was thinking. I've no idea at all. I'm just back and you are looking for a reason to quarrel. That stinks."

"What stinks?" She stands up and faces Gu Ming: "Be frank with me. For one thing, did you ever actually apply for the marriage certificate in the first case? For another, what is going on between you and An?"

Gu Ming cannot restrain himself from stepping backwards. Not knowing whether to laugh or cry, he exclaims, "How old are you? Still so jealous."

"Only because there is no certificate."

"I'm not the one who should take the blame for that."

"If it is not down to you, whose fault is it? You know that only too well."

"I don't."

"Don't act the fool."

"You are more mental than my patients. I'll give you an admissions notice tomorrow. You ought to be put in confinement there."

"This is what you really want, isn't it?" Xie sneers. "You've longed for ages to give me the push and go off with that An

115

instead. Come on. I'm not scared. I'm not scared by anything!"

The daughter takes up the noodle bowl and tries to make her mother have something first and then calm down.

Xie refuses and lets the bowl fall to the floor, shouting, "We can't live together any more, let alone have dinner."

Gu responds, "Just as you've said, let's end it. You have done in our marriage just for the sake of that certificate. No certificate. That's fine. No relationship. Fine! You go and find whoever you like! You've been making things so rough for us these days. As you please!" While saying this, he takes the photo frame from the wall and flings it onto the floor. The frame is broken into shards.

The daughter hurries to collect the pieces, declaring, "You behave. How is all this going? How?"

"How? Ask your dad. By the way, who is to say whether he is your father or not!"

The daughter bursts out laughing: "If he isn't my father, what have you been up to?"

"He's been cheating on me all these years. There is no certificate at all!"

"What is the point of me cheating on you?" Gu asks. "It is none of my business. We've been living together happily and well. What on earth are you thinking?"

"I've just woken up. I've opened my eyes. I've recovered my legal consciousness. I've learnt to protect myself!"

"You never closed your eyes before either," Gu insists.

Xie cries as she shouts, feeling wounded.

In the meantime, the daughter has unclipped the back of the photo-frame and removed a piece of paper that was concealed there. She unfolds it and it turns out to be the marriage certificate of Gu and Xie. She says, "Mum, you can stop now. Look what this is!"

The couple is stunned.

Xie receives the certificate and clasps it in her hands, being enveloped with sharply conflicted emotions, "… just for this paper. Just this paper…"

"Who could have guessed that your mother would have slid it into the back of that frame?" Gu reflects. "It is just as the line goes *What you're seeking left no trace. It beat you like an invincible army, hardly to be guarded.*"

"We wouldn't have found it if you hadn't broken it," the daughter adds.

"My girl," Gu says, "For the sake of your future you should make sure your certificate is put somewhere safe."

"I nearly became an illegitimate child."

Xie doesn't know whether she should cry or laugh, intoning with embarrassment, "How come…"

Virtuous Beauty the Bear

Virtuous Beauty is a bear and a female one at that. Twenty years ago she was rescued from the depths of the mountains by a geological team. Back at that time, she was no more than one month old. Why the mother bear dumped her among the haphazard stones by the stream nobody knows. The cub, paralyzed as it was with fear and being mentally at a loss, was mistaken by Old Sun, the cook of the team, for a black moggy from a peasant family. He brought her back to their campsite and tethered her beside a sack of flour with the intention of using her as a mouser. At dusk, the lads came over to tease the "black cat." The "black cat" contorted her mouth and bared her fangs so the lads might know that this dark creature was not in fact a feline but a bear. Sickly and weak, the cub curled herself into a ball and couldn't even raise her head. Later, one wokful of Old Sun's flour paste infused sufficient vitality into her that she rallied and leapt and pulled all kinds of zany faces. The lads then recognized that the baby bear's lifeless frailty was down to malnutrition rather than disease.

A fortnight on, the baby bear had grown to be a dozen or so pounds. When held in a person's arms, her behaviour was no longer as affable as it was before since she ceased to nestle against one's chest like a little bird. Her soft fine down started to stiffen and grow prickly. Her temperament worsened in tandem with her accelerated food consumption. Besides frequently provoking the dogs which belonged to the villagers from nearby, she also developed an interest in the bleak sparse corn on the cob which grew in the mountains and frequently poached some away. The peasants came to claim compensation and the debtor was usually Old Sun. Everyone, including the Team Leader, believed that Old Sun's laxity was the cause of this trouble and it served him right that he should have to cough up. The baby bear was extremely friendly towards the members of the geological team and would gladly return every debt of gratitude. Anyone in a uniform was free to stroke, touch, tease and play with her or even lift her by the hind leg so that she might stand on her head. On the other hand, whenever a ragged peasant came within 100 metres of her, she would begin to growl and then straighten-up, preparing to pounce. Once, a peasant by the name of Mountain Egg swapped clothes with Old Sun as a test, but the cub still pounced on him. It then dawned on the lads that the animal sized people up not from their clothing but from their smell. The stench of the kitchen smoke that clung about the mountain folk alerted her to her mortal foe.

In Old Sun's reasoning, this must have had something to do with her formative experiences. Like a man, a bear has its memories too. Looking at that baby bear who brandished her forepaws and roared angrily at the mountain people, Old Sun commented, "This fellow must have been traumatized as a cub and is heading towards becoming a monster itself." The others, however, disagreed with him and jokingly gave her a name that was elegant, cheerful and serene – "Virtuous Beauty." Virtuous Beauty was actually already the name of the Team Leader's virtuous and beautiful wife. The men in the geological team by and large met with difficulty when trying to find a woman to marry. The Team Leader had his virtuous beautiful wife, and this made his colleagues envious of him to the effect that they wished eagerly that they could have a Virtuous Beauty, or one of her ilk, to keep them company. Now the bear cub provided an object of hilarity which helped to dispel the dejection they experienced both inside and outside their tents. What was more she knew no distinction between men and women. Whenever there was a meal, she revelled in it; wherever a quilt was around, she would burrow underneath it. She had really brought great comfort to those lonely bachelors. Hugging the warm-bodied "Virtuous Beauty" in their arms allowed them to drift into dreams. It was as if they were sharing a bed with her agreeable namesake, except that this "Virtuous Beauty" breathed a little more heavily and snored a little more gruffly.

By the advent of the cool autumn when the geological team returned to the city from their fieldwork, Virtuous Beauty and the team members were inseparable. In order that they could more readily take care of each other, the team members brought her back to the city. Virtuous Beauty's rural household registration card had been exchanged for an urban one, so to speak. She was at liberty to feast on grain bought at the market price. It was simple and easy. She didn't need to hand over municipal taxes and so forth.

It was at this time that the keeper Lin Yao first came into contact with Virtuous Beauty. On that particular day, all the field members of the geological team escorted Virtuous Beauty to the zoo as though they were seeing off their younger sister. As they were entering the zoo, Virtuous Beauty rode around Old Sun's neck and looked east and west as cockily as a triumphant returning hero. Had her mouth not been crammed full of roasted sweet potato, she would have been roaring in fevered excitement. Virtuous Beauty was welcomed into the bear sanctuary, which simultaneously received a plethora of gifts from the members of the geological team – their leftover canned meat, sausages and refined white flour and such like. Lin Yao didn't set much store by these things. On the contrary, he even wanted to decline their hospitality. He knew that Virtuous Beauty, who had been spoiled rotten by the geological team, was facing the prospect of slumming it on the normal animal rations of the zoo and would suffer the spiritual torture that would come with losing her freedom. Men were capable of understanding everything. They could adjust and control themselves. But what about a bear? Lin Yao realized clearly that the gloating members of the geological team couldn't have made a more stupid move.

Sure enough, scarcely had the baby bear been shut in the cell when rage erupted on both the inside and the outside. Virtuous Beauty, who couldn't accustom herself to the narrow restricted space, rammed her body against the cage time and again, hard and with violence. Later on she gnawed at the bars until jets of blood spurted out of her teeth and mouth and the soft-tissue sarcoma on her left forepaw was chafed bloody. Her "relatives" outside the cage would not stand for that. Reproachfully, they asked Lin Yao why such a little cutie had to be incarcerated and stripped of her freedom. They said that in the mountain wilderness they regarded Virtuous Beauty as a loyal puppy. Virtuous Beauty, who had never been locked up, had become used to humans. She ought to be gamboling and playing like a child on the lawn at the zoo. That would be an added tourist attraction. Lin Yao replied that if this were the case, it would mean that the roads in the zoo would have to be off limits and there would only be a sporadic flow of visitors – nobody would dare enter again.

All of these events transpired more than twenty years ago. Back at that time, Lin Yao had barely come back to the city from the production brigade where he was sent to be rusticated and he had only just married Drizzle Lu, who was assigned to the same production brigade as him. Back at that time, Drizzle Lu was still a common or garden worker and hadn't yet gone to Japan to study. Just as with the newly-caged Virtuous Beauty, everything had barely started for her.

Virtuous Beauty is now already old. Lying motionless in one corner, she has neither eaten nor drunk for fully four days. She is not hibernating. She is disease-stricken. Owing to the long-term effects of being fed by humans, she has lost the habit of hibernation. It is not only she but the many in her brood that refuse to hibernate. Those members of the geological team who once shielded her never came back after they saw her being locked in the iron cage by Lin Yao. Perhaps they have forgotten about her. Perhaps thereafter they were never to again bump into a catlike bear in the mountainous wilderness. Or perhaps they have, but they never again wanted to consign it to a cage that would obliterate its "brute nature."

Lin Yao rides his bike back home after work and his mind is haunted by the plight of Virtuous Beauty the bear. He has turned forty, an age at which according to ancient Chinese philosophy he should no longer feel perplexed by worldly affairs. He still looks young and dynamic, especially when he goes about the zoo in his beige jacket (this is actually his working uniform) doling out food to Virtuous Beauty. Her perfect cooperation makes the process no different from a wonderful circus routine. Standing upright to receive her dues, she is a masterful audience-pleaser. She pivots around in circuits to salute the men and women outside the railings, the soft-tissue sarcoma on her forepaw glistening in the sunlight as if she has grabbed a black pebble in her hand. Her short thick hind legs move clumsily and her big fat rump and strong thick waist sway like a village matron who has given birth to numerous children; all of these manoeuvres elicit bursts of laughter. The problem now is that nothing has passed her lips for four days and even her gums appear drained of blood – a symptom of acute anaemia. That afternoon, Lin Yao went to look for the leaders of the zoo to report Virtuous Beauty's situation. The leaders instructed the Head of the Breeding Section to deal with this problem. The Section Head said to Lin Yao, "Old bears are all like this when they have reached the end of their life. When you and I are old, we might not be in such good fettle as her." "You can't wash your hands of it," Lin Yao retorted. "When she was well, Virtuous Beauty brought a lot of splendour to this zoo. We mustn't act without conscience." "The operational funds of the zoo are pinched," the Section Head went on. "It's already hard to cope with the daily expenditure on drinks alone. Ticket revenues are very limited. Now everyone is busy. Who still has the frame of mind to look around a zoo? If you really want to do what is fair for Virtuous Beauty, just let nature take its course. Watch over her. It is her good fortune that she won't be disembowelled and her paws won't be chopped off by a peddler."

Breathing in the aroma of the Chinese plum blossom, it suddenly dawns on Lin Yao that he is home already.

Lin Yao's father-in-law Lu Junqing planted blossoming Chinese plums everywhere in the courtyard of the Lu family. Those uniformly yellow flowers, all pure and plain, make the large compound feel like a mausoleum and send a chill to the bottom of people's hearts. The gate of the Lu Mansion is rangy, tall and stately. Though the carvings on the bricks have become fragmentary and the lacquer is peeling away, the magnificence remains intact. The withered grass which flutters on the tile grooves and the round slippery edges and corners of the stone steps show distinctly the imprints and marks left behind by time. The past glory of the host family can still be discerned from those buildings constructed from clay bricks, stacked up flush with their corridors in front and lean-tos at the rear, and from the stone drums with beautiful delicate engravings which flank the gate. People in this vicinity refer to this compound as the "Lu Family Mansion." During the Cultural Revolution, the mansion was commandeered by a particular unit of the city's Revolutionary Committee. They stayed there for the duration. Subsequently when policies of reparation were implemented the mansion was returned to its original master. This explains why, in contrast to other large compounds inhabited by civilians, the buildings within have not suffered considerable damage. No small kitchens or earthquake-proof sheds or other similar buildings have sprung up either. The former appearance has been preserved comparatively well. Commendably, sewerage and other sanitary systems have been introduced so that the washrooms can even boast flush lavatories – a marriage of the ancient and the modern. The Lu Mansion has seen one momentous stride forward. The spacious compound consists of the front and rear courtyards where three blocks and a back garden stand. The blocks are linked by roofed passageways. A moon-shaped gate leads to the eastern and western side courtyards respectively. The courtyards are paved with square bricks and the sinuous paths in the garden are embedded with pebbles – all meticulously designed. Three secondary parlours stand at the northeastern corner of the back garden and hide among the groves of blossoming Chinese plums – the serenest spot within the compound. When the great-grandfather of the Lu family was still alive, the parlours were where political business was discussed. The old gentleman was a senator at the beginning of the Republic of China period (1912-49) and took charge of many state affairs for example accepting the local people's petitions, advising the government in the letter of the law and others, delivering query letters to the State Counsel and actions of that ilk. Therefore, the eastern parlours were a confidential centre in which to hatch strategies. Back in those years when the Lu family prospered, guests filled the mansion. Whenever a close relative or a friend arrived to negotiate something important, they would all be invited over there to chat. Despite being manifestly out-of-the-way and placid, back at that time the eastern parlours were indeed where the action was to be had.

Now the parlours on the east are inhabited by Lin Yao. Married to Drizzle Lu the couple has dwelt there for twenty years. At the outset, he could never get accustomed to these three rooms in which carved board screens formed virtually the only partition. The moment he entered, everything inside was on show as clear as day. Even the double bed that should have been hidden away in some inconspicuous place sat in an arresting position by the western wall, making visitors feel that a drama was about to be staged. He suggested that the carved partitions should be dismantled and replaced by walls of solid wood. His father-in-law would not consent. He insisted that parlours were parlours and they shouldn't be changed because they were now occupied. Once those carved hardwood screens had been dismantled, the artistic value would be lost and those parlours would no longer be fit to be called parlours. If Lin Yao couldn't grow used to living there, he could move to the eastern side rooms in the front courtyard. Anyhow those rooms were unoccupied and it would be convenient to come in and go out. Lin Yao mulled the matter over and still felt that it was better to live in the parlours. For one thing it was quiet there and for another, if he moved to the eastern side rooms, he would be assuming the position which was traditionally set aside for the favoured son-in-law of a Chinese family,ᵍ something he didn't want to do. He thought that where the Lu family was concerned he was not a favoured son-in-law but a hired hand at best.

Lin Yao wheels his bike to the rear section of the compound. In the moonlight, the shadows of the trees are dancing. He needs to bisect three courtyards, pass through the moon-shaped gate to the east and trot around groves of flowers to reach his rooms. He is very familiar with the route. He thinks that were he to have to follow another one he would be certain to lose his way easily. The courtyard is too deep. Since the government returned the mansion to them, the bulk of the compound has stood unoccupied. His father-in-law Lu Junqing and his mother-in-law live in the front courtyard. The second block is taken up by Lu Junqing's long-widowed second elder sister-in-law, who others address as their Second Aunt. The third block belongs to Lu Junqing's son Thunder Lu. Thunder Lu went to the United States three years ago and the block has been empty ever since. The residents of the Lu Mansion are sitting pretty in a compound that couldn't be more spacious. And this at a time when the citizens are caterwauling about the shortage of housing and the city government procrastinates over how to increase the average allocation of living space by a fraction of a square metre per person. The compound is vacuous and the echoes sound loud. Weeds are re-branding the courtyards into a wasteland. Lin Yao and his father-in-law have to spend overmuch time trimming and neatening the place up. Anyhow, they are short of hands. Barely have they finished plucking the weeds in the eastern courtyard when those in the western courtyard have shot up like mad again. The Chinese plum trees ought to be pruned, the vine trellises should be sprayed with water, the fallen leaves should be swept away and the drainage ditches dredged ... Even though they slave away like this, the garden still looks bleak. On top of this, the gate remains clamped shut throughout the day and the residents sense their seclusion from the outside world. Tourists frequently halt in their tracks and peep in curiously through the cracks in the gate, surmising that this is a tourist attraction which has not yet been opened. Once the cast and crew of the TV series *Strange Tales from the Liaozhai Studio*[h] wanted to rent out their place but Lu Junqing declined. He said that the compound was already solitary and desolate enough. If some fox spirits and ghosts were invoked in here, wouldn't things become messier still? The camera crew was overwhelmed with disappointment. It was never easy to find such a location they exclaimed. Since the Lu family had not agreed, they would have to build a set themselves. What a pity! It was such a fine mansion.

Lin Yao skirts the groves of blossoming Chinese plums and discovers that the electric lamp in his room is on. He senses a tingling in his scalp. His mind wanders to the female spectre who according to the pen of Pu Songling could remove her own head in order to comb her hair and to the female fox spirit who for four centuries has cultivated the way of immortality in Ji Xiaolan's *Diary of Yuewei Thatched Cottage*.[i] His heart throbs. Only the parlours stand in the garden. If anything grievous were to befall him, nobody would be able to answer his call for help. Though people might respond, they are no more than two or three dodderers and couldn't offer much by way of assistance. It is better therefore that he deals with it himself. Lin Yao hides in the shadows of the flowers and picks aside the twigs to look towards his room. His father-in-law is spreading out an electric coverlet on his bed. Feeling a stream of warmth shooting through his heart, he strides in and calls out "Father."

Lu Junqing straightens up and says, "You should lay a fire here. The garden is too damp. There used to be a pond behind the parlours. The water might have dried up a long while ago, but there is still all this moisture. Don't get ill."

Lin Yao refuses, saying "I only sleep here at night. Drizzle is not here. Why should I start a fire?"

Lu Junqing responds, "I knew you wouldn't, so I have brought you this electric blanket." Lu Junqing then asks Lin Yao how that bear is. Lin Yao answers that she is still in a bad way. Lu Junqing suggests, "You might as well try honey and powdered milk."

"Where can you get powdered milk nowadays?"

"Grind rice into powder and steam it yourself. This is a trick your Second Aunt taught me today and told me to pass onto you."

"Second Aunt is a gourmet. She is not only well-versed in what humans eat but in what animals eat too."

"When your great-grandfather was still alive, the Lu family entertained guests every day. One thing that set our family banquets apart was that we hired no chefs. The hostess led the daughters-in-law to the kitchen in person and, naturally, the flavour was unique. No dishes in the restaurants could hold a candle to them. Among all the daughters-in-law, the most outstanding was Second Aunt. These past couple of years, age has crept up on her and she hasn't been willing to move about and lift her hands. But in the past she truly was great."

"Second Aunt's steamed duck with bamboo shoots and ham must be the delicacy among delicacies in the Lu family cuisine. I have feasted on it only three times since I married into this family."

"This steamed duck with bamboo shoots and ham might end up not being passed down. Drizzle isn't willing to learn to cook it, let alone Thunder. Gone …" While he is speaking like this, he shifts towards the exit but then turns around and adds, "Put some more on top at night."

The telephone rings at this point. It is Drizzle calling from Tokyo. She tells Lin Yao that a typhoon is ravaging Tokyo. Lin Yao probes what a typhoon is like. Drizzle explains that it a blustery storm …

Shaking his head without ceasing, Lu Junqing passes comment on how she is "making a call from so far away only to tell about a spot of wind and rain." He adds, "The telephone really has brought convenience. Tokyo must be 10,000 miles away from here. Calling from 10,000 miles away only to fill us in about wind and rain …"

II.

Everyone is overtaxing their nerves about money.

The zoo's economic situation is akin to that of certain large or medium-sized state-owned enterprises. Such businesses mostly depend upon government-allocated funds and to begin with their capital turnover is tricky to maintain. While the leaders of the zoo fret about how to find sources of revenue and how to diversify operations so that the institution won't be engulfed in economic whirlpools, this financial embarrassment may yet consign thousands of captive birds and animals to be put on diets. Hollow legs are a must for the time being.

The deficit grows bigger like a hole being gradually excavated and everything has sunk into a vicious spiral. The team in charge of the large beasts of prey first submits an emergency appeal. Under their watch the tigress is experiencing a growth spurt. Every day she consumes eight pounds of choice beef, two pounds of cow's milk, forty vitamin C tablets, twenty vitamin E tablets, six raw eggs plus a well-dressed chicken, which in total cost more than 100 yuan. However, one might as well say that she is in need of shedding some pounds. Tigers are animals under First Grade State Protection and take top priority among all the top priorities in the country. Just imagine: without one or two tigers to keep up appearances, would an urban zoo still be worthy of being called a zoo? A meeting is held and supplies for the other animals are reduced in order to protect this top priority. The panda enjoys "aristocratic" treatment in the zoo. Every three days a great batch of fresh pine-flowered bamboos will be transported here from the mountains, small gifts will frequently be donated from national foundations and it is a common occurrence for aid and concern to trickle in from overseas. She might be counted as one among the first batch to garner riches. When foreign guests come to visit, under most circumstances she will be deployed to welcome them. These years, she has been spoiled rotten and so her temperament has changed greatly. Seemingly simple and plain, she harbours a growing number of schemes and tricks in her heart. Whenever golden-haired, blue-eyed guests appear, she thrives on their attention and puts on thousands of naïve faces. Next the foreign guests will dip into their pockets to offer up patronage. She, of course, gets a cut of the cake. Her home is duly repaired and air freshener is sprayed in order that she will snatch one more jot of charity next time around.

What a poor wretch Virtuous Beauty the bear is. She is an animal under Second Grade State Protection. In the mountainous areas, bears are not rare animals and they even fall victim to poachers. China Central Television may have exposed the criminality of those who hunt Northeast China tigers, but nobody has rebuked the people who slaughter bears with the purpose of ripping out their gallbladders. If it were not for the interference of that geological exploitation team, Virtuous Beauty would have never come here. The mountains is where her land of freedom is to be found ... In that land she may be sliced or slain but that would be her own destiny and a situation apart from the present one. When he thinks about it in these terms, Lin Yao can't refrain himself from reviling that grinning Old Sun who allowed Virtuous Beauty to ride upon his neck as he strutted towards the breeding team. Lin Yao wonders what would come into Old Sun's mind if he could see Virtuous Beauty's present plight. Today, Lin Yao is covering Jade Li's shift. Virtuous Beauty lies in the corner all the time in the same posture as when in her infancy she was tethered beside the flour sack by the geological team. Her neck is pulled in and her claws retracted. Lin Yao opens the small door leading outwards. The wintry sunlight comes streaming in and lands on Virtuous Beauty's shaggy hair, highlighting in the brightnesss a halo consisting of numerous dust particles. Lin Yao peers out through the small door. A man and a woman are leaning against the railings of the Bear Mountain. It seems as though they are on a date and most probably their concentration is not focused on the bear. Under these circumstances, Lin Yao hopes very much that Virtuous Beauty can take advantage of that precious serenity to sun and stretch herself. The rampant mites and fleas bite her body all over and are not discreet about it. When she is in good health, he can apply liquid medicine to give her a rub-down. But not now. Too weak to stand up even in a draught. Virtuous Beauty is more fragile than a "pretty sixteen-year-old girl."[j]

Jade Li fetches over Virtuous Beauty's lunch in a basin – several steamed bran and vegetable bread buns. "Wasn't that yesterday's fodder? Lin Yao inquires. "Why is it being served again?"

"They gave it to me," Jade Li replies, "so what can I do. The bosses insist that the funds allocated by the state and the income from tickets must be used to protect the top priorities. Virtuous Beauty is an omnivore. Her food has to be mixed in with the monkeys' food. The monkeys are not meat-eaters so she'll have to do without meat."

"Bullshit! Monkeys and bears belong to separate families. Letting a bear eat a monkey's food. If it goes on like this for very long, she's bound to go down with anaemia."

"This is what they gave me, anyhow. She has to like it or lump it."

Lin Yao goes to the office of the Section Head with the basin and scatters the steamed bran bread buns on the desk. Then, rapping the desk, he asks the Section Head, who is filling out a form, "Is our zoo so big but we can't support a bear?"

The Section Head responds, "You should be clear on this. She is an old bear, a granny bear, a grandma of the bear family, and has had a few off days."

"She is not old," Lin Yao rejoinders. "She can still live as long as she is well-nourished."

"You go over and have a rest," the Section Head answers. "Why get so worked up about an old bear. In the mountains she wouldn't even have those bran buns to gnaw on. She is being kept by a communist society now."

Lin Yao emphasizes how Virtuous Beauty's food must be kept separate from that of the monkeys.

The Section Head persists, "It can't be done. We only have a small quantity of operational funds. Should it all be used on feeding the bear? What about the giraffes, then? What about the gorrilas? And what about that Malaysian elephant? They were all donated by foreigners and every three or five days they will send their representatives here to check out the situation. They simply cannot look like ravenous wolves before those folks."

Lin Yao answers, "Virtuous Beauty is the lone aboriginal."

The Section Head says, "Yeah. And under special circumstances aboriginals are expendable."

Devoid of cheer, Lin Yao leaves the office and spots that Red Flag Chen is feeding his monkeys on the distant Monkey Mountain. The cheerless Red Flag Chen and his cheerless Guangxi monkeys bring out the best in each other. Red Flag Chen and Lin Yao are on good terms. When he doesn't have anything to do, he frequently drops by at Bear Mountain. Sometimes he even plays a round of chess. When it is time to take his leave, he walks off with a few pieces of steamed bread to take care of his monkey children and grandchildren. A few pieces of steamed bread are barely enough to fill the cracks between Virtuous Beauty's teeth but should form a welcome nocturnal snack for his monkeys. Lin Yao is unwilling to go back to the bear sanctuary. He doesn't want to see how Virtuous Beauty is suffering. Recalling what Second Aunt suggested the night before, he scoots out of the zoo to a shop to buy some powdered milk.

Of course, no powdered milk is available. Nowadays children are all being pampered and the era of dining on milk substitute has long since passed. Deep in worry Lin Yao mills around in front of the counter. The saleswoman is an elderly lady. Looking at Lin Yao, she inquires, "The baby's grown bigger and it wants a taste of something different?" Lin Yao nods his head absent-mindedly. In fact he doesn't have any experience of bringing up a baby. His wife Drizzle Lu resolved that she wouldn't have one of their own because she wanted to go abroad.

The saleswoman takes out a sachet of *Star* nutrition power and suggests, "Try this. It is ground from rice. Mix it together with some egg and it will be more nutritious than powdered milk."

Taking a glimpse at the price, Lin Yao grunts, "Too expensive."

"What kind of a father are you?" the saleswoman utters reproachfully. "You even bellyache that food for your child is too expensive. A bag of imported milk powder for babies costs more than 100 yuan and this one costs only eight. Can you still say it is *expensive*?"

Feeling too embarrassed to tell her to put the bag back, Lin Yao has to say, "Then that it'll have to be."

The saleswoman puts the nutritional powder into a plastic bag and gets ready to take the money.

"I want ten bags," Lin Yao says.

"What?" The saleswoman's eyes open wide.

"Ten bags." Lin Yao makes the sign of the cross denoting

the number ten in Chinese with his fingers and repeats this at leisure.

"I guess you must be a first-time father," The saleswoman hazards a guess. "And you haven't a clue about buying things for your baby. Get one bag to begin with. Come back for more if baby likes it."

"This one has a gigantic appetite and needs four or five bags at one sitting."

"A baby boy or a baby girl?"

"A girl."

The saleswoman exclaims, "A girl that is so good at gorging herself? You're not using it for some kind of experiment, are you? To tell the truth, the more you buy, the happier I shall be. I wouldn't mind if you choose to mix it into paste and slather it on the wall to stick up big-character propaganda posters."

With those ten bags of nutritional powder in his hand, Lin Yao heads to another counter to purchase a bottle of honey. Not until that is done with does he go out of the shop, being fixed by the puzzled gaze of the saleswoman's eyes.

When it is time to be fed the nutritional powder, Virtuous Beauty opens her eyes for the first time in the past few days and raises her head. Perhaps the aroma of honey has refreshed her memories about the smell of the mountain wilderness and stimulated her appetite. Virtuous Beauty licks at the paste in the basin laboriously. Finally her strength can no longer sustain her. Out of exhaustion she once again rests her head on the ice-cold cement ground and closes her eyes. Lin Yao thinks, "At any rate, Virtuous Beauty has gotten something into her stomach. Nutritional powder and honey can give her a few calories. It will be for the best if this kind of food can be made to last one week. Perhaps it can still save her life."

On his way past the Monkey Mountain after work, Lin Yao discovers that Red Flag Chen is tossing oranges into the ape enclosure. Red Flag Chen greets him. Only then does it occur to Lin Yao that Red Flag Chen hasn't been to the bear sanctuary for several days. "Why haven't you come to pinch any steamed bread?" he asks.

Beaming, Red Flag Chen replies, "We have strode in advance into the well-off society." With these words, he singles out several big oranges from the basket and hands them to Lin Yao.

Lin Yao takes a look at the oranges in the basket. Bearing only a few marks from mechanical handling, they are not in bad condition. Monkeys and humans as well can derive enjoyment from them. He peels one and pops a segment into his mouth, asking, "Today is the monkeys' festival?"

"A festival, my arse." Red Flag Chen replies, "These guys have a master now."

"They've been sold?"

"Adopted." While speaking like this, Red Flag Chen tips his lower jaw towards the primate enclosure.

Lin Yao can spy that a sparkling bronze plate is hanging in a striking spot upon the enclosure with several distinct black Chinese characters, which read:

Adopted by the Friendly State Trading Company

"This is a novelty," Lin Yao comments. "They are not children. Will the monkeys be rehoused in that company?"

"There is no need to take them away," Red Flag Chen replies. "It wouldn't take more than two or three of them to turn their whole office building upside down."

"So how exactly have they been adopted?" Lin Yao asks.

"They give us money and we hang a plate up here for them."

Lin Yao pries, "Why of all things should this *Friendly State* company adopt the monkeys?"

"It is said that they have hit the jackpot by exporting tree bark and leaves. They figure that they must have hurt the monkeys' feelings by stealing away those trees. Their General Manager feels guilty. What's more, his mother was born in the Year of the Monkey, so he thought to adopt them."

"Why couldn't the General Manager's father have been born

in the Year of the Bear? If this were the case, my Virtuous Beauty would have someone to depend upon."

"This is another way out," Red Flag Chen advises. "Now anything can be sponsored. Oughtn't people have some outlet to release the compassion that is stored up in their hearts? Adoption has been used up and down the country, not just in one zoo. You are ignorant and ill-informed."

Lin Yao retorts, "One plate here and one plate there. It doesn't make the zoo look too shabby or the opposite."

Red Flag Chen enlightens him by saying, "Your way of thinking is behind the times. What era must we be living in that you still care so much about keeping face! Hitler's vow of sponsorship may as well be hanging up there, just as long as the animals can live well and the monkeys can still feast on oranges."

Lin Yao and Red Flag Chen sit outside the railings, chatting as they peel and enjoy their oranges.

The Guangxi monkeys sit inside the railings becoming festive as they gnaw at their oranges.

Red Flag Chen continues, "It's said that Bright the tiger will be adopted as well – by a Chinese American. Nobody knows how that arrangement was fixed between them."

His heart restless with anxiety, Lin Yao feels indignant over Virtuous Beauty's fate. Adoption is being upheld as something as glorious as becoming an elected role model. Having read his mind, Red Flag Chen says, "A bear is not cute and sweet, especially an old, toothless one."

"Who said that?" Lin Yao raises his voice immediately. "You haven't spent much time with her!"

Red Flag Chen defends himself, "Nonsense! You could grow attached to a rat if you spent enough time with it."

"You're playing the devil's advocate."

Enlightened as he has been by Red Flag Chen, Lin Yao thinks that he should go and seek help from others. The first option that springs to his mind is the *Star* Nutrition Powder Factory.

He retraces his steps to the bear sanctuary, looking for that bit of wrapper that might have the address emblazoned on it. Jade Li has already covered his shift and is preparing Virtuous Beauty's supper. Staring at the nutritional powder, he yelps, "Eight yuan for one bag. Eighty yuan for ten bags. A few meals will swallow up your wages. This isn't good."

Lin Yao tells him about his idea of going to the *Star* Factory to solicit sponsorship. Jade Li observes that his younger sister-in-law is in charge of the public baths there. Tomorrow they can go after her and ask her to help with the introduction.

They fix an appointment so that they will visit the *Star* Factory together the following day.

After having entered the gate, Lin Yao bumps into his mother-in-law in the courtyard. Mother-in-law says, "We've made some dumplings today. Second Aunt mixed the filling with her own hands. You can have supper here; no need to cook for yourself." Lin Yao agrees and slips over to one of the parlours to collect a bottle of Japanese Ozeki saké that was brought back home by Drizzle last time.

When he enters his father-in-law's main room, he immediately feels that the suite of redwood furniture has caused the atmosphere to become much dimmer. On the western wall stands a dressing mirror. Owing to its ancient vintage, the glass reflects seven hues of light like an oil slick in a puddle on a road. A time-honoured wooden clock drags its weak hands forward – *tick*, *tock*. It marks the time for your reference only but this has no grounding in fact. A big writing desk stands before the window. A sheet of white felt is spread out on it with writing brushes, China ink, rice paper and inkstones on top. The Chinese plum blossoms in the vase are in bud. His father-in-law Lu Junqing bends over the writing desk meticulously adding stamens and pistils to the blossoms on his picture. Lin Yao doesn't know the first thing about painting, but he knows that his father-in-law is a very accomplished painter and enjoys considerable fame in artistic circles. However, to clarify the point, that has nothing to do with raising a bear – it is another kettle of fish entirely. He and his father-in-law are on good terms though can scarcely find common ground in their conversation.

Lin Yao deposits the saké on the dinner table. Mother-in-law is laying out bowls and chopsticks. Second Aunt pushes the door open and makes her entrance. Despite the fact she is pushing eighty, the woman is still hale and hearty, skinny and diminutive yet not withered, and her mind is still comparatively lucid.

On catching sight of her, Mother-in-law says, "I am going to tell Lin Yao to take your arm here. The brick paving in the courtyard is covered all over in green moss – so slippery."

Smiling, Second Aunt replies, "I know every route by heart. I know clearly in my mind which places are slippy and which are not."

Seeing that Second Aunt has come along, Father-in-law tosses aside the writing brush and trots to the dinner table. Spotting the bottle of Ozeki saké, he knits his brow and complains, "We still ought to drink some strong liquor. Quaffing Japanese spirits with Chinese dumplings gives people the feeling of being a turncoat."

Lin Yao says, "The saké is only twelve per cent proof. It's not hard to down."

"But it tastes like water from a footbath," Father-in-law insists.

The saké is thus exchanged for a bottle of stiff spirits. The dumplings are served – only three plates of them, a dozen or so upon each one. Father-in-law asks why the dumplings are so few in number. Mother-in-law replies, "It's the filling. Can you gorge yourself on thirty-odd or fifty-odd of these?"

"What filling might that be?" Lin Yao inquires.

"Put them in your mouth and then guess" is Second Aunt's response.

Lin Yao takes a bite. The meat is fine and tender and slightly bitter, being shot through with an inexplicable fragrance. With care, he studies the dumpling in his hand but still cannot fathom what the filling is.

Mother-in-law explains, "It is chicken, pigeon and chrysanthemum."

Now, Lin Yao knows that chrysanthemums are edible and can be used to make dumplings. Small wonder that those pots of flowers have vanished from Father-in-law's room.

Second Aunt says, "The Empress Dowager Cixi was very fond of dining on white thick-petalled chrysanthemums. In the past the palace had a kind of chafing dish called the Chrysanthemum Hotpot. The chicken and duck broth inside was used to scald chrysanthemums – it was designed exclusively for the old Empress Dowager. Later on, the eunuch head chef Zhang Lande left the palace and passed on the recipe to Great-grandfather Lu. From then on it became the *piece-de-resistance* of the Lu family's table. That little gold-nugget-shaped dumpling that is tipped into the hotpot at the last moment has a filling of pigeon and chrysanthemum."

Father-in-law pipes up, "Dining like this is the one foolproof way of stirring up a celebratory atmosphere and inviting in pure elegance. The culture of the dining room is like painting – very abstruse. Many still can't get to the bottom of it even though they've studied it for a lifetime."

"A delicacy from the imperial household – no wonder it has to be so meticulously prepared," Mother-in-law comments. "The only problem is that chrysanthemum dumplings aren't suited for an onslaught from a pack of greedy guts. If a few train-wrecking navvies were to drop by, they could demolish all the chrysanthemums in the city at one sitting."

Lin Yao knows that Mother-in-law was the daughter of the boss of the Benevolent Benefactor Hall Apothecary by the city gate. She is far less cultivated than Second Aunt who was a princess originally. It is inevitable that her words tend to come across as rude and vulgar. Nevertheless, she knows how many beans make five far better than Second Aunt – ten Second Aunts put together would be no match for her.

III.

The next morning, remembering that he has an appointment to go to the *Star* Factory, Lin Yao rings the bear sanctuary as soon as he gets up and asks about Virtuous Beauty's situation.

"Fine," answers the sleepy-eyed Jade Li on the other end of the line.

"What do you mean by *fine*?"

"She's gulped down a whole wok of that nutritional-powder paste."

"What's she doing now?"

"Same old thing. Lying down there."

The two make an appointment to meet under the southern overpass at nine. Before putting down the receiver, Lin Yao stresses, "Don't tell others what we are going to do, especially that chap at the Monkey Mountain. We are beggars. If we come away with nothing it will be a matter of shame."

"Still you can't draw your face down," Jade Li comments. "Beggars didn't stand among the lower nine schools even in the old society, let alone nowadays.[k] Are those ad-solicitors and salesmen any more pathetic than us? They feel nothing but you loathe that we're too shabby? An economic society means that face should be ripped off and crammed into the crotch …"

Jade Li still rattles on. Lin Yao hangs up.

The two men reach the nutritional powder factory and rendezvous with the Manager. The Manager was also a student from the "Three Old Graduating Classes"[l] and was rusticated to the same county as Lin Yao. They have never met before but have heard tell of each other. Thus, they quickly strike up a conversation.

"I am not interested in adopting a bear," the Manager says,

"If our baby's nutritional powder became known as 'the *Bear* brand,' what parent would be prepared to part with their money for it and what child would be prepared to open his mouth to eat it?"

Jade Li gives a greatly exaggerated report about the present crisis faced by Virtuous Beauty and beseeches the Manager that Virtuous Beauty might receive short term aid from him.

"I can't," the Manager replies. "A bear needs eight bags of *Star* nutritional powder every day, which means eighty bags every ten days. Now the price of grain, eggs and oil keeps on rising. Every bag of powder produced loses me point one six yuan. If things go on like this, this small factory will never be able to make ends meet." Consequently, neither side can find anything to say. Lin Yao had never expected that they would have reached the end of their conversation within three words and that he would be saying "See you later" now. After they have said "See you later" they may in fact never see each other again. Everything that constituted Virtuous Beauty, including her life, will soon be gone. "… I … I want … to take a look at your workshops. I've never visited a food factory before. I don't know …" Lin Yao doesn't know how he has managed to force out words like these.

"You are most warmly welcomed," the Manager says. "I will escort you over."

From his brief dealings with the Manager, Lin Yao senses the directness and concision of the man's actions and words. The crew-cut man who likes gesticulating in the course of conversation is one of his peers, but the magnificence that Lin might have been able to exhibit has ended up being comprehensively crushed.

When they reach a workshop, the Manager uses various pieces of jargon to introduce the production line. Lin Yao nods his head without stopping and pretends to be listening but deep in his mind he is thinking about how to divert the topic back to Virtuous Beauty. Pointing at the workers who are operating the machines in the midst of a cloud of flour, he says, "Foreign production equipment and technology should be introduced. This equipment is too outdated."

"We very much hope that this can be done," the Manager responds. "But for one thing we are short of capital, and, for another, we can't find a suitable partner to cooperate with."

Lin Yao halts in his tracks and says, "I can help you, but you must be sincere in return."

"His beloved one is a researcher in Japan majoring in Economics and she knows a lot of entrepreneurs," Jade Li adds hurriedly.

"Really?" The Manager also halts in his tracks and fixes Lin Yao seriously.

Lin Yao nods his head.

The Manager says, "Let me make a loose promise: If we start up a joint-venture enterprise with a foreign investor at some point in the future and we are able to put a little aside, the first thing I will do is to adopt Virtuous Beauty. What is more, no matter what product is produced, the brand name must have something to do with bears. That way it will commemorate the trigger that brought us to know each other – the bear."

Lin Yao says, "It's a deal. You will be sure to earn something to put aside."

The men wander to another workshop. Sighting several piles of nutritional powder under the machines and at the corners, Lin Yao asks, "Is none of this edible?"

The Manager answers, "This was all swept from out of the machines when they were cleaned. Not edible."

"Give it to us." With the aforementioned suggestion as the padding, Lin Yao feels that his lungpower is a little stronger. "Give us it for our bear to eat."

The Manager says, "Perhaps it is edible for the bear. But you should sift it in case there might be earth clods, metal and such like."

Upon hearing this, Lin Yao feels so appreciative he doesn't

know what to say. Jade Li is also very excited and thanks the Manager profusely. The Manager says in embarrassment, "Just a little bit of waste stuff. I don't deserve your thanks. Had you said earlier that this is reusable, the problem would have been solved, wouldn't it?"

The Manager tells a worker to fetch a broom. Jade Li declares that he will do the sweeping himself. He does the job meticulously so that the broom reaches into every last corner. Watching how he crouches under the machines, Lin Yao's heart suddenly feels a spurt of sourness and his eyes moisten a little. His facial expression is caught by the shrewd Manager, who, patting him on the shoulder, says, "I should call you 'Brother.' You are a good man. At least after so many years your heart is still tender and hasn't been rubbed so it's become callused."

"That's because I am always dealing with animals."

Jade Li has swept the nutritional powder into one pile and is now bagging it by handfuls. Next, raising the flour sack, he declares to Lin Yao excitedly, "Must be fully thirty pounds here."

Lin Yao says, "We will come back and sweep again in a few days time."

"There is no need," the Manager maintains. "I will ask the workers to take heed and gather it themselves. They will send it over to you when an agreed quantity has been bagged up." With these words, he takes down several bags of nutritional powder from the production line and hands them to Lin Yao and Jade Li, saying, "These are for your children, not for the bear."

The Manager helps Lin Yao to tether the nutritional powder onto the back seat of his bike and sees them off as far as the factory gate.

Lin Yao inquires, "Faffing about for half a day, I still haven't got around to asking your name."

The Manager replies, "My name is Ding One. Ding is the surname. One as in 'one, two'."

Jade Li says, "If a representative needed to be elected, your

142

name would surely give you a head start. According to the strokes of the surname, it would always come first."

Ding One retorts, "If production still can't be kicked up a notch, I won't be able to keep this managerial position for long. And I still dream of being elected what-a-representative?"

Lin Yao says, "That is not for certain."

"Don't be too pessimistic," Jade Li offers consolation also. "The future is bright though the road leading to it is snaky."

The two sides shake hands to say farewell. Having walked quite a distance, Lin Yao is still murmuring Ding One's name.

The duo reaches the gate of the zoo. A crowd is gathering around there quarreling. The small window of the ticket kiosk has been shut. Little Rice, the admissions girl, is sitting in the doorman's room shedding tears. Jade Li is courting Little Rice. He immediately parks the bike and asks her what's wrong. Little Rice blubs, "Isn't it me who is to blame? The zoo leaders arranged for people from outside to hold this exhibition of famous cats here and another five yuan have been added to the ticket fee. It's not as if I've pocketed the money for myself. Why do they all roar at me?"

A tourist shouts from outside the gate, "We are here to see the zoo animals, not those cats. Our family keeps four cats – I don't care."

A peasant with his grandson in tow also takes up his words, "You all say that we peasants are filthy rich. I sold four litres of corn in order to pay for bringing my grandson to the city to watch the tiger, but you insist on making me watch the cats. There are so many cats that they are tripping people up and can't be shooed away. I said I didn't want to watch cats, but wasn't given any choice. The tickets for the zoo and the cats are being sold together. Two cat tickets cost me one litre of corn. After I go back and tell the others, the villagers will laugh at me because I've stuffed myself bloated by doing noting worthwhile.

Jade Li of course sides with Little Rice. "The tiger also belongs to the cat family. It's nothing more than a big cat. Watching the tiger after watching the cats, you can detect their differences more clearly."

"What kind of nonsense is that?" Another tourist barges in. "According to your logic, the zoo could also keep ducks, pigs and rabbits. In their holidays, people could bring their children here to figure out which one is a rooster and which is a hen."

A cadre-like man comments, "This should be reported to the authorities. This is an arbitrary charge and an unauthorized imposition; this is a shameful practice."

Jade Li wants to say more. Lin Yao yanks him away. Lin Yao feels that the leaders are being put in an embarrassing position too. Everyone knows that there is no rhyme or reason as to why a zoo should host a cat exhibition. But what methods have they at their disposal? Today the leaders are acting like this – thickening their faces to beg food for the bear – because they have to do that.

Jade Li says, "Little Rice should be pitied. A crowd has ganged up against her and she was forced to crawl into the doorman's room. This season the ticket income will drop further."

"In a word," Lin Yao concludes, "we are all being dragged down by money."

While Lin Yao is cooking the paste for Virtuous Beauty, Jade Li comes in from the kitchen with a big wok full of bone broth. He tips the better half of the broth into the paste generously and says, "Bone broth is a great tonic. Time to build up Virtuous Beauty properly."

Consequently, Virtuous Beauty's bowels become loose that very afternoon. This acute diarrhoea makes Virtuous Beauty, who to begin with had no energy to raise her head, struggle restlessly in the cage. Lin Yao knows that this is down to the stomach ache. In great agony, he watches her moan like a man but can't offer her any help. In the past he could have stepped into the cage at ease but not today. A tortured-with-pain, disease-stricken bear is irascible; she will change her face easily and not recognize anyone.

They make a call to the medical department and Dr. Du arrives. He observes that the diarrhoea could kill Virtuous Beauty in one or two days.

Jade Li's face alters when he hears these words because it was he who served Virtuous Beauty a big wokful of bone broth. Strictly speaking, he is the "arch-villain."

Dr. Du says, "How can a bear whose stomach and intestines are extremely weak stand such oily food? You love her and hope that she will survive, but in fact you've sped up her death – this is what we call 'more haste, less speed'."

Jade Li sweet-talks Dr. Du ceaselessly and Lin Yao pleads without stopping as well, pointing out that Virtuous Beauty is a delightful bear.

Dr. Du says nothing. He produces an iron syringe, grabs Virtuous Beauty's neck and digs it in. Virtuous Beauty resists very unhappily, her two claws fanning this way and that, unwilling to yield. A Mongolian doctor is a Mongolian doctor. Dr. Du pushes the liquid medicine into Virtuous Beauty by dexterously taking advantage of her wiggling.

Lin Yao asks, "What kind of medicine is it?"

"An anaesthetic," Dr. Du answers. Next he tidies up his medical chest and gets ready to leave.

"Only a shot of anaesthetic?"

"When the medicine has taken affect, cart her over to the infirmary," Dr. Du replies. "She needs to be hospitalized."

Jade Li probes, "You won't do it together with us?"

"I need to go to Monkey Mountain," Dr. Du responds.

"What's wrong with the monkeys?"

"They've got loose bowels as well."

Jade Li surmises, "Could it be that Red Flag Chen thought to follow suit after spotting me fetching the broth?"

Lin Yao says, "Leave his monkeys out of it. Think how we should transport this monster first."

"We have no choice but to ask Red Flag Chen and his gang to help."

"Didn't you hear that their monkeys have loose bowels too?"

"Last time when a zoo in the South wanted some monkeys, we all went over there to help but they even didn't invite us out for a meal. They owe us."

While the pair is talking, Virtuous Beauty, unable to hold on any longer, staggers around in ever-decreasing circuits, her eyelids gradually becoming droopy and her breath increasingly short and rapid.

"Go summon up some guys," Lin Yao orders. "After a while, when the medicine starts to wear off nobody will be able to bring her to heel if she wakes up halfway there."

"Who should I go and look for?"

"The leaders."

Jade Li scoots off like he is taking flight.

Lin Yao steps into the iron cage and strokes Virtuous Beauty's back. He opens his palm. Inside is a handful of bear's hair. A mortally-diseased man's hair will likewise fall off by the handful, Lin Yao thinks. Gazing at the shaggy hair in his hand, he doesn't know how long Virtuous Beauty can survive and feels extremely frustrated.

The zoo leaders arrive with several hired hands. The hired hands are terrified and refuse to enter the bear's den no matter how they are cajoled. They insist that their contracts do not stipulate that they have to come into direct contact with ferocious beasts. If they must do it, more money is needed. This is a very risky job.

Lin Yao placates them, "Don't be scared. She has been injected with anaesthetic."

"What if the medicine hasn't been effective enough? The hired hands answer back, "What can be done if she wakes up? You're her handler. She won't attack you, of course. She'll only bite at us."

Lin Yao says, "Virtuous Beauty is a good bear."

The hired hands riposte, "A good bear still bites. Even a dog bites."

The leaders make a decision on the spot that another ten yuan will be given to each hired hand and if anything happens, the zoo will compensate them in full for any damage.

"Get going," Jade Li pronounces. "If she wakes up in a bit, you won't be able to get away in time even if you run."

Upon hearing his words, those few hired hands that have stepped in stampede with a *whoosh*. "She won't wake up in a hurry," Lin Yao assures them. "Hurry up and push the handcart in."

The handcart is pushed in. The guys haul Virtuous Beauty into the cage on the cart in a melee. The cage is very small, barely big enough to accommodate a bear. Now it has become Virtuous Beauty's "sickbed."

Many tourists gather around when the handcart is being wheeled to the infirmary and exclaim, "Ah, a bear's died." "When she was alive, she was easy to pass by. But after she has died, she's become such a big heap."

The hired hands tug at the bear's paws and wave them at the tourists, "She is still alive!"

The tourists scatter in all directions and the hired hands appear newly cocky.

Virtuous Beauty is admitted to the infirmary. After a general anaesthetic has been administered, she now lies in the cage in the one corner of the room receiving medical treatment. Lin Yao and Jade Li take turns to "wait on her at the sickbed" besides coping with their daily work at the bear sanctuary. They are unspeakably miserable during these few days. Two Guangxi monkeys are hospitalized as well. Since they are at the absolute peak of their fertility, they are entitled to be sent in here for treatment. The monkeys are shut in a cage. Having been injected with who knows what medicine, they are very docile, lying there like a man with their eyes wide open and pitiably gazing at the in-coming and out-going people. Lin Yao is most afraid to see such eyes, innocent and naïve, beautiful and pleading like Virtuous Beauty's. Red Flag Chen also comes to see his monkeys. Lin Yao asks him if he too gave some broth to the monkeys. Red Flag Chen answers, "It would be so good if they could have broth to drink. It was those oranges that screwed them up."

Lin Yao asks how oranges can give monkeys diarrhoea.

Red Flag Chen replies in indignation, "They have all been sprayed with pesticide. A man knows he should peel them. Some monkeys also know that but some swallow them whole. Diarrhoea is only an ailment. It is their good luck that none have died from poisoning. In the future, if apples are sent here, I bloody well need to sit beside the aviary peeling them for these ancestors."

"They are our ancestors and we come from them," Lin Yao says. "We are duty-bound to serve our ancestors." Even though he expresses it in this way, he thinks that adoption has its disadvantages too just as every coin has two sides.

Lin Yao sits down beside the cage to write a letter to his wife Drizzle, entrusting her to find a cooperative partner for the *Star* Food Factory. He especially emphasizes the Manager's promise to Virtuous Beauty as well as stating that the guy was a buddy who was sent to the same county as him to be rusticated on a production brigade. Virtuous Beauty's life is hanging upon this strategy and he needs her all-out assistance. After the letter is finished, on a whim, he rubs off a handful of the bear's hair and slides it into the envelope. At the end of the letter, he adds a postscript, "Virtuous Beauty is seriously ill. One stroke of the hand takes off this much hair. How can the sight of this not chill the heart?" After he is through with the letter, he looks at Red Flag Chen. Something bad has seemingly befallen the monkeys. The hired hands are dragging one dead monkey out of the cage. The monkey's arms dangle lifelessly and her small head hangs down like a baby fast asleep.

Lin Yao goes over there. Red Flag Chen still stands there with his back to him.

Red Flag Chen sobs, "She was with child."

Lin Yao knows that Red Flag Chen's eyes are flooded with tears.

IV.

It is snowing. Chinese New Year has arrived.

As usual, the banquets to mark the end of the year are presided over by Second Aunt. In the past when she cooked, she would do the purchasing herself. At that time the Lu family prospered and she was in the prime of her youth. When she went to the street to buy delicacies from mountain and sea, she never asked about the prices but only required the best of the best and was very strict about the quality. She could ascertain clearly which sharks fins were padded out with sand and which swallows nest had too many feathers. Back in those years, she was well-acquainted with the bosses of all the shops which sold seafood and mountain produce. No one dared to hoodwink the professional Second Aunt. The banquets of the Lu family had been managed by Second Aunt for so many years. As time passed by, the cuisine to entertain the guests conformed to an established routine: six dishes to accompany the liquor and eighteen main course dishes plus soup and sweet snacks. However, by now Second Aunt is not capable of pulling off this turn. This year, her niece from her maiden home Tranquillity Jin has happened to come over to visit her. Second Aunt pushes the boat along the water current and instructs Tranquillity Jin how to cook several traditional Lu family dishes. Tranquillity Jin is a laid-off worker. She used to sing the female lead, known as the "pleated indigo garment,"[m] in a Beijing opera troupe. Later she went to work in a pottery and ceramics factory. The factory was sluggish and changed the line of production. She was laid off. Now she stays at home idle the whole day long until annoyance and perplexity set in.

Tranquillity Jin's presence adds a heavy dose of liveliness to

149

the dinner table on New Year's Day. Having formerly been an actress, Tranquillity Jin is vivacious and not at all reserved. The old gentleman and ladies love her very much. Having heard praise being heaped on the Lu family cuisine for half a day, Tranquillity Jin suggests, "Why don't you make use of the large compound and these delicacies to run a restaurant serving Lu family specialities?"

All those present are surprised.

Tranquillity Jin says, "My aunt's cooking skills should all be winkled out. If they don't get to be handed down that will be a great loss."

A doubtful Lu Junqing observes, "Second Aunt can't even take care of herself. How is she supposed to manage the Lu family's so-and-so cuisine?"

Tranquillity Jin adds that she can come over to help. Her aunt may use her tongue and she will be the one to lift her hands.

"In my opinion, Tranquillity Jin's idea warrants consideration," Mother-in-law says. "The Lu Family Cuisine. This is a good prospect. Who doesn't want to sample the cuisine served at a feudal bureaucrat's home in the old society! Many dishes turned out by our Second Aunt's hands are novel and unique. Outsiders have never even heard tell of them much less seen them. For those Chinese folk who are more and more particular about what they eat, this should prove extremely amenable. Since we have such an advantage, we should make full use of it."

Father-in-law expresses reservation, "We Chinese all know that the eight styles of cooking – Sichuan cuisine, Guangdong cuisine, Shandong cuisine, Jiangsu cuisine and so forth – are classified geographically. However, if we group them according to how they came about Chinese cuisine would include imperial dishes, feudal officials' dishes, civilian dishes, imported dishes, national dishes and such like. At the moment, feudal officials' dishes are not yet widely-known. What is more, the Lu family is short on manpower ..."

"My aunt will give the instructions," Tranquillity Jin suggests,

"I shall take charge of the purchasing and cooking. Anyhow I am idle at home right now and it is better for me to find something to do. We only need to hire two little girls from the labour exchange and that should be enough."

Despite not having spoken a word, Lin Yao is swayed.

Later, the members of the Lu family spend another whole day comparing notes with Tranquillity Jin. Tranquillity Jin draws up the plan. Second Aunt outlines the menu of the Lu Family Cuisine. Every night only a single one-table banquet will be available in the form of a family dinner party that entertains no more than twelve guests. Banquets can follow one of two forms: the formal and the informal. A formal banquet is one staged in the main rooms of the front courtyard; an informal banquet is held in the parlours of the back garden.

After a period of tightly-scheduled preparations, the Lu Mansion changes remarkably from within.

First of all, Tranquillity Jin takes up her station at the Lu Mansion. Secondly, the elderly Lu Junqing and his wife move from the main rooms to the eastern side courtyard. Lin Yao vacates the parlours, moving into the small southern rooms in the outer courtyard.

At Mother-in-law's behest, a construction team repairs and refurbishes the main rooms until they are brand new. The partitioning walls which had created three rooms are torn down to open-up one space. The small suites to the east and west are redecorated as lounges. The big round table that has sat out of use in the utility room for several dozen years where it was buried by dust and cobwebs is also invited out, wiped shiny and spread with a snow-white tablecloth. Wooden chairs and small squat tea tables are deposited in the western lounge. A portrait of the Lu family's ancestor in his Second Grade Hat Button[n] is hung above the long narrow table opposite the door and in-season fruits are presented as offerings. The moment a guest enters, he should be awestruck by the dignity and grace of this opulent ancestry.

The parlours are decorated around the theme of elegance. A *Painting of Angling on the Ice-covered River* created by the host is hung on the wall flanked by a couplet written on two sheets. The first half of the couplet reads, "Regard honour and shame as common as the blossoming and fading of the flowers in front of the courtyard and never feel shocked;" the second half of the couplet reads, "Take staying in one's position and retirement as being as interchangeable as the rolling-up and unrolling of the clouds beyond the skies, staying always broad-minded." A large rectangular table stands in the eastern section of the parlours with eight scented rosewood chairs to match. The writing desk in the western section remains next to the window with the Four Treasures of the Study – writing brushes, ink-sticks, rice-paper and an ink-slab – on top. A hardwood flower shelf stands behind the writing desk. A pot of four-foot-long foxtail fern cascades down like a painting made by splashing ink and reflects a burst of vitality. All these inform people that the host will never allow himself to become lax about his own self-cultivation and a guest has to stow away his rudeness and vulgarity.

Planned meticulously by Second Aunt and Tranquillity Jin, the Lu Family Cuisine showcases its unique style and specializes in delicacies from mountain and sea cooked out of dried raw materials. The original taste and flavour of the cuisine in a feudal official's house are preserved intact. Raw rarities from the sea are seldom used because in the past there were no fridges and it was almost impossible to keep them fresh. If a bureaucrat's house or even the imperial palace wanted to dine on mountain delicacies and sea dainties, they would most probably rely on dried raw materials which had to be soaked in water before being used. These might include sharks fins, abalone, sea cucumbers, swim bladders from fish, sharks lips, bears paws, and camel humps and such like. The diners should be made to feast on gourmet dishes cooked slowly and meticulously over a fire that is neither too fierce nor too gentle and prepared by working the ingredients in accordance with their natural properties; what they relish is the comprehension and recognition of the Chinese culinary culture in a serene state of mood. They are allowed to understand the profundity and abstruseness of the 5,000-year-long Chinese culture. This represents not only a treatment of delicious food but what is furthermore a kind of spiritual nourishment.

Most of the funds to purchase dried raw materials and for re-decorating the compound have come from the proceeds of Father-in-law selling his paintings and from the gifts of "filial gratitude" Drizzle and Thunder wired from abroad. Lin Yao and Tranquillity Jin have no money but are willing to do the legwork and to contribute in other ways. They are regarded as shareholders as well and will receive a share of the dividends. Mother-in-law has declared beforehand that the profits from the first year won't be divided but will be re-invested in their entirety. One half of the profits in the second year will be allocated according to the share of the stock each one holds. The Lu Family Cuisine will be introduced to the market gradually like a rolling snowball. As the others all know only too well she is an excellent steward, who has her apothecary-boss father's teachings to thank – a person from a small family has a small family's shrewdness. When at midnight she plucks the balls of the abacus so they clatter melodiously within the Lu Mansion, the others are all convinced that this amounts to the sound of a booming fledgling business. Second Aunt's cooking skills and Mother-in-law's calculations have made it possible for the Lu Family Cuisine to become commercialized. What will soon serve as the cashier's desk is set up in the small doorman's room. An old-style abacus is used and the ledger is recorded in the yellow account books with red squares. All these lend an air of antiquity that is in perfect consort with the manner of the Lu Family Cuisine.

Everything is ready, only they haven't opened for business yet. In Lin Yao and Tranquillity Jin's view, firecrackers should be set off and a hoarding should be hung out. Father-in-law puts his foot down resolutely. He emphasizes repeatedly, "The Lu family is *not* running a restaurant."

"But it is to all intents and purposes a restaurant," Lin Yao argues with his father-in-law.

"It is a restaurant in all but name," the old gentleman insists, shaking his head.

Mother-in-law smiles, only she doesn't say a word. Not until a long while later does she say slowly, "It is a good thing that this is not a restaurant. The Lu family can't run a restaurant, either."

Lin Yao and Tranquillity Jin are puzzled.

Mother-in-law explains, "Of course all our efforts can't be allowed to go down the drain. To folks from outside none of us will declare that we are running a restaurant. We must only put it about that the Lu family is entertaining guests with a feudal official's household's delicacies. Whoever wants to savour them must book a reservation three days in advance. The patriarch, who has the final say in the Lu family, will also show up to keep them company. Otherwise, please excuse us for ignoring the order." The others all think this idea is original and unique but none knows if it will work.

Sure enough, in spite of being in business for several days none of the passersby knows that this is a venue for dinner parties. The two little hired girls have nothing to do. Mother-in-law instructs them to prune twigs from the trees and sweep the courtyards. The Lu Mansion is tidied up until it is devoid of dust.

Ding One sends for Lin Yao, giving the word that the Japanese *Himori* Food Stock Company – introduced to them by Lin Yao's wife Drizzle Lu – will send hands to inspect the factory the day after tomorrow. Ding One invites Lin Yao to go over there to help greet the guests.

Lin Yao says, "You shouldn't be blindly optimistic. Nine out of every ten inspectors talk nothing but crap. Some domestic enterprises take advantage of this and try to establish a bogus joint-venture company even though no business agreement has been sealed as a matter of fact. After the company has been registered, the foreign investors will have their stake refunded and they will get favourable terms with no strings attached."

"I won't do that," Ding One answers. "I want to kick the *Star* Factory up a notch. No matter what favourable terms are given if no high-grade products can be produced all will have been in vain."

"Ding One, you are great," Lin Yao exclaims. "I didn't figure you wrong."

The Japanese delegate arrives punctually on 15th January according to the lunar calendar – that is to say on the Chinese Lantern Festival. Lin Yao instructs Jade Li in advance that he should let Virtuous Beauty stay like a rascally child in the infirmary for several more days but not leave the hospital in a hurry. That way, by hook or by crook she will be able to cadge some quality food to eat. He goes to the *Star* Factory in person early in the morning.

What dismays Ding One and all the working staff of the *Star* Factory is that a thick snow is drifting down that day. The Japanese delegate tramps across the muddy surface of the road and then wets and messes up the floors of the workshops and the office buildings which all the workers have been sweeping diligently for several days. The Japs are headed by a small old man called Tatsuzo Yokomichi. Exhibiting a black face, this Yokomichi walks to and fro about the workshops and casts his beady eyes first at the windows and then at the ceilings but never once at the machines. Ding One feels full of remorse because he has always focused on everything down below but failed to attend to the ceilings that have become weighted down with dust and dirt. For this reason, he wants to divert Yokomichi's attention and repeatedly describes to him the investment environment and preferential policies implemented by this city. He says that this is a wheat-rich area of Northern China, so is uniquely placed to process food made out of wheat. Added to that, the cityscape and cultural relics are counted as among the most beguiling throughout the country.

Yokomichi gibbers away in Japanese. The interpreter makes clear that "The roofs of the factory buildings must be torn down and rebuilt. Such ancient broken-down sheds are not up to the needs of production."

Ding One replies that this is precisely what he plans to do.

Yokomichi investigates several other spots within the factory. Ding One has selected a tall slender beauty to hold the umbrella for Yokomichi and has told her to follow him closely. The snowfall is picking up in vigour and adds a white coating upon everyone. All the people have retracted their necks. Yokomichi still looks graceful, pointing his finger here and dabbing his foot there and striking a majestic posture, simply because he has a beauty to hold the umbrella for him. What a poor wretch that umbrella-holding beauty is. Clad in a thin cheongsam that has been soaked through by the snow, she grits her teeth as she fights back her shivers and braves the cold snow. She complains not even once for the future of the factory is at stake. Lin Yao wants nothing more than to dart over there and direct a stiff punch at Yokomichi's arrogant face. However, for the sake of Virtuous Beauty, he has to close his eyes and pretend that he hasn't seen anything.

The evening dinner party to entertain the Japanese delegate is held at the Lu Mansion. This was at Lin Yao's suggestion. The Japanese are informed that the Deputy Manager Lin Yao is descended from a feudal bureaucrat's family and that he has entrusted his family to cook some dishes for these guests from a kindred state to savour. It is a purely private matter and nothing commercial. These words seemingly pique Yokomichi's interest.

That evening, several sedan cars park at the gate of the Lu Mansion, introducing much splendour to the compound that has been desolate for so many years. The moment he sets foot

upon the stone steps before the compound, Yokomichi, escorted by Ding One and Lin Yao, feels stricken with awe by the
austere stateliness. The huge vermillion gates that recede backwards deeply give people a sort of neat majesty like a bow that
has been pulled taut but not yet released or a gentleman who
will never yield through he is in a position of retreat. In other
words, this is enough to dwarf and humble any visiting guest.
The ice-cold flat round stone drums – their shape gives full
expression to their arrogance and sternness – stand mute on
both sides of the gate. All of a sudden, none of the crowd dares
to speak loudly. Yokomichi might also have sensed something.
He corrects his tie and puts on a respectful face.

A square boulder lies below the steps on the right side of
the gate. Yokomichi inquires about what was its use. Lin Yao
explains that it is a horse-mounting stone. The foreigners don't
know what a horse-mounting stone is.

Lin Yao goes on, "One would step on this stone before slipping one's feet into the stirrups. In feudal times it was a symbol
of lofty status. A household that was entitled to have such a
horse-mounting stone was classified as belonging to the Second Grade or above."

Yokomichi probes about what "the Second Grade" means.

Lin Yao answers, "If a Second Grade feudal official did not
serve in the Court he was on a par with a governor."

Yokomichi immediately looks at the Lu family with new eyes
and addresses Lin Yao as "Lord Lin" instead of "Mr. Lin."

One mounting-horse stone works its magic as spontaneously
as when a shadow is cast down from a bamboo pole the moment it is planted. This injects Lin Yao with confidence when it
comes to broaching the subject of establishing a joint-venture
enterprise and operating the Lu family cuisine. Furthermore, it
endows him with optimism about Virtuous Beauty's future.

They enter the gate, skirt around the screening wall and reach
the main courtyard through a gate decorated with overhanging
floral patterns carved in wood. The courtyard has been swept

clean so there is not a trace of the snow. A set of couplets inscribed in wooden boards hang on the columns in the passageway:

A gentleman is disposed to like glossy ganoderma *and orchids;*
An ancient sage's heart resembles pines and cypresses.

Two bright red shining palace lanterns contribute to the overall festive atmosphere of the compound on the night of this auspicious day. A full moon has barely risen above the ridges of the eastern buildings which are decorated with animal figurines. Woodwind music floats over from who knows where. Those few foreigners from the other side of the eastern seas are so astonished that they seem to forget what year it is now.

Lu Junqing is already waiting in the passageway. His white beard buoyant, his hair like a crane's feathers but his face resembling that of a baby, he is the very image of an immortal. Lu Junqing clasps his hands in front of his midriff to greet Yokomichi. In a fluster, Yokomichi clicks his heels snappily and straightaway makes a deep bow before Elderly Gentleman Lu. The elderly gentleman says, "No need to stand on courtesy." Then with a smile he steps to one side and invites Yokomichi to come in.

After entering the room, Yokomichi spots the portrait of the ancestor of the Lu family on the wall. He bows to it once more, earnestly as if he has met up with the ancestor in person or with the Japanese Mikado. Only Lin Yao feels that this is funny.

The guests and the hosts take their respective seats in front of the small squat tea table. The subject that Elderly Gentleman Lu has chosen to discuss with the Japanese is how "a gentleman must be cautious even when he is alone." How can the Japs carry on such a rarefied conversation of the type that not even young Chinese men of the present day could not comprehend? Elderly Gentleman Lu appears more unfathomable. He is smiling, he is courteous, he is wise, he is integral, he is graceful and the others can only admire him for it.

A little girl in a small piped jacket serves six dishes full of dried fruit – amber sugar-coated walnut kernels, stir-fried cashew nuts, crunchy sweetmeats, sugar-coated starched peanuts, honeyed kumquats, sliced melons and pure tea. The tea service consists of lidded white porcelain bowls from Dehua County in Fujian Province and within those bowls is brewed the finest tea from the summit of Mount Meng in Sichuan Province.

Yokomichi lifts the lid from the bowl and after barely one sip declares loudly, "Good tea! Good bowl!"

Elderly Gentleman Lu fingers his beard and smiles.

Lin Yao and Ding One smile inwardly but do not let this show on their faces.

Tranquillity Jin informs them that the evening dinner is ready. People then walk to the dinner table.

When it is time to take their seats, they defer to one another. Though a round table doesn't have seats of honour, as the host Elderly Gentleman Lu sits down on Yokomichi's right side and Ding One takes the seat to his left in order that the conversation might flow easily.

When the big assorted *Red Phoenix Saluting the Sun* platter is served, the foreigners all take photos and fawn about how that they cannot find the heart to dig in with their chopsticks.

The two little girls serve the dishes in turn – all of them rare eye-opening novelties. A small pot of high-class Shaoxing° yellow liquor sealed with yellow clay is carried in. The sealing clay is slapped away before the very faces of all present. Fragrance immediately overflows and makes the people salivate. One little girl warms the liquor and then fills everyone's cup. Elderly Gentleman Lu raises his cup and invites the others to join him, "Please –"

After one cupful of liquor has been downed, Yokomichi can't wait to tuck his chopsticks into a plate of braised pork with cherry juice. This dish is prepared as follows: First of all, lean pork is sliced into cubes the size of a cherry and then simmered over a gentle fire in a small pot together with cherry juice for seven hours. Not until all the juice has been absorbed into the pork and the meat becomes ruddy like cherries, should it be brought off the simmer. The pot can then be lifted off the heat and the food be scooped onto the plate. The dish is sweet, nutritious, tender and full of fruity flavour – a perfect accompaniment to the liquor. The other plates of fish smoked with Japanese cinnamon fruit, dried scallops cooked with crushed garlic and such like also have their own characteristics. The lukewarm Shaoxing liquor makes the faces of the Japanese who have little head for alcohol redden like peach blossoms. Yokomichi can no longer put on airs but must ask Elderly Gentleman Lu in which earthly branch of which heavenly stem[p] he was born. The answer is that Elderly Gentleman Lu is two cycles – twenty-four years – older than him. Therefore he pays more attention to his manners and prefaces every word he says with *ojisan,* the Japanese term for an "uncle."

The first course is braised sharks fin in rice wine sauce.

The second course is arhat lobsters.[q]

After they are done with the braised abalone with soy sauce, the little girls serve each one of them a small pure white tea cup full of clear water. None of the others knows for what it is used. Afraid that they might display their ignorance, no one dares to move but waits to watch what Elderly Gentleman Lu will do. Elderly Gentleman Lu uses the water in the small tea cup to rinse his mouth and then spits it into an already-prepared container. A girl hands him a towel, which he uses to wipe his mouth. Now the others know that the lukewarm water should be used to rinse their mouths out and all follow the host's lead in doing likewise.

Ding One asks, "We're in the middle of a hearty dinner. Why then should we rinse our mouths out?"

The elderly gentleman answers, "The next course is swallows nest steamed in pure broth – a dish to be sampled slowly. How can you feel how splendid it is if your mouth is filled with the aftertaste of very spicy food? You must rinse your mouth to better appreciate it."

While he is explaining, a lidded soup tureen decorated with a gold tracery design is served. One girl lifts the lid to one side. Below the pinkish sliced ham is the swallows nest steamed in chicken broth. Every slice of swallows nest is transparent and crystalline and the diners easily work up an appetite. The little girl divides it up among them. Lin Yao takes one mouthful. Indeed, it is delectable. Such a pity that there is only one small bowlful and with two swishes of the ladle it is done. He stares at the pot again. It is clean. He can't help applauding the chef for her precise calculations.

The dinner party ends with a sweet repast which includes walnut cream and bean paste and sweet potato pancakes.

A great feast for the eyes and for the mouth. The foreigners from the other side of the eastern seas are filled with admiration for the cuisine from a Chinese feudal official's household.

Before taking his leave, Yokomichi wants to meet up with the chef who has organized this dinner party.

Elderly Gentleman Lu replies, "My older sister-in-law personally went to the kitchen to arrange this banquet. My older sister-in-law is already seventy-eight. She has been a member of the Lu family since she was sixteen years of age and has cooked for numerous high-ranking officials and eminent personages, among whom many have come simply to burnish her fame."

Since Elderly Gentleman Lu has spoken like this, Yokomichi is adamant that he must meet this Second Aunt. Someone is sent to the kitchen to invite her over. One little girl relays her word and says, "Second Aunt is tired and has already gone back to rest."

For half a day the Japanese fellow feels the pity of this.

Elderly Gentleman Lu escorts the delegate to the decorated gate and halts in his tracks. Lin Yao tells Yokomichi that according to the rules of such a large household, if the host sees the guests off to the decorated gate, he might be regarded as having gone an awfully long way. Generally he will stand in the passageway and clasp his hands, which is his means of bidding farewell. Back in that year when the great grandfather of the Lu family saw off the Grand President Li Yuanhong (1864-1928), he ground to a halt in the middle of the courtyard without yet having reached the decorated gate.

Hearing this out, Yokomichi hurriedly turns around and bows to Elderly Gentleman Lu to express his gratitude. Then he says to Ding One, "Very good. I have come to China several times but this is the first time that I have truly been to China. Mr. Ding, my appreciation of your sincerity stretches down to the bottom of my heart. Our future cooperation will indeed be pleasant."

Ding One catches the overtones to Yokomichi's words and cannot help congratulating himself quietly.

After having seen off the foreigners from the other side of the eastern seas, Lin Yao and Father-in-law go back to the hall and find an envelope on the dinner table. They open it and take a look. Inside is 300,000 Japanese yen. This must be Yokomichi's unspoken present to them. Perhaps he thought that as the Lu family is not running a restaurant it would be improper to settle the bill before their very faces. On the other hand, they couldn't dine without paying. Therefore, he left behind a "humble gift" appropriate to expressing his courtesy to the "Second Grade."

That very night the "humble gift" of 300,000 Japanese yen is recorded in the ledger by Mother-in-law, this being the first item of income since "the Lu Family Cuisine" has been in business.

v.

Virtuous Beauty's diarrhoea abates. When she comes back to the bear sanctuary from the infirmary, she is still somewhere between life and death, her teeth are falling out one by one and she is losing her hair tuft after tuft. Lin Yao's heart is filled with hope as he awaits the news from Ding One. Jade Li has heard from his sister-in-law that Ding One has signed a contract with the *Himori* Food Stock Company to establish a joint-venture enterprise. The Japanese machinery has arrived together with four Japanese operatives.

Soon afterwards, Lin Yao receives an invitation card to attend the "Ceremony for the Commencing of the Cookie Production Line at the *Sun and Star* Food Corporation." At that moment, it is necessary for him to rid Virtuous Beauty of all those mites and fleas. So, he entrusts Jade Li to go instead.

When he arrives back from the *Star* Factory, Jade Li has two boxes of cookies clamped beneath his armpit, and he says that Ding One has told him to bring them with him. Lin Yao asks him how the ceremony went. Jade Li answers, "Ding One, that son of a gun, knows how to whip things up. He invited many movers and shakers over there and hired a gang of trumpeteers and drummers. Those foreign drums and trumpets really created a clamorous din. The workshops have been made-over as well. Big buildings cover small ones. The machines are uniformly white. The workers' uniforms are white too and every one of them wears face-masks and caps to boot. Disposable muzzles and caps that will be discarded after being used once have been imported from Japan. As soon as the movers and shakers cut the red silk ribbons, the conveyor belts of the machines started to rotate without any sound. After a while, many black or white titbits began to appear on the belts and the workers packed them into small iron boxes …"

"Ding One didn't say anything about the adoption of Virtuous Beauty?" Lin Yao inquires.

"He was as busy as a ghostly servant fanning a fire with his breath," Jade Li replies. "It was not the right place to talk about adoption."

Gazing at the two boxes in Jade Li's hands, Lin Yao asks, "Do you still remember? Ding One promised us that as long as a joint-venture corporation could be established, his first product must have some connection with bears."

Jade Li is dubious, saying, "These cookies ... they can't possibly have anything to do with bears. Lin Yao, you shouldn't take it too seriously."

"I might not take it too seriously, but he ought to. My word is my bond. This is a basic principle for how two guys from the 'Three Old Graduating Classes' should treat each other. I said I would find a foreign businessman for him and I did it. He promised that he would adopt Virtuous Beauty and I am waiting to see what he will do." While talking like this, he rips the transparent duct tape from the seams of the *dim sum* boxes Jade Li has brought back. "Let's see what kind of stuff Ding One is turning out."

"Cookies. Ding One told me that it is cookies. The name sounds a little bizarre."

"Cookies mean *dim sum*. Ding One the son of a gun is playing cryptic, a stupid dog striking a wolfhound's posture."

The iron boxes are opened. Lin Yao and Jade Li are too surprised to utter a word.

The cookies in the boxes are a kind of tiny *dim sum* in the shape of stout, rotund bears filled with profuse amounts of cream. The little white bears' arms are outstretched horizontally and their legs are clamped tight together; the black bears must have chocolate in them, their legs are splayed and their arms stick to their bodies. Their round eyes are two pieces of sparkling sweetie – very bonny. Lin Yao and Jade Li draw the black and white bears out of the boxes and line them up along one edge of the table. They alternate between black and white so that in the line of little bears, one has his arms reaching out horizontally and then the next has his hanging down. Legs are clamped shut and then are wide open, so it seems that they are moving in a bloc. If one were suddenly to catch sight of them an intriguing animated effect would be perceived.

Scratching his scalp, Jade Li says, "That son of a bitch Ding One really is good. It is never easy to hit upon ideas like this."

Lin Yao comments, "This really does have a connection with bears."

Jade Li adds, "Anyhow he has kept his promise."

"Let's see what he will do next" is Lin Yao's response.

The beautiful little bears dance on the tabletop. Neither of the two men can find the heart to eat one. Only Virtuous Beauty has feasted on two – one black and one white – of her kind.

The blossoms of the Chinese plum have fallen and the winter jasmines are in full bloom. The Lu Mansion is still a yellow expanse.

Business is unexpectedly brisk mainly because Mother-in-law has contacted the Tourism Bureau and made sure that the Lu Family Cuisine is installed as a distinctive feature for the local tourist industry. Not only foreigners but locals too come to savour the feudal cuisine of an official's household in a feudal official's homestead. Although the prices are shockingly high, the diners all conclude that the dishes are worth every penny and regular return customers are frequent.

Lu Junqing sketches in the daytime and keeps the dinnertime guests company at night. When men of letters and notables arrive, he also needs to compose poems according to existing rhyme patterns and draw pictures, present songs and make up complimentary poems, appreciate flowers and drink liquor to demonstrate his elegant airs and graces to the utmost. Every night eminent guests fill the room and without fail a lavish banquet is staged – one table per day, sometimes in the main rooms and sometimes in the parlours. Sometimes they might even hit upon an original idea and set up the table beside the rockery under the flowers in the garden when a full moon is in the sky. Raising their cups, they invite the moon to join them. A large crowd is formed by the diners if their shadows are taken into account. They never feel forlorn in this poetic atmosphere. Moreover, writing brushes and China ink are to be served anytime at the Lu Mansion. Those who are seized by artistic inspiration can leave behind all kinds of inked treasures if they so please. Those items of calligraphy deemed as "treasures" will be mounted on paper and hung high, whereas those that are mere "splashes of ink" will be sent to a recycling station together with the empty wine bottles – the proper place for them both. The fame of the Lu family spreads. A TV station sends a crew to shoot a feature film with the title "Splendour Re-created by a Laid-off Woman Worker." Before Tranquillity Jin steps into the lens, the audience have already been made to feel intrigued by the sharks fins, swallows nests, tree shadows and walls carved with flowers. The fame of the Lu Family Cuisine is pegged up another notch. Those seeking to make reservations are compelled to wait their turn and most banquets are priced in excess of several thousand or even 10,000 yuan. The rifer the practice of using public funds to wine and dine becomes, the more the Chinese catering business thrives. On the streets, the "Sunflower" Restaurant, the steamed corn bread joints, the eating houses of the Dai minority people, and the Korean bar-becues have created all kinds of styles and patterns of eating. Nevertheless, the cuisine served by the bureaucratic Lu family is the first one truly to meet Confucius's requirement that "It should be impossible for grain to be husked more finely and impossible for meat to be cut more thinly." A private kitchen with a distinguished chef is better than a public restaurant. Once the people become familiar with the cuisine of the feudal official's household, all kinds of folk take it as a great honour that they should have the chance to savour it. If one feels like eating something, dine on that which is wholesome and se-rious. Thus, with generosity everyone throws big handfuls of silver onto the counter of Lin Yao's mother-in-law.

Tranquillity Jin gives full play to her *métier* as a one-time Beijing opera actress. Drawing upon old relationships, she contacts her former male or female disciples in the opera troupes. Those people can neither find it in their heart to abandon the arts nor find any way to earn money. When they have reached the end of their rope, Tranquillity Jin happens to come and invite them over, saying that they can go to the Lu Mansion at night to sing *a cappella* opera arias in exchange for a free meal and hourly pay. Many of these guys possess a body full of skills but to no avail. The opera troupe doles out only sixty per cent of their expected pay and requires them to make up the difference themselves. It is a regular occurrence for them to attend funerals to ply their musical instruments and sing. Now such a fine opportunity for work has cropped up they feel they wouldn't have been able to have gotten this even if they begged. Of course they all promise gamely. Some are still incapable of dropping their airs and graces, yet they cannot stand the sight of their pockets being empty and, when all is said and done, airs and graces are no replacements for rice. They think back to how in the old society there was the saying that one should "play a selected scene." To do as much was hardly considered a shame. Therefore, they come along with hearty spirits. *A cappella* opera arias are added to the nightly banquets. The Lu Mansion emulates the wonderful scenes featured in the *Painting of a Nightly Banquet at Han Xizai's Official Residence*, an artwork that depicts the lives of scholar-bureaucrats in the Five Dynasties.[r] All the diners are mesmerized.

Tranquillity Jin is brainy and quick on the draw. She duly becomes the inheritor of her paternal aunt's cooking skills and adheres to them strictly. Constraints of time are factored in, but this mindfulness serves to enhance the art of creation. The Lu Family Cuisine takes on a more and more refined character. Another chef is hired to meet the needs and he is responsible for cooking the mainstays of the menu. When a traditional Lu family dish is to be prepared, Tranquillity goes to the stove in person. At first, Second Aunt would stand nearby giving directions. Later she never supervises her but hides herself away at home. With a heart completely at ease she no longer ventures out.

Anyhow, Lu Junqing is advancing in years and can't keep the guests company night after night. One seat is left unoccupied at the table together with a bowl and a pair of chopsticks to the effect that the host is here. His attitude remains the same – I am not running a restaurant. When someone special arrives, he will step out, take several symbolic bites and throw out some nonsensical poems such as "The deep compound is unoccupied and a courtyard full of blossoms and drizzle is locked up in vain." Such trifles will, without exception, arouse a spurt of feigned artiness from everyone around. Shaking their heads they all seem to have been implanted with the sorrowful seeds of melancholic love and the scene comes across as comical.

The silver totals in Mother-in-law's account book are rocketing up. One table one night can no longer satisfy the increasingly pressing demand. Customers have to wait in line and book a fortnight in advance. Lin Yao suggests to Mother-in-law that they should add another single-table banquet and at the same time do business in the daytime.

Plucking at the balls of the abacus, Mother-in-law replies, "Then the Lu family will really have become a restaurant." She continues, "Before the People's Republic of China was founded in 1949, to the west of the Temple of the Fire God there was a chap called Leftovers Wang who sold baked pancakes in pig's offal broth. He only had one shop frontage. Customers came in an endless stream and his small eatery was always crowded with people. Business was brisk enough to make others envious. Whoever wanted to enjoy Leftovers Wang's baked pancakes in pig's offal broth had to wait for half a day by the stove until they were so impatient it was as if their hearts were actually being singed by the fire. Later someone suggested to Leftovers Wang that he should purchase the three-room Fire God Temple next door with the sole purpose of extending the shop frontage. For one thing it would be more spacious and for another people wouldn't need to stand waiting by the stove. Leftovers Wang did as was suggested, re-decorated the shop frontage and hired new hands. Who could have guessed it but that business went from bad to worse each day and later nobody would even darkened his door. Do you know why?"

"Did he offend the gods?" Lin Yao proffers. "But surely that is mere superstition." Mother-in-law explains, "The key to Leftovers Wang's booming business lay in the fact that the shop was crowded and customers had to wait. The customers stood there watching others gorging themselves. The more they watched, the more impatient they grew; the more impatient they grew, the less likely they would be just to shovel the food into their mouths. When they finally squeezed their way onto a seat and packed one bowlful into their stomachs, they would hold it especially dear because it cost them so much. Doing business is like your father when he draws pictures – you should play to your advantages and curb your limitations. The Lu Family Cuisine has come this far mainly because the large compound and the special flavour have met with approval. The diners are particular about the dining atmosphere. The harder it is for them to wait for their turn to come around, the more dignified they will appear. You can come and eat whenever you want to. Even so, this is not the steamed buns stall at the western entrance to the street."

Lin Yao feels ashamed that his Mother-in-law has greater foresight than he does. In truth, he is an amateur businessman. From this point on, he seldom concerns himself with the Lu family cuisine but devotes his undivided attention to Virtuous Beauty the sickly bear.

It couldn't be said that Virtuous Beauty has been malnourished of late. The large quantities of leftovers from the Lu family have mostly been brought to her in doggy bags by Lin Yao. Every day when he goes to work, a large plastic bag is borne upon the back seat of his bike. The fat duck and tender chicken passed down from the table are conveyed to the bear sanctuary from the Lu Mansion in an endless torrent. Virtuous Beauty has regained her strength considerably. Jade Li says, "According to the current situation, whether Ding One adopts Virtuous Beauty or not is no longer a pressing issue."

"A promise is a promise," snaps Lin Yao, "whether it is something pressing or not."

Jade Li says, "It is reported that Ding One has earned big bucks. The city is going to list him as one of its Ten Excellent Entrepreneurs."

"This time the strokes of his surname will be put into good use."

Jade Li laughs.

Tranquillity Jin comes by with a string bag, saying that when she cleaned the fridge, a lot of out-of-date food had to be swept out. Afraid that it might be left there to go rotten, she has brought them here for Virtuous Beauty.

Upon Tranquillity Jin's arrival, Virtuous Beauty appears restless. She growls in a low voice so as to intimidate Tranquillity Jin. It is also the first time that Tranquillity Jin has come into such close proximity with a bear. Even though she is standing on the other side of the iron railings, she is still frightened and steps backwards without hesitation.

Seeing through Tranquillity Jin's timidity, Virtuous Beauty becomes more spirited. She actually stands up and reaches her paws out through the bars. Catching sight of this, Tranquillity Jin turns around with a loud cry to run away but is intercepted by Jade Li. Jade Li comforts her, "She is teasing you on purpose." Not until now has Tranquillity Jin stopped running and collected herself to take a look at Virtuous Beauty, complaining, "After coming back home, Lin Yao always murmured *Virtuous Beauty*, *Virtuous Beauty*. I thought Virtuous Beauty was like a puppy. I had never expected that she would be so big, standing there like a pagoda. Whoever falls into her clutches would surely not survive."

Lin Yao replies, "That is not the case." With these words, he reaches in a hand to grab Virtuous Beauty's head. Seeing that Lin Yao is willing to play with her, Virtuous Beauty sticks her mouth outwards and grunts gently too. Lin Yao says, "She is kind by nature. Look at her eyes: so beautiful!"

Tranquillity Jin also plucks up her courage and edges close to the railings to take a good look at Virtuous Beauty. Who would have expected it, but barely has she reached out her head when Virtuous Beauty deals her a slap. Tranquillity Jin is frightened into taking several steps backwards.

"What's wrong with this fellow?" Jade Li queries, "she is not like this at ordinary times. Last time when Red Flag Chen brought his daughter here, she and the girl had a very good time."

"You smell of kitchen smoke," Lin Yao points out to Tranquillity Jin.

Tranquillity Jin sniffs at her overcoat and replies *yeah*. This morning she had this garment on when she fetched some kindling from the fruit trees, and later she used the kindling to roast a duck.

"That figures," Lin Yao exclaims. "Ever since she was a cub, this fellow couldn't stand the smell of smoke and fire. Hurry. Take off your clothes and wash your face."

After she has washed her face and taken off her outer apparel, Tranquillity Jin approaches the railings again. This time Virtuous Beauty is much more composed. Patting her head and then pointing at Tranquillity Jin, Lin Yao says, "This is Tranquillity Jin. A friend."

"You have taken her as a child. Does she know what a friend is?"

"How can she not know what a friend is? Her IQ is the same as that of a three-year-old child, only she doesn't know how to speak."

"Really." Tranquillity Jin draws close to the railings again.

Lin Yao takes out half a sausage from the string bag Tranquillity Jin brought here, hands it to her and tells her to feed the bear.

With fear still lingering in her heart, Tranquillity Jin bleats, "She will swallow my hand as well – yes or no?"

Lin Yao sweet-talks her, "Never. She already knows that you are a friend. If you don't believe me, have a try."

Tranquillity Jin edges close to Virtuous Beauty with the sausage and Virtuous Beauty has already opened her mouth intelligently.

Tranquillity Jin hesitates.

Lin Yao says, "Feed her. She is waiting."

"She really won't bite?"

"She won't."

Finally Tranquillity Jin plucks up her courage and tosses the sausage into the huge mouth that is gaping open only one foot away. Virtuous Beauty chomps and grunts heartily. Happiness brightens up her small eyes, which reminds Tranquillity Jin of the black button-like eyes of those small flannelette bears sold in the shops. You really can communicate with such clever animals. Tranquillity Jin for the first time has the sensation that looking towards the bear is no different from facing a man. She touches the furry palm that has reached out through the railings and spots the pigeon-egg-sized soft-cell sarcoma on it. Because Virtuous Beauty often licks at it, the round, jet-black and smooth sarcoma has become as glossy and slippery as a small pebble. She feeds her some more food. Virtuous Beauty walks around one circuit happily and again sits down in the former spot, stretching out her warty palm as if she is begging; perhaps she thinks that Tranquillity Jin admires the sarcoma on her palm as a choice feature. Tranquillity Jin feeds her more food and takes the opportunity to touch that shiny sarcoma again. Virtuous Beauty reads through Tranquillity Jin's facial expressions. When she has received clearly the message that Tranquillity Jin really loves her, she turns one more circuit on the spot.

Lin Yao says to Tranquillity Jin, "She likes you."

"I like her too."

Lin Yao enters the iron cage and uses an iron brush dipped in disinfectant to groom Virtuous Beauty. Virtuous Beauty grunts in comfort and her head sways to and fro. Sometimes when she intentionally gives Lin Yao a push or a head-butt, she has the perfect semblance of a naughty boy playing with an adult. The harmonious, hilarious scene between man and bear inside the cage entices Tranquillity Jin. She asks Lin Yao if she can also come in. "Never," Lin Yao warns her.

"But you are in there." She is unwilling to back down.

"I can, but you can't. I have brought her up since she was a tiny scrap like this. She is familiar with me." With these words, he pries open Virtuous Beauty's mouth and sticks a hand in there. Sure enough, Virtuous Beauty only grips Lin Yao's hand in her mouth but doesn't throw the heft of her jaw into it.

From now on, Tranquillity Jin is apt to go to the zoo to pay Virtuous Beauty a visit whenever she is free together with some delicious foods. She has fallen in love with her from the bottom of her heart.

VI.

The Lu Family Cuisine is booming and the production turnover of the *Sun and Star* Food Corporation is also shooting up in a perpendicular line. Ding One frequently throws a banquet at the Lu Mansion to entertain guests and tosses around money by the tens of thousands. No longer is he the tightfisted little guy who got so serious over a couple of bags of nutritional powder. His well-ironed suits and expensive brand-named ties are all imported. His gradually-bulging general's stomach has been stuffed with he doesn't know how many delicacies from sea and mountain at the Lu household. Consumers adore the baby-bear-shaped cookies and they have been rewarded the title of being a national quality product – the demand is exceeding the supply. The factory buildings are no longer their former shabby selves. Bright wide workshops are newly constructed in the development zone … After being elected an Excellent Entrepreneur, Ding One has become busier and he comes to the Lu Mansion more frequently. His bike has been exchanged for a common-or-garden *Santana*, something which actually elicits choruses of praise for him. People say that he is modest and prudent and runs the household in a frugal manner. The word on the street has it that he will become a candidate for the next People's Congress. In a word, the roads leading to the business world and the officialdom both stretch out very spaciously before him.

Tonight, when Lin Yao is helping Mother-in-law to staple together all kinds of invoices and receipts behind the desk in the cashier's room, Ding One comes in to settle the bill. In total it is 7,400 yuan. Biting at the toothpick in his mouth, he says, "I need to book an abalone banquet for next week."

Mother-in-law answers, "One abalone banquet can't be done without 15,000 yuan. Nowadays a single Grade One dried abalone imported from Hong Kong costs several hundred yuan."

Ding One says, "10,000 yuan and that's it. You should spend when you have to. Begrudging giving out silver sometimes might prove the ruin of a great cause."

Lin Yao cuts in at this point, "You should spend when you have to …"

Ding One raises his head and exclaims with sham surprise, "*Ayah*, Lin Yao is here too. I wondered who it was …"

Lin Yao gets straight to the point, "Ding One, shouldn't Virtuous Beauty have the benefit of your patronage too?"

Ding One answers, "Of course, I have always kept this in my mind. So long as the factory is reaping benefits I shall adopt Virtuous Beauty." Dabbing at the cheque written out by Ding One just now, Lin Yao challenges him without mincing his words, "Now the benefits are not good?"

Ding One swallows one mouthful of saliva and defends himself, "It is a superficially prosperous skeleton that has been gutted from within. A big tree breeds only a strong wind and widespread fame brings more social distractions – everyone is fixing their eyes on you." Ding One sticks his face towards Lin Yao and whispers, "I won't mince matters. In the past I could sweep out several bags of waste nutritional powder for you, but now if you were to ask me to do that, I couldn't give you even half a bagful. The machinery designed by the Japs doesn't waste even half a mite."

Lin Yao presses, "Then you mean Virtuous Beauty's plight won't be considered?"

"I haven't said that. I have always kept Virtuous Beauty's welfare in my mind. Once …" Even Ding One himself feels that the promise is pale and lifeless. He can't summon up enough courage to get through his words. Lin Yao is not a child and doesn't need to be fobbed off.

Mother-in-law also raises her eyes to peer at Ding One from over her reading glasses, which adds to his unease.

Lin Yao is still hunting him down. "When can your factory be said to be reaping real benefits?"

Ding One replies, "You were present as well when the negotiations were being conducted. The profit is split thirty-seventy between us and the Japanese side. We get only thirty per cent of the profit, but, heading a *Joint-venture Enterprise* panel, I have to stick out my belly and strike the posture of a big boss representing the Chinese side. Only I know the sour bitterness that lies within. Project Hope seeks patronage and you have to dip into your pocket. The fourth outer ring-road is to be constructed and all the units need to contribute money to help. A cultural square is to be built in the centre of the city proper. This is a programme for the public good. The leaders have given the word and they expect an immediate echo. The Bureau of Electricity says that power utilization in the district where our factory stands is soaring and the high voltage wires must be replaced. 30,000 or 20,000 yuan is not sufficient to deal with that …"

The more Lin Yao listens to Ding One pouring out his woes, the more chilly his heart feels. He shivers in a violent and cold fashion, knowing that Virtuous Beauty's lot is now hopeless.

Spotting that Lin Yao's face has turned ugly, Ding One takes hold of his arm and consoles him by saying, "I know that you helped us engage a joint-venture partner for Virtuous Beauty's sake and your friendship will always remain lodged in my mind. Lin Yao, your business is my business. Next month I will negotiate with a foreign businessman about setting up a workshop to ferment black rice vinegar. When the deal is concluded, I shall adopt Virtuous Beauty immediately." Then, slapping Lin Yao's shoulder, he bleats, "Get on your brother's wavelength. Your brother is not his own master now." While speaking like this, Ding One is somewhat emotional and tears are sparkling in his eyes.

Lin Yao doesn't notice that Ding One has now left. Plucking at the balls of the abacus, Mother-in-law says to him, "Surrender that false hope you have in this Ding chap. A businessman's words contain too much water. I did the maths roughly just now. He has spent 300,000 yuan here since the first day he came to our household to dine. What family property can stand such squandering? The way I see it, you should think out another way for your bear and don't believe that there is only tree to hang yourself from."

"I can't find a single tree right now," Lin Yao laments. "Much as I want to commit suicide I can't find anywhere to hang myself from."

Mother-in-law concludes, "Then your bear is buggered."

Lin Yao feels that his windpipe has been blocked with a huge lump and he is so choked he can't regain his breath. He raises his foot and staggers to his room slowly and weakly, his body being sour and soft as if his sinews have been yanked out.

VII.

Lin Yao has been floored by a disease.

The resulting diagnosis says that it is the dreaded haemorrhagic fever. Lin Yao is caught in a bitter struggle between life and death. Drizzle Lu calls home twice a day to inquire about his situation. The Lu family can't spare anyone to wait at his sickbed. Tranquillity Jin stays in the hospital for the better part of the daytime besides managing that single-table banquet at night. Lin Yao weathers a high fever, urinary shortage and coma and finally survives narrowly. He is one round thinner like a snake that has barely shed its skin. Lying on that sickbed, he turns his face to the window weakly. Outside, water is dripping down the eaves gently, the aroma of earth fermenting in the rainwater drifts in from the courtyard and the snow-white buds of magnolia flowers are trembling in the drizzle. This is a spring drizzle, Lin Yao thinks. Spring has come. He has made two calls to the bear sanctuary, but nobody answers. Jade Li has come to see him several times. When Virtuous Beauty is asked after, he answers, "Same old." His chief caregiver is his doctor. The young doctor majoring in infectious diseases is getting ready to use Lin Yao's case to investigate if haemorrhagic fever, the main route of infection for is striped field mice, can also be transmitted by means of the fleas and mites on a bear's body.

After he has been discharged from hospital, Lin Yao further recuperates for the better half of a month. Finally he can get down from the bed and walk around. By hugging the wall, he drags his feet out of the door. It is a sunny spring morning. A crabapple is in full bloom in the courtyard. A delicate white butterfly, seemingly having sensed that it must have come out too early, is landing on the crabapple sheepishly. The sunlight shines onto Lin Yao's bloodless face. Having barely pulled through, Lin Yao is so frail he can hardly stand steadily. His body swaying, one hand gripping the doorframe and the other hand shielding against the eye-prickling sunshine, he gazes at the courtyard blankly for half a day. New lawns have been laid. The fragmented old square bricks on the paths have been replaced with new ones and many grasses and flowers are growing on either side. The main rooms and the eastern and western side rooms have been lacquered anew. Even the couplets on the wooden boards of the columns have been traced with gold leaf again. The present-day Lu Mansion is as ostentatious and extravagant as a princely household.

Lin Yao staggers forward slowly. After turning around the moon-shaped gate, he spots that Tranquillity Jin and Chef Li are slaughtering a snake outside the kitchen. The thick strong serpent wriggles and struggles in Chef Li's hands, until he nails it mercilessly onto a column in the passageway. The moment Chef Li loosens his grip the snake rolls up into a flower in great pain and its tail whips the column forcefully, producing a crisp resonant sound. The more it struggles, the more pain it suffers. The snake must have gone mad. Tranquillity Jin says to Chef Li, "Why don't you make quick work of it instead of letting it hang there and thrash about?"

Chef Li answers, "The snake is too thick and powerful. I can't hold it still."

Tranquillity Jin orders the little girls to go over there and lend a hand. Screaming, they run a mile. Tranquillity Jin goes over and grips hold of the snake in one foul stroke. Chef Li's knife slides down smoothly and relieves the snake of its skin gently. The gutless and skinless snake's shiny white body is still rolling and churning. Witnessing it from afar, Lin Yao feels a wave of dizziness and hears the whir of bees buzzing; he wants nothing else but to vomit.

Lin Yao hauls his swaying body to go to work.

It is the time for spring outings. Gangs of cheering and frolicking pupils add great liveliness to the zoo which had been so desolate. The Monkey Mountain is always a hotspot for the children. Lin Yao knows that this is the busiest season for Red Flag Chen and his colleagues. The arrival of the kids signals the start of a festival for the Guangxi monkeys. Bread and sweets will rain down there and seventy per cent of the monkeys will end up with dyspepsia. Besides quarantining those monkeys that have loose bowels, Red Flag Chen and his colleagues need to clean out seven to eight cartloads of refuse every day to boot.

Lin Yao can see that the *Friendly State* bronze plate is still hanging high on the aviary. The children also read out the name of the *Friendly State* Company while delivering commentaries on the temperament of the Guangxi monkeys.

Compared with Monkey Mountain its neighbour Bear Mountain is denuded and forlorn. Lin Yao scoots over there to take a look. There is no sign of the bear except for two or three piles of bone dry dung. He takes a detour to the rear to push at the door. The door is locked. He sticks his face to a crack in the door and calls out "Virtuous Beauty" loudly. Two sparrows are scavenging in the empty and spacious bear sanctuary. On hearing his shouts, they flutter their wings and zip up to the crossbeam.

Lin Yao finds one of the leaders of the zoo. The leader tells him that Virtuous Beauty has been sold to a civil circus.

Hearing this, Lin Yao is speechless.

Seeing his facial expressions, the leader explains repeatedly, "A black bear's life expectancy is twenty-five years at most. Virtuous Beauty has been living in the zoo for more than twenty years and is a dying old bear. She moves sluggishly and can't attract any tourists. What's more, she has all kinds of diseases and was source of the haemorrhagic disease. Who will dare go near her now? Selling her to the circus was a decision made collectively by the zoo leaders. It is also her best way out. The boss of the circus has promised that she won't be required to perform or practice waving a pitchfork. She will be locked in a cage as a way of keeping up appearances. People will watch her and she will serve as a living ad."

Lin Yao challenges him by asking, "Why didn't you consult me about this?"

The leader says, "You were in the grip of that disease and not even capable of taking care of yourself. How could we consult you? Jade Li handled all of the business connected with Virtuous Beauty."

"When she was young, how many tourists did she win over for the zoo? Back at that time, the Bear Mountain was crowded

179

with people three deep on the inside and three deep on the outside. Now, couldn't you just permit her to die a natural death quietly in the zoo?"

"Lin Yao, cool down. If Virtuous Beauty were still here, she would fill our quota for bears. Now she has gone. We can apply for a young lively baby bear. As a leader, I can understand your feelings only too well. If a lost cat can cause its owner several days of heartache, it should be so much worse when a big bear is lost."

Lin Yao growls, "You don't know animals."

"In this respect you should learn from Jade Li. You see: he has already gone over to the landscaping team to work happily with them."

Lin Yao finds Jade Li in the zoo. Jade Li is pruning sprigs of holly with a pair of garden shears – *chow, chow*. Lin Yao calls out, "Jade Li –"

Jade Li doesn't make a sound but continues working with his head lowered.

Lin Yao says, "Jade Li, I am talking to you."

After half a day, Jade Li responds, "I am listening."

"Was Virtuous Beauty sold out through your very hands?"

"You are right. It was me that crammed her into the cage."

Lin Yao roars, "How could you find the heart to do that?"

Jade Li pays no attention to him and goes on shearing the holly – *chow, chow*. The garden shears work quickly and ferociously. Jade Li is gritting his teeth.

Lin Yao yanks over the shears and flings them to the ground. Jade Li stoops, picks them up and resumes his shearing job without taking one look at Lin Yao.

Feeling that Jade Li is not right in the head, Lin Yao turns around and walks away in a huff.

Jade Li calls Lin Yao to a halt. He explains, "… When you were disease-stricken, nobody brought food to Virtuous Beauty. When she left, she didn't even have the strength to grunt … She gazed at me imploring for help. I couldn't save her but could only gawk at those Henan guys transporting her out of the gate ... Virtuous Beauty carried on staring at me until she reached the gate, but I stood there without moving ... an animal would not sell its friend, though I have."

Lin Yao plops down on the curb of the path feebly.

Jade Li crouches down to wrench Lin Yao's shoulder, saying, "I, Jade Li, have my affections and a spirit of chivalry too. Lin Yao, I have sworn a vow that from now onwards Jade Li will never raise a bear again. I can't stand the torture."

His eyes bulging, Lin Yao sits down on the ground for half a day and nobody knows what is on his mind.

Jade Li suggests, "You should join the landscaping team as well. The job is tiring and sweltering. Nobody likes it. But the environment is quiet and there is no need to deal with the animals – it is very suitable for us."

Lin Yao murmurs, "I shall get Virtuous Beauty back."

"That's impossible. How can you find the circus?"

"I will go to Henan Province first to find the main pitching-place of the circus and then grope for the melon along the vine. A bear can't be just hidden away in any old place."

"The way I see it, the chances are slim."

"Just wait and see."

With that "wait and see," Lin Yao disappears as if swept away by a wind. He neither asks for leave nor informs his family. After several weeks, the leaders of the zoo feel it necessary to emphasize discipline and instruct the breeding section to take note of Lin Yao's daily absence from work, declaring that if he goes three months without clocking on it will be taken that he has voluntarily tendered his resignation. Later on they feel that this is not the appropriate course of action and place a missing person's advertisement in the newspaper, enjoining Lin Yao to come back to work as soon as he claps eyes on the paper.

However, no news is forthcoming from Lin Yao. He has vanished into nothingness as if he never existed at all. His wife Drizzle Lu makes several calls home and always gets the same answer: we are looking for him.

The business of the Lu family has not been affected by Lin Yao's departure and the single-table-a-day banquet advances steadily.

Ding One's *Sun and Star Food* Corporation now not only produces baby-bear-shaped cookies but also vinegar fermented from Chinese black rice, Japanese-styled fried pancakes, peanut and cow's milk powder, *Mind Clearing* instant milk tea, and a raft of such perishables. Business is booming. It is said that the monthly prize money of a member of the working staff is double that of the Mayor's salary. As for Manager Ding One's salary, he has reached the standards promised at the primary stage of socialism.[5] A dozen or so "Ding One Elementary Schools" have appeared in the surrounding suburbs and counties and the impoverished mountainous areas and a "Ding One Nursing Home" stands in the east of the city proper – all donated by *Sun and Star*. When the aged gentlemen and ladies in the nursing home chit-chat while sunning themselves after their meals, Ding One is their main topic of conversation. They are old and have someone to provide for them. When they have water to drink, they never forget from whence it flows – the aged gentlemen and ladies, whose startled hearts have barely calmed down, feel duty-bound to thank and pine after their provider of clothing and food, Mr. Ding One. Some literate idlers then write manuscripts, which are copied out in turn by the residents and mailed out in all directions. Anyhow they are idle and it is better to have something to do. One aged lady who was once a music teacher even composes a song *Hello, Ding One* and teaches the others how to sing it. The singers are passionate and sincere and their hearts are full of love. Ding One truly is a gentleman.

Ding One's great deeds of kindness also reach Jade Li's ears. Now he is not in the mood to be fussed with Ding One. He simply admires his agile mind from the bottom of his heart. The promise of adopting the bear still resounds in his ears but it has never been honoured. Instead many schools and an old people's home have been built. This is where Ding One's brilliance lies. If he adopts a bear, that bear won't write any manuscripts to sing his praises, nor will she sing *Hello, Ding One*. A big wad of bills can at most be exchanged for an inconspicuous bronze plate in a bleak place. How could Ding One possibly do this? Jade Li finally comes to his senses and realizes that Ding One is a friend but at the same time he is a businessman first and foremost.

Today, Ding One drives to the Lu Mansion and says that Yokomichi will come to sign a contract again and has pointed out especially that he wants to dine on the Lu family cuisine. Ding One inquires if there are any dishes amidst the Lu Family Cuisine that he has never savoured.

Thumbing through the menu, Mother-in-law answers, "But you have eaten almost all the Lu family dishes."

Ding One studies the menu and the items are mostly old faces.

Mother-in-law suggests, "We might go and ask Second Aunt."

The pair walks to Second Aunt's room. Ding One asks what Lin Yao has been busy with recently. Unwilling to mention Lin Yao's French leave, Mother-in-law parries, "Still busy with that bear of his."

Ding One promises, "Next time when I come to have dinner, I shall also bring a cheque. I have promised to adopt Virtuous Beauty but never kept my promise. I don't know how Lin Yao must be cursing me in his heart. It is time to do something good for the bear."

Mother-in-law smiles but says nothing.

Hearing out Ding One's request, Second Aunt says after thinking it over for half a day, "The Lu family's cuisine is high-class by itself. In the old society one tableful of dishes would cost more than the expenditure of one well-off rural household in one year. And not just anybody can afford the current prices."

"Second Aunt," Ding One beseeches, "help me think about it again. Are there any dishes that I haven't relished before?"

"Talking about dishes not yet relished, sure there are some. I am afraid there is nowhere you can get the raw materials, though."

"Second Aunt, you underestimate me. In this day and age, I can lay my hands on anything except for the stars and the moon. I could buy an atomic bomb as long as one is on the market."

"Back when I'd barely stepped over the threshold of the Lu household there were a couple of dishes I followed my mother-in-law in cooking. We made them several times back then but never again later on."

Ding One inquires if they are high-class and novel.

"I am sure that nobody has ever savoured them before."

"Spit it out quickly: what are they?"

"Bear's paw stewed in refined broth and deep-fried camel hump *al dente*."

Ding One claps his hands and exclaims, "Second Aunt, you are great. Fantastic!"

Second Aunt reminds, "The paw should be the upper left one, which is the most precious because the bear often licks at it. The hump should come from a white dromedary – tender and nutritious."

Ding One promises, "Second Aunt, just wait. Within one week I will lay my hands on these two things."

VIII.

The sun in the western sky is sinking. The long rays of sunshine are struggling and slathering their last touch of elegance onto the buildings at the Zhao Family Market Town. The sky and the earth have been dyed a bizarre and eerie hue. Raising his head to peer at the sun which squats down lower and lower and

184

looking again at the small town rendered completely strange owing to a change in hue, someone says, "Why does the sky look so freaky? An earthquake must be on the way."

One old man answers, "It is what they call 'evil light.' The Old Lord of Heaven is throwing a tantrum. I have come across this only once or twice in my life. When evil light appears, some mishap is bound to happen ..."

A swarthy, angular, haggard Lin Yao clad in shabby clothes walks out from the creepy light. The original colour of the hiking shoes on his feet can no longer be distinguished and the soles have snapped broken. He tramps his way through the floating dust of the road surface and raises a trail of it in his wake. Every footfall is heavy. A coating of white skin has broken out on his chapped lips. Strings of blood are sparkling between his lips. His eyes have become unfocused and nonchalant owing to exhaustion and befuddlement. His ratty hair and shaggy moustache have become entangled and stained all over with the same dust of exile. In the path of other people's attentive stares he flounders onto a town street and halts before a small eatery that sells pulled noodles.

"Any noodles served in soup?" Lin Yao asks.

The boss of the noodle shop answers, "Yeah. One yuan fifty a bowl."

Lin Yao struggles into the greasy chopstick joint and deposits himself before a camphorwood table, saying, "Two bowlfuls."

The boss replies, "Money first."

Not heeding those distrustful eyes, Lin Yao fishes out his billfold from his trouser pocket, draws one banknote out and places it on the table.

Seeing that the other party is not a beggar, the boss's heart is put at ease and he now becomes warm and chatty. He probes, "Sir, do you want the thick noodles or the thin?"

Hearing the boss address him as "Sir" sounds funny to Lin Yao. He reacts with, "Have you ever seen a gentleman dressed up like this and reeking of the smell of firewood smoke?"

The boss retorts, "How could I not have done. The Reform and Opening-up policy has been in place for a few years now. Doesn't every kind of gentlemen drop by at the Zhao Family Market Town at some time or another? The wealthier they are, the more impoverished they look. Now having a destitute appearance is the fashion. A pair of jeans may be brand new but they have to have two holes cut in the knees. Folks want to copy for themselves the kind of gentleman's appearance you have."

Leaning against the wall, Lin Yao is dog-tired and doesn't want to say one more word.

The boss is not through with his comments yet. "I know you must be travel-weary. If you are tired, please just take a rest here. Even though you do sport a bushy beard, you might not be older than me. Two months ago one guy who was studying the Yellow River on foot reached my shop and looked a more pathetic wretch than you do. Totally whacked as he was, he couldn't even spit out one coherent word."

Soon the steaming soupy noodles are served, two big bowlfuls with a coating of oil floating on top. Lin Yao snatches up the chopsticks and starts to gorge without so much as a "Thank you!"

A din of drum music comes from afar.

"In there a circus on the street?" Lin Yao stops chewing.

The boss answers, "Been here four or five days. There are only these few households in this town and we've all gone over to watch it. But plying gongs and working drums they still don't leave. Who will dip into their pocket to watch it for a second time?"

"Do they have a bear?"

"Yeah. A big one, locked up in a cage. It crouches down there all day long."

On getting wind of this, Lin Yao tosses aside his bowl and runs towards the pounding gongs and drums without saying anything. The boss trots out and reminds him, "But your bundle of stuff is still here!"

"I'm leaving it here for safekeeping."

"Look at this guy," the boss comments. "Even though he's whacked half to death, he is still in high spirits – a circus nut."

The *Great World Circus* from Fuyang[t] has taken up its pitch close to the Zhao Family Market Town.

Beyond the fences of textile, a dying black bear is being locked inside an iron cage. A number of children press around it, stabbing the creature with sticks. The bear, whose eyes are closed, doesn't move a muscle.

Someone shouts, "The bear is dead. Using a dead bear to hoodwink people. How lame."

The children echo, "Dead! Dead!"

"Who said she is dead?" the boss of the circus says, swaggering over with a cigarette clamped between his teeth. "I will let you see if she is dead or alive." With these words he struts to a nearby food stall, sears a poker until it is red hot and then jabs it at the bear for all he is worth.

The black bear experiences convulsive spasms then roars and leaps up so as to pounce at the onlookers with her gory basin-sized mouth wide open. The iron cage clanks as it is rammed. The children stampede in all directions out of sheer dread and no longer dare come close. "Who says that she is dead?' the boss cackles. "She just doesn't want to pay you any attention. The fun is being staged inside: *Zhang Fei Sells Pork, Li Cuilian Hangs Herself, A Threatened Turtle Flips, Men and Snakes have a Dogfight* … Four yuan per person. The operas will take to the stage in turn and the house won't be cleaned in between …"

When Lin Yao reaches the beast's cage, the black bear is already crouching down. The smell of scorched skin and flesh hasn't dispersed completely and a plume of black smoke is still rising from the bear's body. Lin Yao goes directly to the iron cage and hunkers down to study the bear. Exhibiting repeated wounds, the bony bear is panting weakly. Big patches of her hair have fallen off, exposing the bright red flesh in many places. Several flies are quaffing the blood as it seeps out, and are smacking their lips ... Judging from her outer shape, Lin Yao can hardly deduce whether she is Virtuous Beauty or not. Facing the bear that is seemingly dead to the world, Lin Yao calls out in a gentle voice, "Virtuous Beauty! Virtuous Beauty!"

The boss of the circus is always standing nearby with his head cocked, watching Lin Yao. Judging from Lin Yao's clothing, words and behaviour, he concludes that this must be a madman. Thus, he approaches and gives Lin Yao a rude and hard shove, ordering him to get his arse out of here.

Caught off guard, that push makes Lin Yao fall into a puddle beside the cage and he is soiled all over with wet clay, stove ashes, garlic husks, and spring onion roots and other dirty substances. The onlookers hoot with laughter.

With his arms folded before his chest, the boss looks down at Lin Yao and taunts, "You have lost your mind because you miss your wife. Seeing a bear you call her Virtuous Beauty?"

Another gust of laughter bursts forth.

The boss of the noodle shop hurries here and helps Lin Yao up from the muddy water. He blames the boss of the circus, "How can you bully a man like this?"

The boss of the circus retorts, "He is deranged."

The boss of the noodle shop says, "He is not. Just now he ate two bowlfuls of noodles in my shop and didn't show the least sign of madness."

Lin Yao says to the boss of the circus, "I'm here to look for my bear and my bear is called Virtuous Beauty. Was your bear bought from a zoo?"

The boss of the circus replies, "I bought her from a circus at Heyang.[u] By that time she had been re-sold more than once. As soon as I bought her, I started to regret it. She's so diseased she can't even stand up."

Lin Yao surmises, "I think she is Virtuous Beauty."

"Virtuous Beauty?" The boss of the circus grins upon hearing this. "Try and call her then."

Lin Yao once again sits on his haunches before the cage and calls out "Virtuous Beauty" in full view of the crowd.

He calls several times but gets no response from the bear. The boss of the circus says, "There are so many bears. How can she be that one you raised?"

"I feel she is and my gut feeling can't be wrong."

"But she doesn't know you."

Lin Yao reaches a hand into the cage to comb the bear's shaggy hair gently and murmurs, "Virtuous Beauty, I know that the smell I'm giving off doesn't feel right when you pick it up. You should still recognize my voice without any doubt …"

Spotting this, the boss of the noodle shop says, "What with the smell of the kitchen smoke, this farmland and your sour sweat, I don't think your dog could recognize you let alone a bear."

The bear opens her eyes lazily once and shoots a glimpse at Lin Yao. Apparently she has recalled something but then apparently she has recalled nothing. She shuts her eyes again.

Calling out "Virtuous Beauty," Lin Yao takes hold of the bear's paws gently and massages them. Presently, the bear stands up out of the blue, empties one paw and sticks it out of the cage. The paw instantly becomes ferocious and horrible and swings at Lin Yao who is squatting by the cage. Lin Yao is not able to dodge in time. The bear's paw whooshes down and the flesh on a half of his face is flayed off. Next the huge paw flies down from above and delivers a hard strike …

Curtains of blood immediately eclipse Lin Yao's eyes, but he doesn't feel the pain. Everything happens like a dream and then alters before he knows what has hit him. However, before darkness falls, Lin Yao perceives clearly that the swinging bear's paw has a sparkling round smooth soft-cell sarcoma on it.

A sparkling round smooth soft-cell sarcoma.

Ding One said that he could buy an atomic bomb and he was not tooting his own horn. Sure enough, several days later he comes to the Lu Mansion with a freshly-severed bear's paw and a huge camel's hump. He has also brought a cheque and a letter of agreement that states his support for the zoo and how he will adopt Virtuous Beauty. He entrusts Lin Yao's mother-in-law to forward them to Lin Yao.

Mother-in-law says, "When it comes to the business of Virtuous Beauty, you should deal with Lin Yao directly. I don't want to have a finger in it."

Ding One inquires when Lin Yao will be home.

Mother-in-law answers that she doesn't know.

Tranquillity Jin doesn't know how to tackle this gory hairy bear's paw and Second Aunt is summoned. Lifting the bear's paw to examine it carefully, Second Aunt concludes, "Yeah, it is the upper left paw. Ding One can get a fresh bear's paw and he's really great. Back in the past, even banquets at a prince's mansion had to use dried bear's paw, which needed to be soaked in water to swell up before being put in the wok. The lowlier Lu family was in the same boat."

On hearing this, Ding One pretends to be indifferent and says, "*Ke*, a bear's paw. It's a piece of cake ..."

"Put the paw in the wok to be simmered over a gentle fire," Second Aunt instructs. "Copious amounts of water should be added." She especially impresses it into Tranquillity Jin that, "When the water ripples slightly but doesn't bubble this should be sufficient. Otherwise, the skin will be broken as it cooks. A bear's paw served on the table with torn skin is like a chicken with its skin scalded off – disgusting and worthless." She continues while walking out, "When it has been simmered for three or four hours and the hair can be plucked off, summon me over. I need to take care of this dish with my own hands."

After the bear's paw has been cooked in the wok for almost half a day, Tranquillity Jin invites Second Aunt over. Second Aunt puts on an apron, fishes out the bear's paw and rinses it with lukewarm water. She then holds it to her chest and picks the hairs out one by one patiently with a pair of tweezers like she is plucking a woman's eyebrows. Tranquillity Jin stands nearby watching.

Second Aunt expounds, "When removing the bear's hair, you must never be impatient. Some rip it off by the handful as if they plucking a chicken's feathers. This method can never be applied to a bear's paw. The skin of a fresh bear's paw when cooked over a gentle fire is softer than paper …" After she has done with the big hair, Second Aunt instructs Tranquillity Jin to use the smallest pair of tweezers to extract the fine dander. She says that her eyes are not good enough now and she can't see clearly. She instructs that after the dander has been plucked out, Tranquillity Jin should rub away gently that coating of black membrane from the paw with her hands. When the paw has been cooked slightly pulpy, the bones and the claws should be drawn out. By the time it is served on the table, the paw will have assumed its former intact shape, the colour will be white and clean, the soup will be clear and bright and the meat will be pulpy and soft …

Tranquillity Jin fetches a small bench and sits down at the door, proceeding to extract the fine dander and to rub away the black membrane. The hairless bear's paw is glossy and smooth like a man's foot. Tranquillity Jin thinks that humans are indeed really strange creatures. Almost all flying fowls or running animals can enter their mouths. The more original and unreasonable the food is, the higher the class is. "It should be impossible for grain to be husked more finely and impossible for meat to be cut more thinly" has changed into "It should be impossible for food to be more original and impossible for meat to be more unlikely." As long as it can be shovelled into the mouth, a bear's paw is no different from a human foot.

Suddenly, her hand comes into contact with a round soft-cell sarcoma. The sarcoma is on the inner side of the bear's paw and is as big as a pigeon egg. Sensing something, Tranquillity Jin turns the paw this way and that to examine it judiciously. Little by little her hands tremble and so does her heart – "Virtuous Beauty!" She tosses the bear's paw back into the basin with a

191

shriek and the disturbed water wets a patch of the floor.

The half-cooked bear's paw that has been tossed back into the basin points balefully at the black firmament with its deathly pale claws. The centre of the paw curves and draws a shocking question mark. This paw was formerly attached to an intelligent animal, who prodded it out of the railings numerous times to convey to people her feelings of warmth, her happiness and her unlimited dependence upon and love for people … She must never have expected that her paw would surface in another form in a wok of boiling hot broth, and then, when its bones had been drawn out and its hair extracted, it would become a delicacy to be sent to the mouths of the people whom she has loved so much.

The man who wants to adopt her is also the one who will eat her.

Tranquillity Jin no longer touches that bear's paw. She unties her apron, slips quietly into Lin Yao's small room and sits down in front of his small bed in a trance. The quilts and coverlets are in a messy heap on the bed. She finds out that the quilts and coverlets have long ago lost Lin Yao's breath and smell. There is nothing except for a waft of moldy smell. Lin Yao has gone far away.

The follow-up work on the bear's paw is completed by Second Aunt.

That night, the bear's paw stewed in clear broth finds no peer either in the past or in the future – succulent and strong-flavoured, served in fresh mouth-watering broth – and it leaves a lasting impression upon all the diners. Later, though a very long period of time has elapsed and they have savoured other gourmet dishes, the attendees of that dinner party will always strike a posture like someone who has circumnavigated the world and proclaim, "This dish could never be on a par with bear's paw."

It took Virtuous Beauty sacrificing her life to earn such plaudits. Under the Nine Springs of Hell she will close her eyes.

Mountain Savage

A sequestered mountain spot is where my figure is to be seen.
I am clad in creeping fig and Methuselah's beard lichen.
Glancing around lustily, a sly grin crosses my face.
This slender physique will surely be admired for its grace.
["Mountain Goddess" from the *Nine Odes* by Qu Yuan (*c.*
340-278 BC)]

I.

On 19th July 2001, a divorce case was settled at a local court
with the result being that the union between forty-three-
year-old Yang Qingya and her husband, Chen Hua was
automatically annulled according to the Marriage Law. Chen
had left home on 12th July 1997, disappearing thereafter, and
was listed as missing.

Nearly fifteen days of continuous rain have brought about
an obvious rise in the brooks upon Mount Laojun and the
mountain rocks too have become distended with water. The
woods are so soft that they are vulnerable to collapse. Plants,
which have been saturated with rain both within and out, are
swaying like aquarist's weeds in a fish tank. The entire mountain
is shrouded in misty steam. No birds sing; no beasts chase. In
the forests, which are filled with an unusual calm, animals are
sheltering under leaves and within caves and clefts, since they
have a hard time in avoiding this autumnal rain.

Encompassing a vast area, the Heavenly Flower Mountains
are a continuation of the Qinba Range, and consist of high
dacite rocks in the south, metamorphic siltstone in the north
and an exposed devonian sequence stratigraphy in the centre.

The ground structure is complicated; the climate is damp and rainy.

The air around him is thick with the smell of weeds, and endless mountains – all wildly green – are to be viewed on every side. He examines his hands and his long fingernails which assume a green hue when viewed upon the surface of the water. There is no mirror in which to inspect his face but he can imagine how green and wild it is.

His blood has become green as well.

He has neither had a haircut nor shaved in four years. His hair tumbles dishevelled over his shoulders and a beard hangs down onto his chest. He has barely retained the form of a human being.

Confronted by the torrential rain he feels frustrated and despondent. However, frustration and despondence are all that he has, for there is not a glimmer of loneliness. He finds copious amounts to spout forth everyday, to the beech tree, to the single-leaved *kingdonia*, to the spider, and to the lizard… They understand what he says and vice versa. There is no barrier to their communication. Raindrops strike the roof of the shack and water trickles down from here and there. It is so wet and cold that he can sense the chill inside his bones.

He simply desires one thing: to get something to eat.

A bowl of hot noodles served in soup, drenched with chilli oil and chopped green onions, topped off with a smattering of spinach. A bowl of steaming soupy noodles. He is so eager to eat spinach as the last time he had some was four years ago. Spinach is rather common outside the mountains while it is seldom to be found here. There is a profusion of foliage. Trees and grasses will not yield to those small, delicate plants which tend to shy away from the vast green mountains… His yearning for hot soupy noodles has been interrupted by the patter of rain. Melodious and exquisite singing now begins to emanate from deep within the mountains. The singing rises with the wind and possesses no words, merely rhythms. Like

194

convulsive sobs, the twists and turns of the melody prove extremely moving and stirring to the soul.

Only "human beings" can produce such a sound.

He listens to every detail, holding his breath in deep concentration. The sound appears to be in close proximity to him, being melodious and lingering. Sometimes it seems to be coming from the hillside, sometimes from the valley floor, sometimes provocatively from behind the shack, and sometimes from among the branches. The sound delights and confuses him, leaving him perplexed and quaking.

It is the mountain goddess.

A mischievous spirit resides in these mountains.

The mountain goddess is the sprite described in Qu Yuan's work as drinking spring water and slumbering under pines and cypresses. It maintains an intimate yet suspicious attitude toward humans. Knowing his determination to seek out a true mountain goddess, Geng Jian, one of Qu Yuan's artist friends, created for him a painting entitled *Figure of a Mountain Goddess*. It depicts a coquettish girl who wears flowers in her hair and sprigs of ivy upon her back, as she leans against pines and cypresses driving leopards and tigers with her bare feet and arms. She looks askance, full of tenderness and inspiration. Geng Jian never had the opportunity to see a mountain goddess. The wild beauty pictured in his painting is undoubtedly the product of his imagination and of artistic license. For an artist, this could be considered a resounding success; for a scholar, such as him, specializing as he has done in modern archeology, it might be passed over with a laugh.

What on earth is a mountain goddess?

This is not known.

Wang Fuzhi, a scholar of the Ming Dynasty concluded that rather being a supernatural entity this was the consequence of an embryo developing deep in the mountains... In the daytime it hides itself within trees and thus can be called a *Muke* or "tree guest."

Having lasted for half an hour, the singing is brought to an abrupt end by a clap of thunder, which returns everything back to dead silence. He stares absent-mindedly at the rain, and seems to be waiting for something with great patience but in a trance. A red-spotted stonecrop stands by the entrance to his shack. A glittering droplet rolls onto a leaf but is reluctant to fall off.

The humidity inside the shack mingles with that from outside. Under the low "bed" stretches a ditch which flows from west to east in an attentive way. From time to time waves are generated within the ditch. The "bed" is covered with weeds and upon these there lies a thoroughly sodden sleeping bag. The four legs of a "table" that has been pieced together from boards are planted into the earth. The table is covered with a plastic cloth. Beneath this is to be found probably the only dry patch anywhere in the Heavenly Flower Mountains. On the table sit his *Nikon* F6 camera together with his research notes and materials. These are purported to have something to do with the mountain goddess. He steps out of the damp shack, stares at the cliff while pausing on the spot and then starts to shout. His scream is distinct from that of the leopards, monkeys and mumbling pandas. Air flows up from his pubic region, passing into that hollow throat before striking the vocal cords. This is the sound made by human beings, full, deep, indulgent and intelligent. Through this sound he is declaring to the mountains which species he belongs to, what standpoint and views he holds and the fact that he is one constituent of these mountains and forests. He is friends with everything in the forests and the mountains, has breathed with all the creatures and shared a common destiny, so he cannot extricate himself from them even for a short while. His "human shout" ricochets off the mountain rocks opposite, and is broken into pieces at his feet, shattering into the grass. Nothing is to be retrieved. He has been waiting all along for a response, for a song he can understand and perceive; but it is in vain.

Today he fails again.

He begins to "cook." The flour has become waterlogged. So too have the firewood and the aluminum pot which is smudged beyond the point of identification. Hot soupy noodles now appear an extravagant demand. Even were he to have a fire, he would be unable to make those tender noodles. He extracts a blob of sticky flour from the bag, kneading it flat and square but being clueless about how to handle it. Such an air of helplessness also pervaded the existence he shared with the always-wretched Yang Qingya and that son who entered so precipitately into his life.

Thousands of times he has recalled how his marriage with Yang Qingya commenced. Still the whole escapes his comprehension. It seems that Yang Qingya's father was the prime mover in facilitating the marriage. Looking at the matter from a purely conceptual perspective, Professor Yang confused the criteria for selecting a son-in-law with those he would employ for choosing his supervisees. Upon graduating the man became Professor Yang's son-in-law. As a specialist in archeology, it is something of a pity that he never studied thoroughly the duties and responsibilities of a son-in-law. Thus his life descended into a total mess. He had no passion for dull materials and data. So it was when he was in the presence of his wife Yang Qingya as well. He barely knew how to deal with tender and sentimental passions let alone his wife who would often writhe around like a snake. He dared not touch her and hid away from her fiery eyes. She said, tearfully, that he was sick and asked him to take a welter of traditional Chinese medicines. Even so, these didn't work. He then acknowledged that he was indeed sick. Tangled up in shame and anxiety, he was always afraid of darkness and of the night ... Seven years ago, he was summoned to join a state-organized scientific expedition searching for "unidentified living objects" in the Heavenly Flower Mountains. He observed pandas mating in bamboo groves and takins copulating indiscriminately under the sun.

He was overcome by a similar impulse, too, imagining his own mate. Now who should that be ...

Definitely not Yang Qingya!

What was more disconcerting was the arrival of his "son." Almost as soon as he got back from the expedition, his wife gave birth in the hospital. This was despite the fact that he had sojourned in the mountains for two years during which time his "son" emerged out of the void. It was so embarrassing. He couldn't fathom this business out. His mother-in-law shared in the conspiracy whereby the circumstances of the pregnancy were kept a closely-guarded secret. At the urging of his mother-in-law, who told him that every husband should be at his wife's bedside, he paid a visit to the hospital. Along he came, bringing a pot of chicken soup that had been thrust upon him by his mother-in-law. It looked so normal ... On the ward he saw Yang Qingya half-reclining, her cheeks glowing ruddy. He saw "his" son too in his swaddling clothes, a little thing that looked exactly like a golden monkey. Yang Qingya kissed the little monkey all over its body, telling him that all infants had this appearance and things would get better later on. As he stood there uneasily with no words to say he came over sick. Grievance, depression, disgust and aversion all flared up in that moment. He came over exceedingly pale and was dripping with cold sweat. Harbouring no embarrassment, Yang Qingya showed intimacy towards the little "monkey" before him, pronouncing her love. Instinctively, releasing this pronouncement caused her to be filled with happiness. He, on the other hand, recoiled from it, detecting a conspicuous challenge therein.

He came to realize his present situation whereby there would be no position for him in that family.

Without any delay, he lifted his travel bag and headed for the Heavenly Flower Mountains.

By that time, the expedition team had already been disbanded as the state did not want to waste any more funds on this uncertain and vague project. But he always felt that something was drawing his spirit and soul there and that some indiscernible force was summoning him to return. Not hesitating for one moment, he turned back to the mountains. His desire to avoid that "monkey" face was not the reason for returning.

He became the sole investigator there.

The mountain had grown far deeper than ever before.

In the Heavenly Flower Mountains, he was to experience a feeling of release and ease brought about by a return to his homeland, a feeling of harmony and tacit agreement, a feeling of happiness and excitement as if attending a pre-arranged appointment. His life belonged to the mountains; his home was there also. He now believed he must be a tree, a blade of grass, a grey-tailed rabbit that wiggles its hare lip beneath a tree.

Or a mountain savage.

He just hasn't run into one of those yet.

There have been plentiful sightings of savages in the Heavenly Flower Mountains. The county annals compiled in the eighteenth year of the reign of the Emperor Guangxu (1893 AD) record that these creatures have resided in the Heavenly Flower Mountains for a long time. Savages were commonly known as mountain ghosts or *muke*, organisms which delighted in singing and grinning. They generally possessed a mild but suspicious character. Around the vicinity of Mount Laojun is to be found a host of cell-like stone caves which appear lofty, sharp, distant and tranquil. The stone caves were home to a number of savages, mostly with a stature in excess of three metres … The portion of the county annals compiled after the founding of the People's Republic of China in 1949 even recounted the story of his father, an aerospace exploration engineer who encountered savages on Mount Laojun.

Under the aegis of a national geological and mining resources survey his father led a small team to carry out ground-marking work at Mount Laojun. It was 5ᵗʰ May 1956. At 4.30 pm, following after the local guide Wang Shuangyin, his father together with two team members, climbed up from Tiger and

Leopard River behind Green Peak, over Walnut Terrace and to Military Camp Ridge half-way up Mount Laojun. That was a beautiful place surrounded by vaunted mountains and high ranges. The ridge was clad with oak trees and red birches, and dense, straight-stipuled *salix* covered the ground. A sense of sacredness and awe was involuntarily generated within the tranquil forest.

Advancing in a column of four, the team walked on. No sound was to be heard as they trod across the spongy leaves. All of a sudden, Wang Shuangyin who was walking at the head of the pack stopped, causing the rest of the team to halt. In the meantime, they all saw the "person" in front of them. His father later described how that "person" was markedly tall, with long hair, fine brown down on his body, having slightly yellow but bright eyes, high eyebrows and long arms … The people and that "person" stared at each other in surprise. Then that "person" fled towards the nearby bushes and at the same time, Father, while aiming at the "person," pulled the trigger and hit its right shoulder. Shaking, the "person" wiped the wound with one hand and that hand became coated with blood. It turned back and looked at the team with a puzzled expression. It grinned and bared its fangs, the eyes being cloaked by the gloom. Father tilted his gun for a second time. Wang Shuangyin pushed the barrel of the gun upwards and shouted to the "man" that he should "run!" It seemed to realize something was afoot and swiftly sped behind a rare maple, without a clatter. They made chase, though scarcely any sign of it was to be found save for the blood on the tree trunk. They searched around the tree but did so in vain. It had disappeared.

Wang Shuangyin said this was a mountain ghost and could not be found because it had been absorbed into the tree. It would not die until that maple tree was felled. A team member added that it was not a mountain ghost but a savage which must be reported to the relevant government bodies. Another team member – from Hubei Province – claimed that such entities were to be found deep in the mountains of his hometown. These often barred the way and repeatedly asked people the same question: "Is the Great Wall still standing?" If you answered "Go build the Great Wall," it would run away at once. It is rumoured that they were the descendants of the folk who had hid away in the deep forests during the reign of the Emperor Qin Shihuang in order to avoid being put to work on building the Great Wall … Father didn't say a word, regretting having fired that shot. Until the final moment of his life, the old man felt guilty that he had been so impertinent, blaming himself to the effect that "it was already fleeing but I still felt the need to do it harm…"

He has thought about this time and time again. If he were in his Father's position, he would never have shot at it. Instead, he would have walked over and extended an honest hand. Likely there would have been a different ending; likely the maple would not have become bloodstained.

Now he has located that selfsame maple tree his father came across before. The *Acer miaotaiense* is a very precious strain in this world. There are only a few across the whole of China. Nonetheless, here is to be found a forest of this precious tree that remains unknown to the outside world. The one behind which the *muke* hid is tall and upright and so thick and strong that three men could barely embrace it together. Its slow rate of growth ensures that there isn't much change. Now it is festooned with moss so the blood cannot be traced.

He has resided alongside the maple for four years though has never been given the chance to see the *muke* emerge from it.

A beautiful clouded leopard often frequents this place as it forms part of its territory. His arrival made the beast uneasy and it demonstrated its power the first few times by threatening him at the gate of his shack and blocking his way to his tour of inspection. He always ducked away from the creature and never courted a head-on confrontation. Later on as it recognized that this man neither had any evil intention nor wanted to compete with him for food or a mate, it grew accustomed to his presence and regarded him as it did the grass and the trees within its territory. He has thereby become a mobile component of the landscape under its watch and an entity it must defend. It is necessary for it to preserve the order and stability of this area. The leopard is duty-bound.

The rain has not yet abated.

A rock rat sneaks into the shack dragging its big wet tail behind. It is his old acquaintance and his closest neighbour to boot. There are two of them, one he has named "Rocky" and the other "Ratty." Rocky is male while Ratty is female. Both of them dwell in the fissures behind the shack. They live a pastoral life whereby "Adam delves and Eve spins" and have become deeply attached to each other. Ratty is comparatively introverted, reserved and shy, acting restrained whenever she comes over for a visit. Rocky is not. He is lively and outgoing, exhibiting a number of bad traits. He frequently climbs onto the table and onto the host's body, showing no respect. The rat that has just entered stalks around the shack in a confident manner, mounting the wooden table and sitting on the can. He watches him with his sparkling eyes. It seems that only in this way can it communicate with him as equals.

He is able to identify this one as Rocky. Ratty is fatter with two brown marks on her forehead. Ratty does not talk in a shrill voice, let alone have the habit of squatting on the can. Rocky likes cozying up with him and might visit him dozens of times in the course of the summer, without any forewarning. Sometimes he even bounds onto his bed, where he impolitely pads against his face with warm paws until he wakes up. What is more, he never retreats without any spoils and always snitches away items of food such as instant noodles and cookies as he leaves. Tirelessly, the rat transports food from his shack one trip after another not caring about how this is perceived. Once he couldn't help but pay a call at their nest, whereupon he found one of his socks in among the crumbs.

They displayed hardly any shame at all in the presence of these stolen goods. In fact, they jumped up and down on the stash, chirping incessantly to the point that it was jarring to the ears. He ended up gleaning another handful of soybeans.

At this moment, Rocky is sitting opposite him. From his serious mood, he can tell that this is a formal visit rather than a casual drop-in. After autumn rains have subsided, the temperature in the mountains will soon decrease and within a month it will snow. Many animals are preparing to hibernate and this time Rocky is approaching to bid farewell. The little thing is inclined to come over and meet with him in earnest at this juncture every year. The custom marks his short and temporary sabbatical from the household. He passes over a fruit drop. Rocky accepts it, tactfully peels off the wrapper and plants it in his mouth. All at once, his cheek bulges in an exaggerated fashion.

He says, "You can't hoard this. You must eat it right now."

With two chirps, Rocky retrieves the drop from his cheek pouch. After a while, crunching is heard from its mouth. He is so excited and happy enough to dance.

A blood pheasant flies over the roof of the shack, squawking. This is a Class A protected animal and extremely exalted and elegant. Ever-graceful, it seldom behaves like this. Some mishap must have befallen the bird. He bends forward, searching for the blood pheasant. Everything seems quite normal. Rocky is scornful of this business as he continues to squat on the can and sneezes. When he realizes that nobody is paying attention to him, he slips a few cold-relief tablets into his mouth and leaps away proudly.

Donning his raincoat, he approaches the cliff edge. The rain is starting to let up. Fog rises from the valley floor. In one hour the fog will have enveloped everything: the trees, the ivies, the moss and his shack. It is growing dark. There is a glittering light over on the cliff opposite, like a lantern or a torch, which moves dimly in a charming fashion. He shouts a few times; the light goes out. Then he can hardly see anything through the thick fog. The crag on the other side is so sheer that even blue sheep don't have a hope of traversing it, let alone people with lanterns…

He turns back and notes a bunch of red sheep-breast fruit honeysuckles at the gate of his shack. Its scientific name is the Standish honeysuckle, a *caprifoliaceae* plant that grows on river dikes of 1,000 metres above sea level. Its shape resembles a sheep's breast, having big globular size. Being succulent and tasty, it is the most moreish fruit in the mountains. It is a mystery to him how a variety of fruit from the foot of mountain should have found its way to 1,900 metres above sea level and be able to form a cluster here. This was definitely not accomplished by rock rats. He picks one. It is so ripe that his hands become drenched in its juice. It feels cool when slipped into the mouth. He crinkles his neck because of the coolness and feels so comfortable that he looks like Rocky did when he just ate that fruit drop.

There are things in the mountains which cannot be comprehended by ordinary logic, such as the inexplicable light, the mysterious mountain fruit and the spontaneous freestyle singing … He must live with the likelihood of encountering something absurd anytime, anywhere.

This is the haunt of the mountain ghost.

II.

The next day it is colder. Frost has formed on top of the shack. As the wind blows, he feels a nip in the air. Overnight, the trees appear to have become sparser. The wingceltis leaves are not as oily and soft as they were the day before and have turned black and dark… Scarlet and light yellow leaves remain visible on the more distant hills.

He knows from experience that winter is nigh.

In this regard, the rock rats have a much keener sense than him.

When the snow falls, his activities will be greatly restricted. He is compelled to go to Walnut Terrace before winter comes to collect some over-winter necessities such as rice, flour, oil and salt from Wang Shuangyin. Old Wang's house is his base and headquarters, as well as a refuge of happiness. Old Wang was once his father's friend.

Obviously there is another important issue with which he and Old Wang have to deal.

He passes down the ridge of Mount Laojun. A bird intones: "Mountain ... mountain guests go back." He seeks out that bird which is trying to persuade him to return to the woods and finally finds it at the apex of a bitter oak: a greyish black little creature, its delicate tail bobs up and down and its head tilts to the left and to the right in a somewhat melancholy yet comical mien as it chants "Mountain guests go back."

Scores of land leeches sway on the tips of the trillium, half of their bodies pointing into the air. They are waiting to launch an attack on the human body. Instinctively fond of fresh blood, the creatures will suck vigorously from whomsoever they catch. This sucking makes their linear bodies engorge to dozens of times their original size. If you don't drive them away by force, they will continue to suck until their abdomens burst. His smell draws closer and becomes more distinct; the leeches relay this information between each other, waiting nervously but with excitement. Their sucking discs are agape and their bodies have expanded inordinately. Closer, closer, at last they see that face which is so familiar to them and smell the sweet and sour odour that emanates from his warm pores. They begin to shudder with anticipation ... Finally, they and the human body pass by. He appears to have known already. He pushes aside the said grasses with a stick and strides over them nimbly. At once, there rises the squall of disappointed leeches bemoaning how unfair it is. They have been waiting here for a month and have been thinned down to their skins. He smiles at the leeches and thinks these little things are too naïve by far: they have been waiting on this exact spot for years, never even contemplating shifting somewhere else...

The same sound that Yang Qingya made when she kissed the "monkey face" is to be heard from the woods. Raising his head, he notices that a tree is bedecked with little monkeys, precious golden monkeys with lustrous glittering fur and small blue faces, which taken in unison are redolent of the sunny sky in autumn. So breathtakingly beautiful. Despite having already caught sight of him they pretend to be restraining themselves so as to present a pleasant surprise. They are let loose with a sudden scream and the wood is instantly filled with a din and cackles. Each of them is showing off; some swing above his head and others intentionally tease him by performing dangerous manoeuvres in his vicinity. They are not afraid of him; nor do they want to avoid him. They are trying to infect him with their glee for in terms of species they are much closer to him. They are relatives, authentic relatives. Pandas don't count, nor do rock rats. They are completely distinct from human beings, so far apart. Confronted with this clamorous but merry group, he unexpectedly casts his mind back to that little "monkey face" in the hospital. He doesn't know and wouldn't like to know who the father of the little thing is. As he is past caring there is no need to set his nerves on edge. The child makes no sense to him and Yang Qingya makes no sense either. Everything should be natural. Flowers bloom and fade, winter gives way to spring. All is brought to an end as it should be.

At the age of four that "monkey face" might now resemble a mandrill.

After having bid farewell to the monkeys, he walks 200 metres further. The ridge turns north east from that spot. He sees the forest of arrow bamboos on the northern slope. In the late 1980s this forest bloomed and then died, being reduced to a desolate "dead sea." Disaster befalls arrow bamboos once every sixty years. The old bamboos turn black and are completely decimated. The seeds of the mature bamboos plop onto the ground and new bamboos sprout, denser and more exuberant. These young bamboos spread and reproduce; they grow vigorously after rain has fallen on the mountain land. Sixty years is a short span, almost the same as his life expectancy. He wonders if they will at least be able to grow healthily for a few dozen years after his death. His life is short, so too is that of the bamboo. However, both grow and live according to different timeframes, a factor which prolongs their existence.

Something swooshes in one corner of the wood. Without seeing it, he knows it is Sansan. Sansan is a male panda he met here on 3rd March the year before last. At that time, he was cavorting with a female panda much bigger than himself. When he came across them, the female was flirting with Sansan by placing her head against the ground. Sansan mounted her hesitantly, finishing in less than ten seconds and then turned away immediately afterwards. Feeling that she had not completely enjoyed it, the unfulfilled she-panda caught up with him and barred the way. Somehow Sansan looked at the female panda and then sat down, with the female circling around him again and again. The female panda got angry and bit Sansan straight on his rear leg. With impressive forbearance, Sansan moved himself and sat down again. The female panda made repeated requests though it cut no ice with Sansan. She lashed out and savaged Sansan on the bottom, causing him to flee in a hurry. Sansan was only an immature medium-sized specimen and was too small to take the initiative. Now he has grown up into a handsome mature panda with bright fur and a well-proportioned figure. He has observed Sansan pursuing the opposite sex outside his domain on a few occasions, engaging in "fights to the death" with other male pandas and being beaten black and blue.

His communication with Sansan is very simple. Except for when he is fighting for mates, he is perpetually humble, friendly and mild-mannered, not as sceptical and cautious as other animals. He is simple-minded. The world is not that complicated to him. His acceptance of him is plain, too, the panda being neither too overwhelmed nor overexcited. On their first meeting, they sat together for a whole afternoon staring at each other. Then both fell asleep and walked away upon waking up. On their second meeting, he gave Sansan a piece of confectionary as he had done with Rocky, but Sansan sat down on it. The *White Rabbit* sweet manufactured in Shanghai was stuck to his posterior for a fortnight. Then came the meeting where Sansan demonstrated how to scale a tree. He climbed up and then fell down, climbing and falling intentionally to please him. He himself tried once but couldn't get down again …

He "swims" towards that noise through the dense bamboo forest. Sure enough, it is Sansan. Having eaten his fill, Sansan places his pair of paws on two separate branches and comfortably leans back against a big rock, snoring. A drop of golden sun shines on him; his black and white fur brightens and becomes clearer, allowing him to appreciate the artistic beauty and the delicacy of the divine force. Sansan has small eyes and suffers from acute myopia but the big dark circles around his eyes counterbalance that sense of regret. Besides, with his clumsy fatness he looks rather like a toy, possessing a child-like innocence which encourages him to hug and caress the animal.

Among all the wild animals, the species closest to human beings might well be the giant panda.

He holds the camera and takes multiple shots of Sansan. The shutter-sound awakens Sansan. He opens his eyes and peers at him like a newly-woken baby, not realizing what is going on. Finally, Sansan recognizes him and greets him with a hum that resonates from deep within his throat. He stretches his paws, strips away a handful of bamboo branches and snaps them off easily. Much as if he were eating sticks of celery, he starts chewing from the root so that all the leaves are left behind.

Sansan consumes one bunch after another. Gamely and in a lively manner, he exerts no greater effort to gather more as he lies in the food. As he eats he defecates quickly making a mess beneath his bottom. After a while, he can hardly find any more bamboo within arms reach. He gets up reluctantly, treads two or three steps and sits down again, stripping and eating. As there is no other panda with which to share it, there is plenty of bamboo. Sansan eats unhurriedly and with ease. He watches Sansan for almost an hour. After eating his fill once again, Sansan reclines on the spot, one rear leg lifted high, his paws resting on his round abdomen. He falls asleep again within his gaze.

Looking at his panda friend, he feels moved to pass comment. The panda belongs to the class of *mammalia*, the order of *carnivora* and the genus *ailuropoda*. A specialized scientific sector has been dedicated to this unique species which is indigenous only to China. Supposedly a huge and fierce carnivorous animal, the process of evolution has seen it make concession after concession. On failing to compete with other carnivores it took to eating grass, and, on being outpaced by other herbivores it turned to bamboo. Bamboo is so rigid and tough that no other animals accept it with relish. And yet the panda did. In order to survive, it swallows its shame and uses its typical carnivorous teeth to consume half its body weight in bamboo. However, the nutritional value of the bamboo is only equivalent to seventeen per cent of the volume eaten. The sabre-toothed tiger, the dinosaur and the mammoth each existed contemporaneously with the panda, but have all become extinct, being turned into ancient fossils which lie scattered at every corner of the world. Surviving nonetheless, the panda has gone onto become the pet of human beings owing to its humility and self-satisfied demeanour, its near-sightedness, and its personality, which serve collectively to mask its laziness and laissez-faire attitude. The sabre-toothed tiger was never to emulate the panda's feat of being able to leave China and be transported all over the Earth. The philosophy of the panda encapsulates the key aspects of the Chinese nation and the essence of the Taoist spirit. "Perfect goodness is like water," implying the characteristic lament of the Chinese people.

Lovely, pathetic, and hateful.

When he gets up, he notes the huge footprints nearby. A row of footprints stretches across the wet ground towards the forest of firs that stands ahead. This indicates that after the rains ceased, around sunrise, it must have walked here, just below his shack. He has missed it again and was in fact just several hundred metres away. He presses his racing pulse and measures the footprints that are so similar to those left by humans: 42 centimetres long, 3 to 5 centimetres deep, with a stride length of 80 to 100 centimetres. It must be a heavy-set specimen two metres in height and 150 kilograms in weight... He cries out to the fir forest and a golden pheasant rises up from therein, dashing to some *eupteleas*. He knows that he has failed to find it again yet still proceeds forward tracing the footprints which finally disappear on the rocks of the cliff. He mulls this over for a while, not knowing where it has gone. Did it fly over to some place, worm its way into a cave, or vanish into a big tree as his father saw that time ... On a nearby bush, he discovers several strands of brown hair and places them with care into his specimen clamp which already contains many more similar materials. In his shack, he has archived over 300 samples of film footage, 1.7 million words of notes and a great quantity of other evidence. Every day he spends in the mountains he keeps himself busy.

Returning back to the grove of arrow bamboo, Sansan is still asleep. He doesn't disturb him and simply passes by. A saying by the American zoologist George B. Schaller springs to mind when talking about pandas: "The panda has no history, only a past. It has come to us in a fragile moment from another time."[v] He thinks this does not apply to Sansan but well applies to *muke*.

He arrives at Walnut Terrace by sunset. Walnut Terrace is a small and narrow precipice upon the mountain side. Altogether three households and eleven villagers reside there.

A small river flows from the north of the village. Water splashes against the rocks, projecting white foam and generating a tremendous sound. The impetus of this flow is out of synchrony with the dullness and quietness of the small village. The footpath which winds down from Mount Laojun is curtailed by the river but two thin logs set over the channel ensure it is passable. Quaking a great deal and being waterlogged from the splashing torrents, this presents a precarious bridge. Two or three cottages, together with five or six oxen, seven or eight acres of land, and scores of walnut trees: these furnish the livelihood of the small village. In a sense, this place is only able to live on as a Shangri-la because nobody of the ilk of the poet Tao Yuanming discovered it and celebrated it in their writing. The season where there is no frost lasts 120 days though this is an unreliable rule of thumb. No one could count on there being any decent crops during the frost-free period. The yield of wheat is about 600 pounds per acre, recouping precisely the seed money; the maize that is planted beneath the mulching film grows sparsely, the greater part of it being foraged by bears and wild boars. The village is situated in the high mountains upon extremely cold land that is usually incapable of yielding vegetables other than potatoes and kidney beans. By chance there happens to have been a good harvest of radishes, a crop considered to be rare in the mountains. The place falls under the administration of the Heavenly Flower Mountains Wildlife and Nature Reserve. Every plant and grass here is protected by the nation. Every animal is afforded dignity; they can eat people while people are not permitted to eat them. They would resort to human flesh only for survival whereas the man who eats them is breaking the law. Mountain folk have become so frustrated on account of this but have no recourse. This marginal arable land is in the process of being reforested with the consequence being that the three households which comprise Walnut Terrace will be relocated two mountains away to Jiang Family Camp by the end of the year. Jiang Family Camp is 130 miles from the county town. That place is accessible by highway, though, and is much more densely populated.

Old Wang's house is located to the northern end of the village alongside the river. Three adobe farmhouses each one with a bright frontage and a couple of shaded rooms to the rear were built quite some time ago when Old Wang got married. Now he is seventy-six. The farmhouse is surrounded by land that has been reclaimed for cultivation over seven generations. The maize harvest has already finished. Stones of different sizes emerge from the bare land, like some strange islands. Beside a head-high blue stone there grows a wild walnut tree. The tree is no taller than the stone, with a twisting trunk, that scarcely seems capable of stretching itself out.

That is an incredible place. He cannot help looking at the tree for longer.

The thatch on top of Wang's cottage has become black. A few patches are covered with plastic tarpaulins and stone. Behind the cottage nestles two barrel-like containers each with a hole in the centre: beehives. In front of the cottage is a flat and clean open space on which potato slices that have been boiled are left out to dry. Potato slices form rations for over-wintering. Out on the verge a brood of chickens are being guided by the mother hen to seek after food; a sleeping cat is being pecked at by the hen as a warning not to touch its children. A skinny dog lies on the steps. It yawns drowsily and walks to the sty behind.

Old Wang is sitting on the ground in the living room, scraping potatoes with a shard of iron. Long sprouts jut out of the potatoes indicating that they are not at all fresh. Old Wang is very skilled at handling shrivelled potatoes. The iron shard in his hand seems to have eyes. It is so agile and never scrapes away pulp; the little potato is soon becoming a white ball. Old Wang doesn't show much enthusiasm upon his arrival. Not pausing, he carries on with his work, and only utters the word "sit."

Old Wang's expressions closely resemble those of Sansan the panda.

He takes a seat and accustoms himself to the darkness inside. There are many frames upon the wall, most of which contain pictures of Old Wang and his offspring. In one frame is a photograph of Wang's late parents. In the image, Wang's father looks earthy and honest and Wang's mother looks honest and earthy. From their appearances one can discern that they were dutiful farmers. On either side of the portrait hang a picture of a popular movie star, one male and one female – like the golden boy and jade girl effigies in a shrine.

Wang's wife is busy cooking on the kitchen range. Thick firewood cut from birch logs is burning under the range. The smell of boiled preserved meat emanates from the big iron pan. Old Wang has now dropped his shriveled potato and fumbles for a c/o letter from behind one of the frames. The letter has already been opened by Old Wang; even though he cannot make out one word of it, he has to open it. Whether literate or not, he must open that message.

The letter relates the laboratory report into a clump of red hair he sent to the forensic unit of the 329 Institute in the city. They have drawn the conclusion that the submitted sample doesn't belong to an orangutan or a human being. This was discovered after pressing and filming, slicing, and conducting an impression examination, blood type material identification, and PAGIEF analysis of the hair keratin. It belongs to an unidentified higher primate … Enclosed together with the letter is a set of forms.

After having read the report, he sits there alone. No one knows what he is thinking about.

Old Wang says that only mountain ghosts have red hair. He knows this much without needing to investigate.

He brings to mind Geng Jian's *Figure of a Mountain Goddess* once again.

Old Wang says that all the preserved meat has been boiled and tells him to take the lot with him tomorrow. He replies that he cannot get through so much, while Old Wang reminds him that even though he might he might fancy some more in the future there will be none. All of the villagers from Walnut Terrace will have moved away by the end of November; by then, this place will have been reduced to a wasteland. The place where generations have lived and grown up will become a wasteland … Old Wang is very sentimental, and has no more words to share. Likewise friend has nothing to say. Old Wang then advises him to find a time to make an appointment to see a doctor since Old Wang believes he is ill but cannot diagnose what disease he has. He bares his white teeth toward Old Wang.

Old Wang says: "Don't growl. You are a mountain ghost yourself. No need to carrying on searching any more."

Old Wang's wife has prepared a dinner of cracked corn porridge together with cowpeas and kidney beans boiled with preserved meat, accompanied by fried potato slices. The spread is so substantial that it looks like a banquet for Chinese New Year. One big chunk of meat can fill a bowl and has to be torn apart in order to be eaten. They drink homemade distilled corn liquor. The liquor is so heady that one cup is sufficient to make them feel dizzy and intoxicated.

Having drunk two cups, Old Wang tells him that the lion's share of the corn was eaten by *muke* this year. He asks how Wang knows that. Old Wang answers that there's no other creature that would bother to break off the corn cobs like that. Once it has started to eat, it will work its way along the whole row, breaking away the green husk carefully.

He proposes that it might have been bears.

Old Wang continues: "Bears don't eat like that. Bears wolf down an entire field but don't go row by row. Bears don't peel off the husks either."

He asks if it could have been wild boars.

Old Wang says: "Wild boars are more stupid still. They butt down the corn stalks and then just chew away idiotically."

He says what this *muke* doesn't know about is drinking. Old Wang answers that it's because it hasn't ever come into contact with alcohol. If it were to, it would become a drunkard as well.

While they are drinking and talking the chickens, the dog and the cat brush about his legs, waiting for their reward. Halfway through the dinner, the cat leaps onto his knee and then onto the table, licking his bowl and popping its head in and off. Wang's wife doesn't eat at the table but mounts the threshold with the wooden ladle used to feed pigs in her arms. She beams at them.

Old Wang reproaches his wife: "I've been telling you my whole life not to ride the threshold but you never listen. Always such a half-bred. A woman like you will be drowned in laughter when you move to Jiang Family Camp."

The wife still rides there and laughs, paying no attention to Old Wang's rebuke.

He notices that her big toe is poking out from the rubber-soled "liberation" shoes and flexing back and forth in a fascinating way.

Old Wang is rather contented with his life at present, especially this year. He sold the cluster of "hen of the woods" mushroom he dug out for 2,000 yuan, a huge sum he has never seen the like of before. He wants to make a new outfit for his wife for when they move to the new place. Despite being somewhat simple-minded, she bore him five sons. Now all five are working outside the mountains, and one has risen to become a township head. Old Wang says he would survive all the same even if he we not to leave Walnut Terrace. "I've never paid less than I should have, whether we are talking about grain or tax. I don't understand why we are being forced to move. Other folks emigrate to America or Canada but we move to Jiang

Family Camp. Moving for farmers is not the same as it is for city folk. They can just flit from one apartment to another. For us it means much more. We have to take the graves of our forefathers, our pigs, a couple of hives full of bees, our dogs and cats, and everything that has a life …"

Old Wang chatters to himself as he drinks not caring whether his guest is listening or not. He does not want to look into Wang's convoluted personal matters, so walks out with a deep red and warm face.

Nighttime at Walnut Terrace is as cool and soft as water. The blue sky is replete with bright stars. The galaxy looms directly above the head, like misty clouds. Satellites are orbiting at a slow but regular pace, one, two, eastward, southward, northward … The human race is everywhere, including the lonely universe.

The surrounding mountains are in complete darkness. Stars twinkle at the forest on mountain top, like leopard's eyes.

Somehow Old Wang rears up behind, looking at the sky, and says, "When the galaxy becomes forked, you wear thin pants and shirts; when the galaxy shifts its angle you wear thick cotton-padded trousers and jackets. Look, the tip of galaxy has reached the northeastern ridge of Mount Laojun. Winter is coming." Hardly has he finished speaking, when a meteor slides across the beautiful sky, then a second, then a third… No one knows from whence these countless meteors have come or to where they will go. They form a splendid, animated scene overhead; something brilliant and wonderful only normally to be encountered in fairy tales.

He excitedly applauds, "A meteor shower! What a beautiful meteor shower!"

Old Wang says plainly, "Someone has died. Many people have died."

The starry sky falls into silence. Old Wang and he stand there motionless, thinking about their own respective concerns. After a while, Old Wang tells him: "Will you take him away

216

tomorrow… I know, sooner or later, you will take him away…"

He looks at Old Wang. His eyes glitter as if the meteors that just passed by now have flown into his own eyes.

Old Wang avoids his line of vision, mumbling, "He will never go with me even though we are brothers."

A muntjac is crying sorrowfully across the river, one wail after another.

Dew descends.

… He doesn't sleep soundly that night.

In the morning, Old Wang and he arrive at the big blue stone, carrying a pickaxe. Wang's wife follows them at a distance, pulling a weird expression. No one knows whether she is crying or smiling.

The big blue stone welcomes them in silence.

The wild walnut tree tilts depressingly. Collectively, the plants around the stone, including the spurreys, the cuckoo-buds, the wood nettles, and the plantains present an unnatural green colour. They have braved the frost and are singing the last elegy amid the gusty wind.

A jay joins the chorus.

Old Wang burns a few pages of a notebook left by his grandson as an offering before breaking the earth. Who knows if this is done for the dead beneath the ground or for the wild walnut tree above the ground … The soil having been churned up, the tree falls down. The dandelions clocks are tossed upward and carried across the river on the breeze all the way to lofty Mount Laojun.

The subsoil is generally rocky. The coffin is thin and rotten. The twenty-three-year-old bones are revealed to possess a mixture of dark green and dreadful white hues. They lie quietly at the bottom of the pit and look up at the pale late autumn sunshine in as well as at the landscape that hasn't altered much after he went to sleep. Old Wang spits a drop of alcohol into the pit, jumps down and passes the bones up to him one-by-one, first the skull, then the breastbone and then the arms and legs. As he picks them up, they gradually grow heavier in his arms. Excited and now nearly out of his mind, he is anxious to leave, even dropping the meat boiled by Wang's wife. Old Wang feels a faint pathos in his eagerness to travel such a long way, and so willingly covers a considerable distance in the process of seeing him off. They pass over the brook and join the path leading to Mount Laojun. Neither of them talks. Old Wang is particularly melancholy, a feeling he has never detected in this rough mountain-dweller. He is surprised at his red-rimmed eyes and wonders what Old Wang is sad about – him leaving, having to move house, or becoming separated from his brother? He asks Old Wang to pause and Wang does so.

Old Wang says, "Greet your father for me. We haven't seen each other for nearly fifty years."

He thinks this man is senile.

Old Wang says, "You look so much like your father. From behind it would be impossible to tell you apart."

He bids farewell to Old Wang and walks up the mountain. After he has covered several twists in the mountains, he turns to find Old Wang still standing there, waving at him.

IV.

A group of takins from over the mountain have assembled to welcome him.

On returning to Mount Laojun, he finds that his shack has fallen victim to an unprecedented raid. Two pillars have been torn up; half of the shack has collapsed. Pots and bowls lie scattered across the slope. Food has been flung about all over the ground and cannot be gathered up. Every last bottle has been upended and every scrap of fabric has been torn. It can be presumed that none of the "evidence" and specimens that he took efforts to collect will have escaped. The intruder seems to have been determined to make life difficult for him: even those plaster casts of *muke* footprints have been broken and bitten, then thrown into fissures or clefts...

Zhuangzhuang did it.

That large, strong black bear still retains a childlike innocence and likes to play mischievous tricks. He might put a stone to block his water sink or steal the honey Old Wang has brought for him. No matter where the honey-pot is hidden, the bear will still dig it out. It is said that dogs have an extra-sensitive nose. As far as he is concerned, Zhuangzhuang's nose is far more acute. He doesn't steal in front of him like rock rats; he grabs stealthily and feels it is normal to pinch something every time he drops by. This time, Zhuangzhuang has consumed too many fermented berries which turned to alcohol in his stomach and made him drunk. Gotten drunk and acted crazily. However, he didn't tear open his own lair but his shack; he acted like those people who curse others rather than themselves when they are drunk.

He goes over to upbraid Zhuangzhuang for what he has done. He doesn't know that Zhuangzhuang was drunk at the time and thinks the joke has gone too far. Living as neighbours, how could the bear be so unfriendly and spoil their relationship? He puts down the backpack. But after having second thoughts, puts it on again. He is afraid that he cannot afford to lose anything more should another Zhuangzhuang be around.

Zhuangzhuang is in his territory, plucking acorns from his favourite oak.

He calls out: "Zhuangzhuang."

Zhuangzhuang pretends not to hear and continues to compete with a thick branch. He shakes the branch so that ripe acorns might fall down. Acorns hail down onto his head, causing a lot of discomfort. After this rain has finished, he cries out to him up there, questioning why he has destroyed his belongings. Zhuangzhuang pays no attention to him, instead climbing higher. The bear treats him as one of his own kind and must be thinking "I have thrown so many acorns down to you. This should be ample compensation for all your losses. Why are you still thundering at me?" Zhuangzhuang is indeed very busy. Everyone is busy this season. Following his bout of drunkenness, he doesn't have time to indulge in deep and profound introspection upon his behaviour. He must have a gathered a vast quantity of food including acorns before winter comes. He has fattened himself up so that he can hibernate until the start of the next spring.

Even though he yells incessantly, Zhuangzhuang still turns a deaf ear to this. In fact he has no way of dealing with this black bear. The so-called "argument" will only go as far as a bit of shouting. If he really were to irritate the creature, he would find himself in serious trouble. He cannot risk death arguing over such a point. It seems that Zhuangzhuang has already been made conscious of his fault and he should better stop now. He doesn't want to waste time on Zhuangzhuang. The hard bones inside his backpack are poking against his back making him nervous but at the same time subconsciously excited. Arguing with Zhuangzhuang is just a warm-up used to rouse his energy, much like the drumming before the opening of an opera performance. The really interesting part is yet to come.

For a few days, he never leaves the shabby shack that is now incapable of keeping the wind and rain at bay. No cooking smoke rises up from Mount Laojun; his shout cannot be heard about the cliff and rocks either.

The rock rats have made ready for hibernation. In spite of their profound sleepiness and their internal clock being pushed to the limit, they approach this shack that has been mangled out of all recognition. Hardly being able to find the old entrance, they jump up and down, chirping, not knowing what to do; a blood pheasant strides over, babbling, then flaps away; Sansan the panda is firmly entrenched in his own land, taking little notice of his friend who he hasn't met for a long time; takins send out their envoy, a strong male takin which stands in front of the shack for three hours before leaving out of frustration; the most frequent guest is Zhuangzhuang, the black bear, who walks around the shack with his round stomach: he feels satisfied with his "masterpiece," having reconstituted the shelter into how a lair should look. The clouded leopard skirmishes with Zhuangzhuang behind the shack. The leopard cannot bear how Zhuangzhuang comes and goes away so freely within his own territory as if he were a personage of note. Zhuangzhuang has sufficient energy and feels like fighting at that same moment. The leopard, being naturally competitive too, cannot tolerate the bear's defiant attitude for long. The two of them tussle doggedly nearby, trampling down a whole section of bush and dislodging dozens of big stones. Even in proximity to this onslaught, the owner of the shack never shows his face…

It is surprisingly quiet inside the shack, while there is an unprecedented clamour outside. In the final few days before the beginning of winter, the animals on Mount Laojun act as though they have been coming along to a fair. Each of them has completed a few laps around the shack, casting an attentive gaze upon it.

They didn't spot him.

v.

He goes down the mountain to Heavenly Flower Town to pursue a matter he considered exceedingly urgent.

This is the first time he has left the mountain in several years.

Compared with the initial time he visited, Heavenly Flower Town has become populated with more bijou hotels and delicate hair salons, boasting more brightly coloured flags and advertisement balloons, and being home to more men who are playing truant and to more shiftless women. Everything seems to float with decadence and transience, lending with the impression that everyone is oppressed, aggrieved and helpless. His inability to assimilate with the crowd makes him the focus of the whole town's attention that day. Ever since he walked out of the forest and planted a step on the cement bridge, he was chased by children. They surrounded him, shouting at him "Savage! Savage!" and pelted stones and sods at him. Men are astonished at his strange looks while women are repelled by his smell.

He looks steadily forward, conducting his business calmly and with a confident bearing.

Upon exiting the post office, he enters a restaurant.

The proprietor of the restaurant shoves him out. Losing his balance, he pitches over into a foul ditch. His clothes which were already discoloured now become filthier. No one extends a supportive hand. The onlookers watch him in a circle, laughing at him, much like a bunch of bastards. He sits up next to a heap of faeces, examining his flayed and bleeding knees with a mind that is now all of a blank. With affected generosity, a woman tosses him half a pancake as if she were feeding a homeless dog.

He rejects it.

The woman suddenly changes face, telling the crowd, "He's bragging by refusing to eat it!"

A group of tourists come over, treating him as a rare object and taking photos of him while whispering to each other: "The savage has come down from Heavenly Flower Mountain and is strolling about the town…"

This is a once-in-a-blue-moon opportunity.

He closes his eyes, without any explanation. It is abundantly clear to him that he has already trodden out of the network of humankind and no longer belongs to this world. That much was confirmed when he walked into the town post office and the clerk was filled with fear as she accepted the 100 yuan note which stank of weeds and was worn and stained green. It seemed that he looked like a ghost from another world and his money was the ghost currency brought from over there. The clerk repeatedly checked the authenticity of the note in the currency scanner and five minutes later when she held up her head, the "savage" had already left.

Now, all he wants is a bowl of hot noodles in soup. A bowl of hot noodles served in soup, drenched with chili oil and chopped green onions, topped with a smattering of spinach – just what he has been imagining for so long.

This wish will not be granted – the people don't permit him the chance.

Confronted with so much strangeness and ugliness, he misses his honest and enthusiastic companions back in the mountains: the rock rats, the blood pheasant, the panda, the black bear, the clouded leopard, the takins, and the *muke*. They would never hurl stones at him and disdain him with scornful and haughty looks.

That kind of look is the preserve of humans alone.

An unkempt owl staggers in front of him and skews across the road. Two kids are haring after it, subjecting it to a vigorous pursuit which will be followed by a fierce mauling. Owls have poor eyesight in daytime. This one is obviously wounded and can hardly fly. People here regard owls as ominous, as the saying goes "If 'night-cat' enters a house, trouble will come at once." Driven to desperation, the owl dives into a woodpile. The kids still stab at it with a stick... He thinks that the preschool education in China is ridiculous. The legend of the "hateful wolf" helps to establish animals as the opponents of human beings. They classify animals according to human concepts categorizing them into "good ones" and "bad ones" or "fierce ones" and "benevolent ones." This logic is cankered from the root upwards. Wolves eat sheep according to their biological need, as is predetermined by the food chain. There are rules and disciplines in the animal world. They are not like human beings, who given the chance, will eat everything except their own species and turn whatever they can lay their hands on into clothing.

Two men in uniforms accost him on the cement bridge leading to the mountain entrance, saying they are going to escort him to the Public Security Management Office of the Forest as they believe that his presence is a threat to the safety of this forest. Dumbfounded, he cannot understand and does not know in what way he is posing interference. He growls at the uniformed men, with a jarringly loud roar. The roar can be comprehended by the black bear and the clouded leopard but not the uniformed men. The fatter one with a big belly takes out a string with which to bind him up. He pushes those two jobs-worths down to the ground and runs around two trees, circling them with a rat-like skillfulness leaving those pursuers in his wake. People shout and kick up a fuss. The two uniformed men who were low-key in their manner just now become emboldened, crying out to the crowd: "Catch him. He is a down-and-out."

He is like that wounded owl.

It dived into the woodpile and he doesn't know its whereabouts. He collides with the belly of the fat one with his head and finds a way to escape.

Like a swarm of bees, his chasers persist in running after him. The cries of "Catch the savage" whip up above Heavenly Flower Town. More and more people join in. It is beyond dispute that a new sighting has now been added to the records of "savages" in this district; the sighting can be validated by Witnesses No. 1, No. 2, No. 3, No. 4, No. 5, No. 6, No. 7…

He flees along any path he can. Somehow he reaches the cliff opposite his shack. The search team forms a ring around the valley. The tumult of people's voices and the dogs barking presents an excitement and tension to all no matter whether they are human or canine. He looks to the opposite slope of the cliff. That familiar scenery: the half-collapsed shack, the tall maple, the dense grove of arrow bamboo, the thick bush;

he is there in the shack, the *muke* is in the maple, Sansan is in the forest, the leopard is in the bush... A sense of intimacy is engendered spontaneously. That is home. Yes, it is home, a home he can return to. He has never been so relaxed and so comfortable. Taking a deep breath, he is inoculated with the scent of mint coming from the bottom of the brook.

Someone climbs to the summit on one side. They see him standing facing towards the setting sun. Wearing a smile on his green face and a golden light beaming upon his body, he steps onto the clouds that are swarming in from below. Soft, white, glittering clouds. He disappears into the clouds...

The wind blows. A babbling chanting with no lyrics, only a rhyme, rises up.

He is not falling but ascending. Like a slow motion sequence in a movie there appears his little shack and the maple, followed by a glade of rhododendrons which dwarf him and then a gneissose granite rock formation beneath which are to be found the dark-coloured mountain folds and a red maple fluttering in the wind.

That is not a fold; obviously it is the stone cave. That is not a maple, either; obviously it is the *muke* in the sunset. He has finally got around to seeing it. It sits by the cave entrance in a leisurely posture, its legs hanging down by the cliff. A huge pair of feet swaying in the air, as it hums a song ... Green surfaces. Endless green. The scent of mint becomes thicker and solidifies ...

Mountain goddess and tree guest.

VI.

A fortnight later, the Institute of Vertebrate Palaeontology received a parcel from Heavenly Flower Town, inside which was a humanoid skull with a brief report attached also. Its contents were as follows:

Item: A farmer named Li Chuntao, female, born in Walnut Terrace, Heavenly Flower Mountain in 1902. While undertaking farm work in a field in the mountains she was captivated by the sight of an unidentified animal that could stand erect like a human being. She disappeared for two months and came back pregnant. She gave birth to a son in December of that year. The boy was named Wang Shuangcai. According to the recollections of local people there, Wang Shuangcai was covered with short brown hair from birth, and had massive feet and long arms. His face closely resembled that of an ape. He was short in stature. The specimen was mute and behaved strangely. He could, however, understand human words.

His brother Wang Shuangyin revealed that Wang Shuangcai died of natural causes aged 23. There were six brothers in Wang's family among whom only Wang Shuangai was "totally different." With his relative's consent, the remains of Wang Shuangcai were exhumed on 19th July 2001. The initial examination results are attached here:

Judging from his leg bones, the deceased was 1.42 metres tall with the ratio of arm to leg length being disproportionate. The skull is 8 centimetres in height; with a low and narrow forehead, and a protruding brow ridge. The brain volume is not big, 2/3 of the size of that of a normal human being. There is a unique and strange structure to the rim of the eye socket: the *glabella* space measures 5 centimetres. 5.6cm is typical for ape men and 2.8 for modern human beings. The *foramen magnum* is smaller than that of ordinary people with a plain *occiput* and an inconspicuous occipital dome, which is closer to later fossils of *homo sapiens* in China and presents features associated with underdeveloped brains.

From the above characteristics, Wang Shuangcai from Walnut Ridge can be determined to have been close in nature to anthropoids ... Further research and examination are requested to verify these findings.

Endnotes

a **Jingyang Ridge** is a site in Yanggu County, Shandong Province. In the narrative of *The Water Margin* (also known as *The Outlaws of the Marsh*), attributed to Shi Nai'an (c. 1296-1376), the locals deliberately try and keep a low profile because none of them is brave enough to tackle the man-eating tiger that menaces their area.

b **The Four Cleanups Movement** was instigated by Mao Zedong in 1963 and lasted until 1966. It aimed to root out perceived "reactionary elements" from within the Chinese Communist Party. As part of this movement, intellectuals retained their posts or study places, though were sent to work in the countryside where they were expected to be re-educated by the peasants. The titular "four" in want of cleansing were politics, economy, organization, and ideology.

c The exploits of the hero **Wu Song** are recounted in Chapters 23-32 of *The Water Margin*. Having been persuaded by a dishonest steward in a tavern that, contrary to local rumour, there is no wild tiger on Jingyang Ridge he drank his fill and slept outdoors. Waking up in a stupor, Wu is charged at three times by the tiger before he manages to restrain the beast with his bare hands, pinning it to the ground and then finishing it off with a sharp stick.

d *erhaung* **and** *erliu* **melodies** are two forms of singing used in traditional Peking Opera. They require careful training and vocal dexterity to master, otherwise the sound is truly cacophonous.

e   **Keiji Yokomichi** was a somewhat stupid character in the 1976 movie *You Must Cross the River of Wrath* (*Kimi yo fundo no kawa o watare*), known alternatively in English as *Manhunt* and *Dangerous Chase*. The film was released in Mainland China in 1978 and, being one of the first foreign films to be permitted in cinemas after the end of the Cultural Revolution, its storylines and characters entered everyday parlance.

f   *Taking Tiger Mountain by Strategy* was a Peking Opera and one of the Eight Model Plays sanctioned for performance during the Cultural Revolution. It was adapted from a factually-based novel by Qu Bo (1923-2002) and is concerned with a Communist revolutionary who infiltrates a gang of bandits in disguise in order to covertly smash its activities.

g   The **favoured son-in-law** is a reference to an episode from the life of the renowned calligrapher Wang Xizhi (303-61 AD). Xi Jian (269-339 AD) of Jiankang (present-day Nanjing) heard that the sons and nephews of the Wang family at Langya (present-day Linyi City in Shandong Province) were all very handsome. He sent a messenger to deliver a letter to Wang Dao (276-339 AD) requesting that he could select a young man from the Wang family to be his son-in-law. Wang Dao told the messenger to go to the eastern side rooms to pick and choose. After returning to his master's home, the messenger reported to Xi Jian, "The young men in the Wang family are all laudable. When they heard that a son-in-law would be selected from among them, they all got dressed up and tried their best to stay dignified. Only one young man was unmoved. He continued to snack on some foreign pancakes with his belly bare. He looked composed and nonchalant." Xi Jian exclaimed, "This one will be my favoured son-in-law!" He inquired who this young man was and was informed that it was Wang Xizhi. He then married his daughter Xi Xuan off to him.

h   *Strange Tales from the Liaozhai Studio* is popularly known as *Legends about Ghosts and Fox Spirits*. It is a collection of 491 short stories written by the esteemed novelist Pu Songling (1640-1715) in the Qing Dynasty and represents the summit of the classical Chinese short story.

i   *Diary of Yuewei Thatched Cottage* is a collection of short supernatural stories written in classical Chinese between 1789 and 1798 in the form of a diary by Ji Xiaolan (1724-1805). Mr. Ji was originally an imperial academician. Historically the book has enjoyed a reputation on a par with *The Story of the Stone* and *Strange Tales from the Liaozhai Studio*.

j   **more fragile than a "pretty sixteen-year-old girl."** In traditional Chinese culture sixteen is the age when females are said to reach the prime of their beauty, though they are admired for their delicacy rather than robustness.

k   The **Lower nine schools** were those professions looked down upon in traditional Chinese society, namely: *yamen* advisors, *yamen* runners, those who weighed with scales, matchmakers, pawnbrokers, the "monsters" of contemporary life (human traffickers, conmen, witches, and so on), thieves, burglars, and prostitutes.

l   **The "Three Old Graduating Classes"** refer to the graduating classes of 1966, 1967 and 1968. Because of the Cultural Revolution, the middle-school and high-school graduates in those three years left school all together in 1968 and created a huge employment crisis.

m   **A pleated indigo garment** refers to the female protagonist in a Beijing opera troupe. The name comes into being because the female protagonist often sports a pleated indigo piece.

n **Second Grade Hat Button** was a form of hat tapering towards a point in the middle and bearing a tassel. During the Qing Dynasty (1644-1911) it signified the ministerial status of the wearer.

o **Shaoxing** is a city in Zhejiang Province in the southeast of China.

p **In which earthly branch of which heavenly stem** means "at which hour on which day in which month of which year." There are ten heavenly stems and twelve earthly branches. It is an ancient way to record the Chinese era used in the Xia Dynasty (*c.* 2100 BC- *c.* 1600 BC).

q **Arhat lobsters** are cooked like this: the first half of the lobsters is roasted into sweet salty red sections with the shells on and the second half of the lobsters is deep-fried in oil into crispy fragrant tender golden-yellow lengths with the shells off. Their upper halves being red and the lower halves yellow, they look like arhats (Buddhist disciples who have reached enlightenment) with a bulging bared belly. Hence the name.

r **The Five Dynasties** refer to the Later Liang Dynasty (907-23 AD), the Later Tang Dynasty (923-36 AD), the Later Jin Dynasty (936-47 AD), the Later Han Dynasty (947-50 AD) and the Later Zhou Dynasty (951-60 AD).

s **The primary stage of socialism** was a key concept in Deng Xiaoping's formulation of Socialism with Chinese Characteristics. When the government adopted aspects of the market economy and private ownerships from the 1980s onwards, it was reiterated that China had been a semi-developed, semi-feudal society when the Communist Party came to power. In order to stimulate the economic base and boost productivity certain policies formerly considered antithetical to Marxism had to be adopted within the short term.

t   **Fuyang** is the ancient name of the present-day Ci County in Handan City, Henan Province.

u   **Heyang** is a county-level city under the jurisdiction of Jiaozuo City in Henan Province.

v   These words are taken from page 287 of Schaller's study *The Last Panda* (University of Chicago Press, 1993), which was largely researched in the Qinling Mountains of Shaanxi Province.

Acknowledgements

The original Chinese version of "What You're Seeking Left No Trace" was first published in *Baihua Zhou*, Vol. 12, 1998. The original Chinese version of "Virtuous Beauty the Bear" was first published in *Fragrant Grass*, Issue 2, 1997.

"Big Fu the Tiger" and "On Camera" were translated by Professor Hu Zongfeng, "A Panda Named 'Little Mite'" and "Virtuous Beauty the Bear" by He Longping, and "What You're Seeking Left No Trace" and "Mountain Savage" by Dr. Zhang Min. Dr. Robin Gilbank cooperated closely in the editing and preparation of each text.

The author and translators wish to thank Jamie McGarry and Valley Press for helping to bring this book to fruition, and the School of Foreign Languages at Northwest University, Xi'an for financial support. Thanks are also due to Dr. J. Graham Jones for his assistance in proofreading and to Dr. Long Jinrong for her help with legal matters.

The cover image for this book is an edited version of the original photograph 'Tunnel Drivers, Qinling Mountain Range, Xi'an' by Matt Ming. Promotional materials for this book include photographs of the author, which were reproduced by kind permission from the Taibai Publishing House.